P9-ECJ-778

DISCARDED
BY
Yuma County Library District

TREASURE WELL

OTHER RECENT FIVE STAR TITLES BY MAX BRAND®:

TREASURE WELL

A WESTERN TRIO

MAX BRAND®

FIVE STAR

An imprint of Thomson Gale, a part of The Thomson Corporation

YUMA COUNTY
LIBRARY DISTRICT

(928) 782-1871
www.yumalibrary.org

THOMSON

GALE

Detroit • New York • San Francisco • New Haven, Conn. • Waterville, Maine • London

THOMSON
GALE

Copyright © 2006 by Golden West Literary Agency.
"Treasure Well" by George Owen Baxter first appeared in Street & Smith's *Western Story Magazine* (6/27/31). Copyright © 1931 by Street & Smith Publications, Inc. Copyright © renewed 1958 by Dorothy Faust. Copyright © 2006 by Golden West Literary Agency for restored material. Acknowledgment is made to Condé Nast Publications, Inc., for their co-operation.
"Outlaw's Conscience" by George Owen Baxter first appeared in Street & Smith's *Western Story Magazine* (7/11/31). Copyright © 1931 by Street & Smith Publications, Inc. Copyright © renewed 1948 by Dorothy Faust. Copyright © 2006 by Golden West Literary Agency for restored material. Acknowledgment is made to Condé Nast Publications, Inc., for their co-operation.
"Clean Courage" by George Owen Baxter first appeared in Street & Smith's *Western Story Magazine* (7/25/31). Copyright © 1931 by Street & Smith Publications, Inc. Copyright © renewed 1948 by Dorothy Faust. Copyright © 2006 by Golden West Literary Agency for restored material. Acknowledgment is made to Condé Nast Publications, Inc., for their co-operation.
The name Max Brand® is a registered trademark with the United States Patent and Trademark Office and cannot be used for any purpose without express written permission.
Thomson Gale is part of The Thomson Corporation.
Thomson and Star Logo and Five Star are trademarks and Gale is a registered trademark used herein under license.

ALL RIGHTS RESERVED

No part of this book may be reproduced or transmitted in any form or by any electronic or mechanical means, including photocopying, recording or by any information storage and retrieval system, without the express written permission of the publisher, except where permitted by law.
Set in 11 pt. Plantin.

LIBRARY OF CONGRESS CATALOGING-IN-PUBLICATION DATA

Brand, Max, 1892–1944.
   Treasure well : a western trio / by Max Brand. — 1st ed.
     p. cm. — (Five star western)
   ISBN 1-59414-394-3 (alk. paper)
   1. Western stories. I. Title.
PS3511.A87T747 2006
813'.52—dc22   2006022175

U.S. Hardcover:
ISBN 13: 978-1-59414-394-6
ISBN 10: 1-59414-394-3
First Edition. First Printing: November 2006.
Published in 2006 in conjunction with Golden West Literary Agency.
Printed in the United States of America on permanent paper
10 9 8 7 6 5 4 3 2 1

DEC 21 2006

CONTENTS

EDITOR'S NOTE

Throughout his writing career Frederick Faust featured series characters in his contributions to Street & Smith's *Western Story Magazine*. Among his creations are Bull Hunter, Ronicky Doone, James Geraldi, Chip, Speedy, and Reata. Three stories about the character Tom Fernald appeared in 1931. Unlike many of Faust's series characters, Fernald is not a legend wandering the West, but rather a sheepherder, who is the laughingstock of the nearby town and at the point of losing his meager ranch to the money-lender. The trio of stories published under Faust's George Owen Baxter byline are "Treasure Well" which appeared in June 27th issue, "Outlaw's Conscience" in the July 11th issue, and "Clean Courage" in the July 25th issue.

★ ★ ★ ★ ★

TREASURE WELL

★ ★ ★ ★ ★

I

Never had Mount Griffon worn a deeper hood of black, or the wind blown a stronger gale across the peaks and down the valley. It tore away the clouds from the top of the great summit and flung them in swift and level flight across the sky, shooting faster than belief. Sometimes a white feather of snow blew level into the face of Tom Fernald, and sometimes hail rattled on his slicker or bruised his blue hands, for he never afforded the luxury of gloves. However, he kept on his way doggedly, thinking of how the little stove would tremble and roar in the shack, once he got home and fired it up, and how the wreaths of smoke would twist upward from the bacon that hissed in the pan, and, above all, he meditated upon the coffee pot and the fragrance of it that now appeared to him as the thought of a drug to an addict. But to a degree, he locked even expectation behind his set jaws, and fronted the storm. He did not urge the horse beyond a dog trot—for there were still miles remaining to him. Often the pressure of the gale blew them to a walk, or even stopped them altogether, the horse leaning forward as if against a wall. Then, shaking its head, it would go on again. And Tom Fernald, shaking his head, also, gravely sympathized with the mustang, and let it have its way. For he understood horses.

The people of the Mount Griffon range had little use for the slow wits of Fernald, but they respected his opinions about horseflesh. This pinto was the ugliest, toughest, most enduring handful of sinew and India rubber that he ever had tackled, although he often picked up a few dollars in spare time by breaking so-called outlaws on the range. Like most bad ones, there was plenty of intelligence in the pinto, and, having once been mastered, it respected this rider, but this rider only. Other men remained for its scorn, its hatred. But to Tom Fernald it submitted, no longer caring to endure the masterful grip of his knees, the slashing sword strokes of the quirt. It kept its malice in reserve, and this gave Fernald a warm feeling of pleasure. He was not a proud man; he lived in a district where a sheepherder could hardly retain pride, but the pinto was to him a silent flattery every mile he rode upon its back.

The horse was stalwart, stocky, rather of the type that one might call pudgy. So was Fernald. He looked plump about the shoulders and chest; only his face was lean. As in the case of the horse, the seeming plumpness indicated strength rather than soft living. He was padded out with muscle, not with fat.

On this day, although the wind was blowing him cold and turning his eyes as red as the red eyes of the horse, an inward content fortified Fernald. For he had money to pay a debt. He had spent two days driving in sheep to town. He had sold them off for a fair price. He had paid off certain annoying debts in the stores, and he retained in his pocket $250. Of that sum he would need to spend $200, he dared say, shortly after his return to the shack. The other $50 would see him through a long spell.

On the whole, he felt that he was distinctly on the upgrade. He knew, now, that he had selected his land wisely. It did not produce grazing of the sort on which cows will fatten, but it was all right for sheep. It was such bad land that he had been able to buy it for $2.50 an acre.

"You'll grow more rocks than cows on that ground," the rancher had told him with a savage grin after the money was paid over.

But from the first he had not been fool enough to hope to

raise cows. Sheep were the limit of his ambition—just now.

So he had put the first of the flock on the ground, and tended it, and struck some years of good prices, and prospered. It was slow, bitter work. He was twenty when he began for himself. He was twenty-six now, and he was only beginning to feel out in the clear. Always there was very little cash between him and despair. But the sheep lived, multiplied with astonishing speed, and now he told himself that, inside of another year or two, he would be able to buy some of the rocky hill shoulders behind his place. That land, again, was useless for cattle—the neighboring ranchers disdained to run sheep—and he could buy the uplands for a song.

Well, one of these days he would prosper to such an extent that he could afford to buy some land with a deeper soil, a soil where he could run cows. And in the heart of Fernald there was always a quiet hope that on a time he would be able to show some of the disbelieving world in which he had grown up that he was not altogether a fool.

Sleepy Tom, they called him. He did not dissent it. He was accustomed to being looked down upon. But the quiet hope was always inside him; he was waiting for some great tomorrow.

He came over the top of the last rise. A driving sweep of snow half blinded him, but, squinting through it, he saw the dim outlines of the shack ahead of him in the hollow.

The pinto understood perfectly, also. It pricked its ears half forward against the blast, and lifted its head. Shelter and food for them both were just ahead. But something else was just ahead, also. It was the silhouette of a rider, almost lost in the flying snow, and coming suddenly upon the eye of Fernald. It swept closer. It was Bill Ransome, Bill the gambler, the reprobate, suspected of many crimes, who sat there with his tall horse angling across the trail and leveling a revolver at Fernald's head.

"Shove up your hands!" he commanded.

Fernald obeyed. He thought of the money in his pocket, and his heart turned to stone, a stone sinking, as though through a well. But it never occurred to him to resist. For that matter, he did not even carry a gun. It was an extravagance.

Bill Ransome rode nearer. "Where's the dough?" he asked.

"What dough?" said Fernald with blue, stammering lips.

He no longer felt the cold. He felt nothing except the cruel face of Ransome.

"You didn't sell no sheep in town, I guess?" Ransome said, sneering.

"I used up all the money, paying debts," said Fernald.

"You did like hell. You never would spend that much money in a year. I know you, Sleepy," said Ransome. "Where's the coin? If I gotta search you, I'll strip you to the bone, damn you, and let you walk home the rest of the way."

"My wallet's in my inside breast coat pocket," said Fernald.

Ransome reached inside the coat of Fernald and took forth the bit of old, limp leather. The hopeless eyes of Fernald followed it as a marooned sailor follows the disappearing outline of a ship.

"Makes you sick, don't it?" demanded Ransome.

"Yeah, it makes me kind of sick," Tom Fernald said slowly.

"How much is there inside?"

"Two hundred and fifty three dollars," said Fernald instantly.

"You count the pennies, don't you? Well, that was just about what I figgered on. You can put your hands down. I know that you don't pack a gun."

"No," said Fernald, his lips and his brain both numb with shock, "I don't carry a gun."

"If you did, would that've stopped me?" Ransome asked. "You damn' sheepherder, spoilin' range with varmints? Would your carrying a gun make no difference to me?"

"I guess it wouldn't make no difference to you," said Fernald.

He looked with mute grief, and with wonder, also, into the face of the robber. The man seemed to be taking from the hold-up more pleasure than the mere acquisition of the money.

"You look like you was about to bust out cryin'," said Ransome. "I kind of half wonder that you don't. You was always a soft fool . . . a regular sheep."

Fernald said nothing; there was nothing to say. He was already looking past the form of the tyrant into the future. A dreadful blank was all that he could conceive there. He had thought that he was embarked in a substantial ship. Now he could see that he had been drifting in a mere paper skiff. Even this slight blow would sink it. Bankruptcy. That was what lay ahead. They had only despised him before. They would suspect him of crimes, now. Bankruptcy! It seemed to Fernald the last disgrace. It blanketed all the joy of the world in a thick mist.

"You never had no spirit. That's what's wrong with you," said Ransome. "That's why you don't deserve to have nothin'. Because you got no guts. That's why I got no use for you. That's why nobody's got no use for you. You never fought none. You always dodged a fight, standin' around with your fool face, when you was in school."

Fernald could remember that. He never had fought when he was in school. Not that he actively feared the other boys, but he never had felt in himself a rage sufficient to make him wish to batter and bruise their faces, as they did to one another. Once— yes, even twice—he had received blows and not returned them. Heavy blows, but he had felt them hardly at all, because even in his childhood there was that same rubbery padding of muscle girt about him, an insulation against the hard knocks of the world.

Ransome went on: "You got no guts. Look at you now, looking like you been shot through the heart, and you've only lost a couple hundred dollars. That's nothin' . . . to a real man. It ain't gonna kill you to lose this."

"It'll bankrupt me," Fernald said, his voice sounding faraway in his own ears, like a spirit flying down the wind. "It'll bankrupt me, I guess. I owe a couple of hundred to Pete Visconti. He'll never let me off."

"You owe it to Pete Visconti? What for?"

"Interest."

"Hold on! Did Pete Visconti trust you for that much?"

"Three thousand dollars."

"Why, dog-gone my heart," said Ransome. "The dirty dog, he wouldn't trust me for even one grand. Like as though he preferred you to me. Well, the both of you can be damned, as far as I care. So long, Sleepy!"

He turned his horse and rode away. The storm swallowed him almost instantly, and Fernald wakened from a daydream of misery to find himself in front of his shack.

He had not urged the horse on; the pinto had simply taken its own way through the wind, and had arrived at the proper end of its journey. Now it shrugged and twisted, to apprize the master that it was time to dismount.

Like a lifeless thing, Fernald slipped to the ground.

II

It was not a handsome shack. He had built it in the days when he knew little about such things. The shelters and sheds that he had constructed in after years for the sheep were much more thoroughly and neatly made, for instance. But nevertheless it seemed to Sleepy Tom that there was a sort of romantic beauty about the wretched façade of the hovel, a sorrowful beauty to be mourned, for soon the place would be as the dead to him.

He took the mustang around to the shed behind the house, and there he was surprised and shocked to see another horse already put up. He recognized the powerful roan horse of Pete Visconti. Aye, but when had Pete ever been late in his tours of debt collection?

Coming out from the shed, once more, he now saw that smoke was curling above the stovepipe that poked through the roof of the hut. He shook his head and told himself that it hardly mattered. As well face the thing at once. Better to have it over and done with, rather than to stand before the dreadful thought for another day or two, like a condemned man facing the firing squad. He dragged himself around to the front of the house, opened the door, and went in.

Visconti was finishing a meal, and drinking coffee. He went on with his occupation, stooping his head toward the cup, as though his hands were too weak to lift such a weight. Only from beneath his shaggy brows he looked up at the owner of the place.

He seemed to Fernald more like a vulture than ever before, with his prematurely bald, red head, his small forehead, his vast hook of a nose, his scrawny neck, and the enormous and unexpected width of his shoulders. Deathless hunger for gain was in his eyes.

"Well, Tom," he said gloomily, "I been waitin' here quite a time for you. I been wastin' about a couple hours of my time. Gimme the money, and I'll start along."

Fernald went over to the little stove, stepping slowly. He did not answer at once because the roots of his tongue were frozen in his throat. And to fill his attention, to rally himself a little, he picked up the heavy iron bar that served him as a poker, lifted the lid off the stove, thrust blindly at the wood, and finally turned with the bar still in his hands.

"Go on and hurry up," said the money-lender. "I'm late now.

Gimme the money. Why don't you buy bacon that's got more meat in it?"

"This kind is cheaper, and fat is just as good as lean, if you're hungry enough."

Suddenly the other grinned, and his face was even more ghastly in its ugliness, smiling, than in repose. The resemblance to the vulture was more perfect.

"Yeah," he said, "and that's how you'll get on. I bet on you. I bet against the rest of 'em, but I bet on you. Because you don't mind bein' humble. I been humble, too. I had nothin', when I started. Now I'm forty, and look what I got. You'd like to know what I got, wouldn't you?" He paused, staring.

"What you have is yours, not mine," said Fernald.

"Aye, that's the way," said the money-lender. "It don't matter to you what other folks have, and it don't matter to me, neither. That's where you're right. I seen that when you first come and talked about money to buy the sheep walk. I let you have it for that reason. Now you got a tidy place. Next year, you can pay off half what you owe. That's why I charged you smaller interest, too. I get ten percent, twelve percent, fifteen percent, sometimes. But I done you a favor."

Fernald looked blankly at him.

It was a strange thing to hear Visconti talk of favors. His business was well known. It consisted of lending scattering sums about the range to small farmers, to ranchers in a pinch, to anyone in desperate need—and with some security. Then, if they failed in a payment, he swooped down on them, vulture-like in action as in appearance. No man in the country was so detested. Rumor declared that no man was so rich. Somewhere about his little house among the rocks, it was said that he had a great treasure buried. For he never trusted a penny to banks. The farms he swallowed, he picked up for next to nothing and sold again for huge profits. He had been doing it for fifteen years, but no bank saw a penny of his hard cash. Certainly he kept the money concealed about his house. But, when he departed on his tours of collection, a hundred times his place had been searched, and always in vain. Five times men had tried to extract the secret from him, gun in hand, and five times they had died, and under the terrible hands of Visconti, and five times he had lived, in spite of wounds.

All of this flowed through the brain of Fernald, as he looked at his unsavory guest. "Yes," he said at last, "you did me a favor, I guess. I remember being surprised, at the time."

"All right," said Visconti, "we've had enough of this here billing and cooing. Now, you fork over the two hundred, and I'll start along."

"I haven't the money," said Fernald.

Visconti paused, rested a hand on the table from which he had risen, and stared. "You lie!" he said. "You went in to sell sheep. You fool, you're lyin' to me."

"I was robbed. Bill Ransome robbed me," said Fernald.

"Why'd you let him rob you?" thundered Visconti. "Why in hell didn't you break his back for him?"

Fernald said nothing. There was nothing to say.

"You think I'll let you off, you coward, but I ain't gonna!" roared Pete Visconti. "I'd take the coin out of your blood, if could do it. That's what I'd do. Why . . . damn you! . . . you fat, worthless. . . ."

He stopped. He had been interrupted by a harsh, gritting sound, and, at the same time, Fernald was aware of a pain in both his hands. He looked down and saw that in his agony of mind he had bent the iron bar into a half circle.

Visconti had seen the same thing, and his eyes bulged in his head. Still staring, he backed to the door. There was something like fear in his face. Only when the door was open, and the outer storm whistling behind his back, did he seem to regain some of his poise, and now he cried: "You could've broke him, like you've bent the iron! You can bend iron, but you can't bend men. You're no good. You're beat by the world. A Chinaman could kick you in the face. And I'm gonna foreclose on you. You hear me? I foreclose . . . tomorrow!"

He slammed the door. The world was darker than his cabin, to Tom Fernald. He had not moved from his place. His hand still gripped the iron, when the door opened once more.

It was the money-lender, wearing a scowl. "My horse has gone lame," he declared. "I'll take your hoss in part payment. I'll allow you eighty dollars for the worthless brute. Is that all right?"

"Yes," said Fernald. "I guess that's all right."

Horse or no horse, it hardly mattered. Anyway, when the foreclosure went through, the horse would be taken from him. For who would bid a penny on such a place as this? It would go to the mortgagee for the value of the naked mortgage. He, Fernald, had no right to the very clothes on his back.

Presently he remembered, however. The pinto was not a safe animal for a stranger to ride. He started to the door, threw it open, and then he recalled the long legs, the might for which Visconti was famous. He had killed men with his bare hands, and it would be foolish to warn him against the mustang. Why, he could probably break the back of the horse. This thought had barely gone through the mind of Fernald, when he heard a squeal of rage, the scream of a furious, pitching bronco, and around the corner of the shack appeared the pinto, with his back humped, his hoofs five feet from the ground, and big Visconti at a crazy angle in the saddle.

But he was not afraid, for all the bucking of the mustang. He had his quirt working. And his lame horse, pulling back, suddenly broke the lead rope and hauled off before the driving of the wind.

It was a wild duel that followed. For Visconti rode well, and very well. The length of his legs helped him, and the might of his hands upon the reins. But against him the pinto pitted as much equine deviltry as Fernald had ever seen collected in the brain of any one horse.

Snow sleeted the ground, like a polishing of thin ice, but the pinto did not lose its footing. He pitched as even Fernald never had seen him fight before. Surely since the battle with its present master, it had been revolving new schemes in its wicked skull.

Just before the door of the cabin, it humped its back, thrust down his head until it almost touched the ground, and began to spin like a squirrel on a wheel, around and around, with a gathering momentum.

Had Visconti been finely seated, when the maneuver began, all might have been well with him, but he had lost a stirrup the instant before, as the revolutions began, and he slewed off to that side of the saddle, unsupported. Desperately he clung. His shouted curses beat against the ear of Fernald, but still his big body sloped farther and farther toward the horizontal. He began to work farther from the saddle, and suddenly he was sluiced out of it like a stone.

Fernald dodged the shooting body, saw the great arms stretched out to break the shock of the fall, saw the contorted body of the money-lender.

Straight at the open doorway he was flung, and Fernald heard a dull, heavy thudding sound.

He turned, expecting a furious tirade of curses from Visconti, but the dim interior of the cabin was lost in silence and in shadow.

On the jamb of the door was a red spot, and Visconti himself lay in a curiously twisted position upon the floor. Fernald drew back an instinctive pace in horror. For suddenly he knew that the money-lender never would rise again.

III

First, for he dreaded the entrance to the cabin, he caught up the horses as they moved before the wind, and tethered them in the shed. Then he went back inside the little house and lifted the huge body of Visconti. He weighed well upwards of 200 pounds, but weights rarely bothered Fernald. This one was a little clumsy; it kept slipping through his fingers like a sack of wheat, loosely filled, but he managed to stretch the dead man on the bed. He laid the head straight; he closed the eyes. Then he sat down to think.

He would have to ride the pinto back to town—a cruel thing to do, after the journey of the day. But better that than to spend the rest of the day, until the storm ceased, alone with a dead man.

So he got up, put on his hat and slicker, and went to look at the fire in the stove, to make sure that it was low enough to be left safely. On the way, he picked up the poker, which he had dropped to the floor; it slipped instantly from his grasp, and now he saw with alarm that it was half covered with blood. There was more blood on the hard, earthen floor of the shack. There was the stain on the jamb of the door. And . . . . He staggered as the shock of fear struck him.

Murder! That was what people would say. For they knew that he owed money to Visconti. Cruel, cowardly murder. And here was the instrument—the bent poker!

He reached out his hand to steady himself against the wall, then snatched it back. There was blood on that hand, and fingerprints on the wall. . . .

He ran outside, picked up snow, rubbed his hand clean. He went back, caught up the iron by its clean end, and, taking this outside, flung it far away. For a moment, he had respite. Then he thought of the bed.

Yes, as he had suspected—there was a red stain upon the topmost blanket. Fool that he had been not to think of that. He hardly dared to sit down. It was as though whatever he touched, whatever lifeless object, would be stained by the presumption of his guilt and rise, on a day, to give damning evidence against him. But the strength of his knees was unloosed, and he had to sink down into a chair. He told himself that he had to think, but think he could not. His brain spun.

The dead man lay there, in the shadow of the corner, with only a red stain and a faint smile visible upon his face. As though in death Visconti was comforted by the knowledge that an innocent man would hang for his destruction.

Aye, who would think of placing the blame upon chance and a bucking horse? Does a horse buck in the center of a small shack and leave no imprint on the ground?

The ground, to be sure!

He got a shovel and trimmed off the surface where the wet appeared, then he trampled this down, very hard. He spent an hour at the task, looking again and again, from every angle, at the spot, lighting a lamp, and scrutinizing again and again.

At last it seemed to him that the place would pass muster. But then it seemed to Fernald that he heard the beat of horses, horses galloping down the trail. His heart stood still. Were they coming already, then, the messengers of the omnipresent law? He strangled. It was as though the rope already had jerked around his throat.

Then the gleam of the rifle barrel shimmered into his vision, where it lay across two pegs in the wall. In the full magazine of it were fifteen shots, and fifteen shots meant fifteen lives, when the pinch came.

Suddenly it was to Fernald as though he had been lifted, as by the thrust of great wings, into a dizzy height from which he looked down at himself and all the world, and he wondered to find himself wretchedly housed in that sheepcote. Were there not better things in life? Ah, far better, and joy beyond dreaming had been found by others. He felt a great leaping of the heart. The fear that had been shuddering in him vanished.

So he placed the rifle beside the door, opened it, and looked out. There was not a rider in sight. The long trail stretched empty and gleaming among the hills. Every winding of it was familiar to him, a thing prized, because so well known, but now he looked at it with new eyes that scanned the farther horizons, and wished to be beyond them.

There's no murder unless a dead body is found, thought Fernald. He had heard that. And now he vowed, calmly, that the body should disappear, and all traces along with it. The iron bar, for instance, which in his folly, in his panic, he had flung for away. He had simply cast it out where strange eyes might more readily find it. This seemed to him as the action of an idiot, or a mere child, a thing done in the absurd distance of infancy. So it was that he now felt about himself and all that he had been only the moment before he grasped the rifle.

That, it seemed, had turned the trick. A thousand times before this he had grasped the biting cold of the steel, but on this day it was as a charm that altered all his being; the thrill of that touch had run through him with an electric current that still existed in him. He felt taller, more powerful, and yet more light; he knew that he was standing straighter. So the way cleared before him, in an instant.

He got the iron, thrust the end of it into the soil until it was thoroughly cleansed, then, with the grasp of his hands, he bent it slowly straight once more. His hands hurt, but he felt that he loved the pain, for it brought back to his mind the fear that he had seen in the eyes of the vulture, Visconti. He understood very well now. Unarmed, the great Visconti had slain men, but for all that there never had been in his fingers such power as this, able to mold the rigid might of iron.

He went back to the hut, twirling the bar in his hand, smiling. Then he picked up the blanket, swathed the body of the dead man in it, and lifted the burden to his shoulder. A good, solid burden, drooping down before and behind. As he walked, his knees knocked against the feet of the corpse and set them swaying loosely. He was surprised at the warmth that remained in the dead thing and came to him through the thickness of his slicker and of his coat down against his own living flesh. But he went on steadily.

Few men in the world could have endured that weight for such a distance, but Fernald, without pausing, stepped up the hill behind the house and over the ragged ground beyond its summit. He knew exactly the place where he would leave the dead thing. There was a certain broken pile of rocks, weathered to looseness, pried at and split and divided by frosts, stirred by the storm wind. It was at the foot of this that he stretched the body.

Over it he stood for a moment, thoughtful. There would be much money in the wallet of Visconti. He never traveled, fearless as he was, without much cash. However, in a sense that money would be contaminated. Fernald stooped merely to turn the body face down, for he had a touch of compunction at the thought of the massive boulders beating down into even a dead countenance.

Then he went behind the rock pile. Just as he had expected, he was able to locate a keystone. Twice he heaved at it until his tendons cracked, but then it gave suddenly and, loosening with it tons of stone débris, rushed down to bury Pete Visconti.

A rabbit jumped up from the base of the ruin and scuttered away, dodging, every leap as though the devil were after it.

And young Tom Fernald looked and laughed again, freely and loudly.

There was still something to be done, but much was already accomplished. The dusk was gathering, and the storm was blackening the twilight. So much the better for what remained.

He returned to the house and examined everything, minutely, with the lamp. There was nothing to betray him, now, except the blood stain on the doorjamb.

He whittled off the telltale spot, and then rubbed earth over the fresh face of the incision until it was exactly the tone of the surrounding wood. So much for that.

Now the horse of Visconti alone remained, and disposal of it caused him to ponder for a time. There was a great ravine not more than a mile away. He might shoot the mustang and roll the body down into the roar of the water beneath. There it would soon be eaten as with teeth. That seemed the best plan.

He went out, carrying his rifle. It seemed strange to him that he so often had walked abroad without a gun in the preceding days. He had learned better practice, now.

So he mounted the pinto and, taking the roan on the lead, went slowly across country—slowly, since the storm was raving, beating, and tearing at them, and because the roan was delayed by its limping.

At the edge of the ravine, he dismounted, raised the rifle, and pressed the muzzle of it against the temple of the horse. The big beast turned its head. He felt, rather than saw, the eyes that waited for him in the dark of the night. And below them the creek was thundering.

Fernald lowered the gun. He had a sense of guilty weakness about this. In the old days, he had been foolishly soft and gentle with animals, but those days were old indeed, and now he moved in the light of a new era, wherein only logic should reign and illumine his way before him. And yet—it was the lameness of the horse, he felt, that undid him. He cursed his foolishness, but even as he did so, a new idea came to Fernald. The mere removal of the body of the dead man, and of all signs of the crime was not enough. Something should be gained, out of all of this thought, this hazard. Chance had struck a vulture from the skies, but surely some man must profit by that fall.

There was the hidden treasure of the miser. There were the hoarded thousands, the tens of thousands that must be hidden somewhere about the house of Visconti. In a trice he had made up his mind that the horse of Pete Visconti must be returned to its own pasture. And perhaps he, Fernald, would take something more than grass from the place.

IV

There were five slow miles across country with the lame horse on the lead before Fernald reached the Visconti place. It was about eleven o'clock of the night, so far as he could guess, when he put the lame roan in the pasture behind the barn. There the wall of the barns itself would give shelter against the storm; unless the wind changed, there was plenty of grass for food, and a runlet of water crossed the upper end of the field. If no man came for days, or years, the horse might still thrive. This thought contented Fernald.

His pinto, he had tethered among flinty rocks a full mile from the house. It was not likely that anyone would know the hoof marks of the pinto, but all things appeared more or less simple to modern investigators of crime. He had heard much about the prodigious feats of the criminal observers. That was the reason he had left the horse so far away. His own boots might make marks on the ground that could be followed, but not for long. The storm would cover over and wash out such mere surface impressions. So he crossed from the barn to the house of Visconti.

It was a shack very much like his own, almost worse built, a little larger, perhaps. The door was locked, but he tore the bolt through the rotten wood, and wondered at a man like Visconti trusting to such a shallow protection. Then he went inside, found a lamp, and lighted it. There were two windows, and neither shutters nor curtains to cover them. Like two eyes they were now shining out into the heart of the night, perhaps conveying an intelligible message to someone. Perhaps one more of the murderous crew who had tried for the life and treasures of Visconti would slip up now. If he did not find the host, that made but a small difference. He might use his gun on the actual occupant, and then trust to his wits in making the search.

However, this danger must be endured for a few minutes. Even murder was not likely to be abroad in such weather as this; the wind seemed trying to pry the roof off the shack. Moreover, the thickness of the storm would prevent the light through the windows from traveling far.

When Fernald had made up his mind that the danger was unavoidable, he composed himself. No real panic had grown up in his mind. It seemed to him that he could never again in his life find such a capacity for fear as he had had before, on this day when he took the rifle from the wall of his cabin. It was in his hand still, a cold but a true comforter.

Raising the lamp, he looked carefully around the shack. The stove was like his own. Two legs had been broken off and wooden blocks served in their stead. The bed was a bunk built against the wall, covered with a heap of soiled blankets. There were two or three common wooden boxes near the bed, filled apparently with clothes and with papers of various kinds. From pegs along the wall hung clothing, most of it half molded green with age, falling to pieces of its own weight, but still retained by the miser even when he could not wear it. Otherwise, there was little in the room except a homemade table, two stools, and a rack containing a good rifle, a double-barreled sawed-off shotgun, and a pair of revolvers. There was nothing more.

Suddenly Fernald knew that the treasure could not be here. It was not far, to be sure. It was somewhere near, so that the master could almost keep his eye upon it, but an instinct told Fernald that Visconti would never hide the money in this narrow space, which was so sure to be hunted over and over by the seekers. *Somewhere near, somewhere outside the house.*

Suddenly he was aware that the storm had fallen. In place of the yelling of the wind, a vast silence covered the mountains, and, through the silence, spies seemed to be creeping up on him.

He put out the lamp, and went into the outer darkness. There he stood, pondering. There was a small woodshed beside the shack, and a little smokehouse near it. There was the windlass of a well just to the left. Otherwise, there was nothing made by man between the house and the barn.

Well, why not the barn, or the granary that stood beside it? Either of those places might be the correct ones, and either of them offered a thousand places where the money might be secluded—in a sack of wheat, or of crushed barley, for instance, since the bulk might not be great. Or it might be stowed in a portion of the mow of the barn, or dug into the soil near it. Yes, or some hollow tree near the house would be sufficient.

He began to feel, gloomily, that his task was a foolish one, and that he could have told from a distance that, where so many had failed, he, of course, could never succeed. However, he would not give up at once. He was striving to think of something—striving to force his mind to act along the lines of the mind of the dead Visconti.

At length, he shrugged his shoulders and gave up the

problem. He was thirsty, thirsty as a man who has been losing blood, so he went to the well, and unwound the windlass, lowering the bucket that went down to a considerable distance before it struck water. Then he drew it up, and pulled the bucket the final arm haul by grasping the rope. So securing the bucket, he raised it to his lips and drank from the surface like a horse from a trough. It was good water, cold as snow and pure as a running spring. *Too good for Visconti,* he told himself.

He emptied it, glad that a rope could not retain finger marks. He thought it rather odd that Visconti, a man so miserly, should use new rope in his well. Perhaps the old one had just broken, however. Yet, even so, this rope seemed two or three times the dimensions necessary to support a well bucket. That, again, was a surprise, a great surprise. Was Visconti sometimes careless in his spending of pennies?

The thought was so novel to Fernald that he sat for a moment on the stone rim of the well, considering the man, his peculiarities. But no one, surely, had ever known him to fail to calculate to the utmost scruple every penny of his money. This rope, then—why was it there? Support a bucket? Yes, or a man. A horse might pull on it as a derrick rope, in fact. . . .

Suddenly he whistled softly to himself, as though calling home an important thought. The next instant he was lowering the bucket. He sent it down to water, then blocked the windlass so that it might not stir, and finally swung himself down into the well, lowering away along the rope.

Several arm's length from the top, he twisted one leg in the rope for support, and then scratched a match and looked about him. All above him, the stones were gray or green with lichens or moss. He looked down, and to the left, a foot or so beneath his hand, he saw what he wanted—a large stone outlined by a dark streak—a streak such as might be left by the frequent removals of the block from the wall in which it stood, the process rubbing away the moss at its edges.

He lowered himself until it was shoulder high, than rapped on it. A hollow sound came forth. He wedged his fingers in at the top and pulled. There was no effect at first, but finally the stone turned outward as on a hinge, and left a little aperture. The heart of Fernald leaped into his throat. For he knew, now, that he had found what he wanted.

Into the hole he thrust his hand, fumbled, and touched the cold, damp surface of oiled silk. Surety became doubly sure. He drew it out—a small packet. And by match light, he examined the contents. It contained, as he had dared to dream, a sheaf of bills. There were twenties and fifties—100 of them closely compacted. That very morning, he would have felt that the contents made a fortune. Now, it seemed little—to a man liable to being charged with murder.

He put the little packet into his pocket and reached into the hole again. There was package after package, and, drawing them out, he stowed them about his clothes. Still his mind was deliberate. Eighteen of those packets he counted before his exploring fingers found the interior of the cavity empty. Then he hauled himself lightly, easily, hand over hand, to the top of the well, and stepped on firm ground again.

But nothing must be forgotten. Perhaps long days would pass before anyone discovered that Visconti had disappeared from his house. On the other hand, the very next morning a close inquiry might be made into everything. The keenest eyes in the world might come and peer about the place.

First of all, he drew the bucket to the top of the wall as he had found it. Then he returned to the house, and relighted the lamp. A dozen of his foot marks remained visible on the compacted earthen floor, and these he obliterated with care, one by one.

As he finished, he looked up to the face of a battered, rusty little alarm clock that stood on the table, and saw that it was after two in the morning. He had spent much time for his search. It had seemed to him a half hour. It was really five or six times as long.

But at last he could leave the place. His nerves had been twitching to be gone for a long time, and now he set off across country at a good gait. He did not go directly to the spot where he had left his horse. It might be that, in spite of his precautions, searchers would discover his trail. If so, he must set them a problem on the back trail. And this he did. It took him an hour of rapid walking, doubling back and forth, before he permitted himself to come to the spot where the pinto waited.

It whinnied softy when the scent of the master came down to it on the wind, and the heart of Fernald jumped. He schooled himself instantly. From this moment, he told himself, nerves must disappear. He must act with calm not alone in the middle of masking darkness, but in broad daylight, with a crowd about him. The least start, a change of color, a careless word, might twist and knot the rope about his neck.

So he mounted the pinto and made the return journey.

As he neared his own place, it no longer seemed to him as a home, but as a weak spot in his armor, a point at which the rest of the world could always find him. So long as he lived here, the law possessed a master key and might walk in upon him by night or by day. However, the last thing that he must dream of was flight from the house, at present. Instead of that, he would have to remain and tend the sheep industriously, patiently, for weeks, perhaps for months.

The sheep! He began to laugh, but with a growling sound deep in his throat.

V

By the way he traveled, it was fully five in the morning when he had put up the pinto. And this he did with care, also. For he rubbed the mustang down so as to remove the traces of sweat, as far as possible, and gave the horse a good feed. Then he went to the house.

The wind had risen again, and with a more threatening howl in its voice than ever. It carried the same stinging streaks of sleet, and the same rattling volleys of hail.

It was too late for anyone to be up; it was too early for anyone to be abroad. Therefore he lighted his lamp with a sense of security so great that he did not even take care to curtain the window with a blanket, which he could easily have done. Neither did he first sit down to the counting of the treasure. It bulged in his pockets. It pressed him with a weight of joy. And he put off the glad moment while he kindled a fire and put on the coffee pot again.

He would not have time to sleep that night or morning. He must be out at his work with the sheep in case chance passers-by should go that way to note him. He must not be found asleep in the middle of the morning. Indeed, nothing must occur to raise question.

When the coffee had boiled, he poured himself out a good tin of it, and sat down to sip, and to work.

Work? Aye, he could work like this forever, drifting treasure through his fingers. Joy kept surging up in him, making him tremble, putting his teeth on edge like a strange liquor. And, in the meantime, he was counting.

In each packet the sum differed. He found one with $50,000. That was the largest sum. The rest varied down to the first one he had taken out, the smallest sum of all. And when he had finished, he had added up this dizzy total of $435,000! It stood stacked before him, the bills segregated according to their denomination.

That was not all he found. There were the mortgages, the little thin sheets of paper on which so many a small farmer had signed away his hopes of future happiness, so to speak, to get the help in the present hour of need.

Well, those signatures would no longer represent a hell of dread. He opened the stove and thrust them in, a handful. His own mortgage was among the rest. As he heard the flame roar suddenly up the chimney, he felt as though his own old life, its cares, its bitter, grimy burdens were being swept away. He turned, smiling, from the stove, and saw pressed against the window the face of the devil. Or was it only the ugly features of Bill Ransome, the robber and ruffian?

The face had disappeared instantly. Now the door opened. A gust of wind entered, and fluttered the bills under the weights that held them down.

How suddenly, how simply retribution had struck against young Fernald. Through his first small carelessness, disaster had reached him. Through the smallest flaw in armor, a needle may reach the heart of the wearer. He saw that all his former precautions were as nothing. By one act he had undone himself.

Ransome stood before him, grinning like a beast, his eyes beastly green as well. He was wet. His face was blue and white with the cold and the exposure of a long ride, but the flare of his nostrils told that it was not of cold that he was thinking just then.

The heart of Fernald grew as calm as a stone. Suddenly he had made up his mind, and the resolve in him was unalterable. He looked at the revolver in the hand of Ransome, and it seemed a foolish little toy—a mere trifle, compared with the vastness of that thing which lay there on the table.

"So you got it," said Ransome. "You got the money out of

old Visconti, did you?"

The use of the name was almost a shock to Fernald, but now
he discovered that the nerves by an act of will may be insulated,
so that disturbing shocks will not actually come home to the
brain. This thrill of horror, he suppressed as it began.

"It takes a sneak to catch a sneak," said Ransome. "Me, I've
combed that place from head to foot, but not a dog-gone dollar
could I find. But you, you sneak . . . you thief . . . you could
find it, all right."

He was working himself up into a passion. Fernald watched
the progress of it curiously.

"I make a touch and get a couple hundred out of you, and
you ain't man enough to defend yourself," said Ransome, "but,
by God, you're man enough to go and snoop around the Visconti place till you find where he hid the stuff, eh?" Then he
asked, lowering his voice almost to awe: "How did it feel,
sneakin' around the house, like that? How did it feel, Tommy?
Kind of gave you the gooseflesh, I reckon?"

Fernald merely shrugged his shoulders. He would commit
himself to nothing.

Ransome scowled again. He pointed to the table, saying:
"How much?"

"Four hundred and thirty-five thousand," Fernald answered.

"Four . . . hundred . . . and. . . ." The sum would not frame
itself upon the lips of the robber. "My God," he said at last,
"when I got trimmed in that poker game, last night, I was pretty
sore. I didn't know it was sendin' me out on the road to find
my fortune. And there she lies. There she is, right under my
nose!" He scowled more darkly than before at Fernald. "Lucky
thing for you, you fool, that you didn't have somebody else look
in on you, somebody that might've turned you over to the
police. That's what would've happened. But me, I'm gonna let
you go. I'll have the coin, and let you go. I won't be a hog,

neither. I'll give you one of them stacks. One of them little stacks, right there next to you. That'll be enough to make a sheep walker rich, I guess." He laughed as he spoke. His eyes were wild with greed and with joy. "Who would have thought," he went on, "that Sleepy Tom was my luck . . . Tommy the coward, the fool." He drew in his breath as though drinking. He swallowed.

"Here," said Fernald, "sit down and have some coffee. Let's talk a minute."

"I'll drink some coffee," said the other. "But what's there to talk about . . . except how you got it?"

"You ought to let me have more than you plan to do," said Fernald. "That's not much. There's twenty piles, Bill. You ought to give me more."

"How much?" asked Ransome, his hands twitching, the gun jerking, also.

"Half, I'd say," said Fernald.

"Are you half a man?" roared Ransome. "How come you to rate half when you ain't half a man? No, by God, I dunno that I'll leave you a penny."

"That's hard," said Fernald.

"Is it? It's better to have no money than to be dead, ain't it?"

"Yes, I guess it is."

"You can bet that it is."

"But you wouldn't murder me, Bill. I guess you wouldn't murder me."

"Wouldn't I?" Ransome sneered. "You think nothin' of cuttin' the throat of one of your sheep. I'd think no more of soaking a bullet in between your eyes. You ain't a man. You're only a damn' blattin' sheep, I guess."

"It's hard, Bill," Fernald said.

"Yeah, you think so now. But you try to make any trouble about this, and I'm gonna come back if I have to come from the end of the earth, and I'm gonna let the life out of you like the water out of a smashed canteen. You hear?"

"Yeah . . . I hear," said Fernald. "But let me have one of these stacks. One of the small stacks, Bill."

"You? I dunno. I oughtn't to. But I'm free and easy. Come easy and go easy. But now that I'm a man with a fortune, I'm gonna be a damn' sight more careful. I'm gonna take care of my coin. Well, I'll let you have one of 'em."

"Which one, Bill?" asked Fernald, stepping to the very edge of the table, as Ransome did the same.

Not a yard separated them.

"Maybe that one in the corner," said Ransome, pointing with the Colt.

Fernald caught the gun hand just below the wrist. It doubled under the enormous pressure of his grasp and the gun squeezed out on the top of the table, falling softly across two money stacks.

"Why . . . you damn' . . . you fool!" gasped Ransome, and reached for the gun with his free hand.

Fernald picked the hand out of the air and held it easily. And when Ransome, amazement more than fear in his eyes, lurched back, Fernald came with him, leaping lightly over the table. The shoulders of the robber struck against the wall of the house, and there he stood, bewildered, twitching, horror in his face. Fernald had to look up at him a little.

He was smiling, and a coldness like death was in his heart. He felt as during that other moment when he thought he had heard the beating of the hoofs of horses along the road.

"You fat . . . you damn' yaller-hearted . . . ," grunted Ransome, and struggled with all his might, jerking up a knee at the groin of the other.

Fernald jerked him to the floor and sat on the heaving chest.

Suddenly the struggling ceased. The horror remained on the

face of Ransome, the bewilderment with it.

"How'd you do it?" he groaned. "Leave go my hands. You're breakin' the bones."

"It'll soon be over, Bill," said Fernald. "Don't you worry just now about a few broken bones."

"Whatcha mean to do, Tommy?" growled Bill.

Fernald smiled down into the brutal face. "What do I do to the sheep, when I need mutton?" he asked.

"Tommy, you wouldn't go and murder an old friend like me that went to school with you?" Ransome pleaded. "You wouldn't . . . oh, my God, you would Tommy . . . !"

"Stop screaming," said Fernald. "It won't last long."

He took both the hands of the other in one of his. Furiously Ransome struggled, but the grip held. Even Fernald was amazed. Big as the man was, he was a helpless child in that grasp.

Then, reaching up his free hand, Fernald took the revolver from the table.

"No!" screeched Ransome. "No, no, Tommy . . . I'll be your slave. I'll be your slave for life! You wouldn't murder me! Oh, God, I'm young, Tommy. I've led a rotten life. If you kill me now, I'll go to hell!"

"You've been in hell all your days, I think," said Fernald without emotion. "Wherever you've been, you've made hell all around you. You wanted to see me ruined today. There's not a man in the world that needs killing as badly as you need it. And you're going to get it now. Your troubles are about over, Bill."

He took the revolver by the long barrel and weighed it above the face of Ransome.

Suddenly the latter ceased struggling entirely. He lay perfectly still, his eyes closed, his face ghastly. The terrible hammering of his heart shook the entire body of the conqueror.

"God have mercy on me," said Ransome. "I been a hound. I

meant someday to change. God, have mercy on my rotten soul."

I'm being a beast, Fernald said to himself. *Even the finding of the money was no better than this. Not as good. I want to kill him. God, how I want to kill him. I want to smash his brains out . . . and he lies there and yammers about God.*

"Bill," he said aloud.

There was no answer.

Bill was whispering to himself, words that could not be heard.

Fernald stood up. "Get up," he said. "I can't kill you. I ought to. I know I'm a fool. But I can't kill you."

VI

He was never to forget, not to his death day, the eyes of Ransome as the man looked up at him, through a mist of terror, out of another world, which seemed already to be receiving him. "D'you mean that, Tom?" muttered the robber.

Fernald replied with a mute gesture.

Ransome got to his elbows, to his knees, to his feet. He stood with his back against the wall, one hand thrown up against his face. There was blood staining that hand. It had spurted from beneath the fingernails under the vast pressure of Fernald's hold.

The latter looked at the picture of Ransome with the same curiously detached interest that he had felt before.

Bill Ransome reached for a chair, found it by fumbling, sank into it, and buried his face in his hands.

"Here," said Fernald, a moment later. "Here's some coffee. Take this. You're done up for a minute."

Ransome shook his head. He spoke without looking up, his grimy, red-stained hands still pressed over his face. "It's kind of a miracle. It's a thing I don't understand. Why should I be alive?"

"Because I'm a fool," said Fernald. "That's the reason. Because I'm only a sheepherder, as you said before."

Ransome groaned. "You had mighty little to do with it," he said.

"No? Who did, then?"

Ransome pointed a finger upward, and Fernald, in surprise, actually glanced toward the rafters, before he understood what Ransome meant. The man seemed to think that that last, dying prayer of his had been heard by the Almighty, and instantly answered.

"You're a fool, Bill," said Fernald. "It's only because there's a weak streak in me. I don't like murder, Ransome. How about you? Here, man . . . drink this coffee."

Ransome swallowed the draft scalding hot, and a second cup after it. He made a cigarette, lighted it, and smoked with great inhalations. Still he looked down, probing into his own thoughts. "Something happened," he said at last. "I dunno what."

"'You've got blood on your face, Bill," said Fernald. "That's one thing that happened. There's a basin and a bucket of water. Go wash it off."

"I've got blood on my face," Bill Ransome said in the same dazed manner. "I've got blood on my rotten soul, too. I been no good. I been the lowest in the world. I been so low, Tom, that if I lived a hundred years, prayin' and doin' good, I never could make up for what's happened. Not for the things that I've done in the world. You ought to've killed me. I ain't worthy to live."

"You're taking it pretty hard," said Fernald. "You'll feel better, after a while. You'll feel well enough to go and tell some of your crooked friends what you've seen here on my table. Or else, you'll tell the sheriff, to get a stand in with him."

Ransome, to the amazement of Fernald, nodded.

"Perhaps I will," he said. "I've been as low as that. Honor among thieves. No . . . I ain't even had that. Maybe I'll be that low again. But I dunno. I got a hope . . . I got a funny kind of a hope. . . ." He paused.

"Look here," said Fernald. "You're gonna go dippy, if you keep on with these here ideas. You quit it, Bill. You've been no friend to me, but I don't want to see you go dippy. I'd rather see you dead."

The other stretched forth a questioning hand. "You wanted terrible bad to kill me, Tom. Ain't that so?"

"Yes, that's so."

"Yeah, I know it. I seen the death in your eyes . . . I seen it your hand, too, all ready for me. But it didn't come down. What stopped your hand? You say it was yourself. I hope that it was something else . . . only I know that there ain't any reason why I should've been saved by anything else."

"Bill, you poor fool," said Fernald, "d'you think that God Almighty is bothering about you. But you'll go crazy, if you start thinking that way."

"He wouldn't let me die," Ransome said solemnly. "He sort of thought that I was too mean and low a man to die. I wasn't good enough to die, yet. It ain't right that what I am should be snuffed out and the soul of him stand for a man, in a man's shape . . . and . . . ?" He pressed his hands against his temples, then drew in a great breath. "I gotta stop thinkin'," he said. "My brain, it's turnin' around and around inside of my head."

"You'll feel better, after a while," insisted young Fernald. "Keep hold of yourself. That's all. Have some more coffee. And then if your hoss is waiting, I won't keep you any more."

"I'll go," Ransome said, rising.

He went to the door, fumbled blindly, found the latch, and opened it. As he stepped out, the storm cuffed him into a stagger. He came reeling back, half a step, and had to lean far

41

forward before he could make headway.

Fernald thrust the door to behind him. Then, looking around him, he saw that the day was beginning. A film of gray covered the single window.

He set about his business, soberly, only pausing at the window long enough to see Ransome ride out into the wind. Still the form of Ransome, bowed in the saddle, haunted him during the day, and the face of Ransome with the red marks of his own blood upon it.

Something had happened in the soul of that man, to be sure. How long would it be before Bill Ransome carried to the town his strange report?

No later than the end of that day, of course. Either the officers of the law would know of the affair, or else—more probably—Bill himself and some of his friends would return to rob the shepherd of his spoils. To withstand them, he could do what?

To run away was to salvage the money for only a short time. He knew that flight almost inevitably is a running into the hands of the law. The long arm of order and right will eventually pick out even the craftiest of criminals.

He could not run. He must remain, surrounded with nameless dangers. And what could his defense be?

He saw the line of it clearly. In the first place, the money must be concealed. Among the rocks of his land, he could find many places, one as good as the other. He would divide the money, say, into three parts of about $150,000 each. If one or even two should be found, something more would remain. If he were imprisoned, he would have a fortune waiting when he at last was released.

So much was clearly the right way to go about his business.

Suppose, then, that the friends of Ransome came to commit the robbery? He would have to be away from the house, lying out somewhere on his place, ostensibly to look after the sheep during this bitter weather, really so that he might not be located. And if he saw them from afar, they would taste some of the contents of his rifle!

He smiled, when he thought of that. He had always been a good shot; he simply could not afford to waste ammunition with misses; he could not afford to go hungry, either. One learns exquisite precision, when it is necessary to clip off the head of a squirrel rather than risk smashing the entire body to pieces with a heavy slug. And if the robbers came, he might be able to give them something more important than money, in the consideration of this world and the world hereafter.

But if it were the law to which Ransome appealed? In that case, he would take the line that Ransome was lying. Upon Ransome's side would be, of course, the mysterious disappearance of Visconti, which would make it probable that the miser had been murdered for the sake of his money.

On the other hand, there was the long life of quiet and hard work for which he, Fernald, was well known. In the entire county there could hardly be found a man less likely to commit a crime of any sort, far less a deed of blood. The good citizens would simply fail to think the thing possible.

This conception made Fernald sneer. They would have a chance, one day, to find out that he was made of metal a little sterner than they thought.

Suppose, then, that all went well—that he avoided the law and the robbery friends of Ransome—then what? Patience and time would help him. He could allow his prosperity to increase by slow stages.

The disappearance of the miser and his mortgage, at one stroke, would of course give him some grounds to appear more prosperous. And when he made sales, no one would know exactly how much he had really made. He could begin to trade more, sell and buy more often, building up a bank account composed, apparently, of the profits of the business, but in reality almost entirely recruited from the buried treasure.

This would be a slow business. But, in the meantime, he could wait for a chance to sell, even a chance that was not greatly to his advantage. And then, moving to a far distant community, moving into a new line of work, he could at once establish himself on such a large scale that soon all of his hidden money would be at work for him.

That was wealth, content, and a cunning victory over the brain of the world.

This was the scheme that he evolved as he ate his breakfast. Then he went out into the blast of the wind. It was as strong as ever. He had not slept all the night through but had been almost constantly active, but, nevertheless, he felt no sense of fatigue. His brain was clear and his body was stronger than ever. For he was equipped with a new confidence that fortified him, and made him as a thing of iron.

So he strode with his stuffed pockets, the slicker whipping about his legs, up among his highlands. He passed the sepulcher of the dead man, and noted with pleasure that all of the rocks had been glassed over with frozen sleet. By the time that had melted away, and the spring was there, who would dream of looking here for a dead body?

Only, in the sky above the spot, he saw a pair of buzzards circling into the wind and with it, with equal ease. They knew, it seemed, what lay beneath them, under the mass of stone.

VII

The heart of young Fernald was on fire. But the eye of Fernald remained the calmest blue gray in the world as the days passed.

He was waiting for fate, for chance, and the comings of

golden hope. And, behind all of those abstractions, he had knowledge of buried treasure and a buried body over the rocky grave of which every day the buzzards still would be circling.

But if they knew, men did not. At least, there was no visit paid to him by Ransome and company. Neither did the sheriff nor any of his men come riding out with guns. One day went by calmly, quietly, like the next. Winter ended, and spring began, and the white retreated far up the slopes of Mount Griffon, and the green thrust and the flowers pricked the green with dapplings of color. But still he was left alone. And the trail that passed close to his shack seemed, in fact, more empty than ever.

Then he went to one of his rocky cairns and opened it, and took out a single packet of money, the least of all, with a scant $35,000 in it. Never before, saving once only, had so much money been in his hands. But he regarded it as a mere penny. Even this was too much for him to put into circulation as his own property in a single day. But he rode to town on the pinto with it, prepared to spend what he could in a solid way.

The town of Griffon was wakening with the warmth of the spring. Old Mrs. Newman sat at her door in the sun. Tod Murphy, the ancient, was hoeing in his garden. In the street, children raced and tumbled, and their yells ran like war cries of red Indians through the thickets of the vacant lots.

But in the midst of all this bustle and life, no one paid the slightest attention to Tom Fernald. They never had. It was a custom, he hoped calmly, that they would persist in.

He went to the butcher, Sam Martin, and tried to sell Sam an installment of sheep, but Martin was overstocked and dismissed him with blunt words. That was a disappointment, but Fernald could not afford to allow himself to be upset by small things.

He walked into Joe Bane's saloon near the butcher shop. After he had made a sale, he always went in there and took one drink of good old bourbon. Never more than one. Perhaps in this way he consumed three or four glasses of whiskey in the course of a year. Now he took the farthest, most obscure corner of the bar, and was so lost in the shadow that it was some time before the bartender saw him and asked his pleasure. He ordered the drink, tasted it, poured it down. It circulated quickly through his veins. A thread of fire was woven into his consciousness; a hot mist struck up across his eyes. But he told himself that this was bad. He must not allow himself to be swept off his feet; he must keep his brain free from any tarnishing. For who could tell when its keenest edge would be tried?

The bartender knew him. He even deigned to waste a few words on this rare customer. He wanted to know how things were going on the farm.

"Pretty well," said Fernald. "How's things around town?"

"Oh, things are all right," said the bartender. "Things are better'n usual. Bill Ransome has gone and joined the church." He laughed softly as he said this. "Ain't that right, Ed?" he asked of a man leaning at the bar.

Ed Walters, tall, lean, brown of face, turned a sour expression of thought upon the barkeep.

"He's done better than go to church . . . he's gone to work," he said.

"He never was much on working," Fernald said quietly.

"Yeah. But he's working now. He's working hard. He's gonna make good. He don't mind when the boys hand him a laugh. He smiles back at 'em. Ain't a day," went on Ed Walters, deputy sheriff, "when some of the boys don't go down to Riggs's blacksmith shop and look Bill over. Bill's covered with grease and dust and soot, but he don't mind. He sticks to his job. He's gonna make good. I never knew that there was so much stuff in him, but it's there."

Fernald, listening, did not smile. But he felt a stirring of a vast contempt in his heart. How base and small and petty was human nature, when such a fellow as Bill Ransome could regard himself as the object of a miracle, a direct act of interposition on the part of God.

"Bill was always a pretty strong fellow," he said.

"He's gettin' stronger," said the barkeep. "I was talkin' with Riggs in here the other day. He says that the second day that Bill was swingin' the fourteen-pound sledge, Riggs seen the hammer put down, and the handle was all over blood. He looked at the hands of Ransome, and they was covered with blisters that had busted.

"'You've gone and ruined your hands, pretty near,' says Riggs.

"'They seem to be a bit skinned up,' says Ransome, and looks down at his hands as though he hadn't noticed them before."

"He was just bluffing, I suppose," said Fernald.

The deputy sheriff swung his head slowly about and stared at Fernald.

"Bill kept right on workin' with raw hands," he declared. "Would you've had the guts to do that, Tommy?"

"Maybe not," said Fernald.

"Then shut yer face," said Ed Walters, "when we're talkin' about real men."

It was a brutal speech, but it did not jar upon Fernald. He had heard similar language used to his face before this, but on this day he looked calmly at Walters and knew that he could take the man in his bare hands and break him. But he allowed none of this knowledge to appear in his glance. He took a sort of fierce delight in the insult. They must not know the truth about the new Fernald. They must not even dream of what he really was under the skin. So he looked back at Ed Walters and shrugged his shoulders a little.

The barkeeper, too, favored Fernald with a glance of contempt.

"Ransome is a man that's gonna be heard of," he went on. "I was to talkin' to the parson the other day. He's a friendly like kind of a man, I gotta say. I never been inside of his church, and I guess I won't till the day that they bury me out of it, maybe. But it don't make no difference to the parson. He treats me just the same. Well, that's all right, and he walks along by me and tells me how Bill Ransome comes over after night, bloody hands and all, and works in his vegetable garden behind his house for nothin', and won't take no pay. An' how Bill is readin' the Bible every night, and workin' over it like a kid in school. You could laugh, maybe, but I say that something has happened to Bill, and, when I say it, I mean it."

He stared at Fernald, as though daring a hostile comment, but Fernald merely said: "Well, I'm glad to hear about Bill turning straight. Him and me went to school together. I've got nothing against him. What else has been going on?"

"Oh, nothin' much," said the bartender, bored with this conversation. "Not since old Visconti was bumped off."

"Hold on," said Fernald. "When did that happen?"

Both men turned and stared at him.

"Don't you know nothin'?" snarled Ed Walters. His temper was never good, and now it seemed more raw than ever.

"He's stuck away off there in the hills," said the bartender.

"Yeah, him and his damned sheep," said Walters, unpacified.

"All he can do is to come into town and slam real men, like Bill Ransome."

The bartender, after all, was a peacemaker, and he seemed to feel both scorn and pity for the manner in which Fernald was absorbing all of these insults. At last he said: "You know, Visconti was killed. At least, he disappeared, and I guess that means that somebody got to him finally. They found his roan in the pasture, dead lame. And they found the house closed, and mold everywhere. Been away for days, it looked like. And there ain't been track nor trace of Visconti ever since."

"I'm glad of it," said Fernald, making his voice burst out strongly.

"Yeah, there's others that are glad, too," said Ed Walters. "I guess you owed him money. So did a lot more. And I'll tell you what . . . it was one of the lot of you that done the trick." He scowled straight down the bar toward Fernald as he said this.

A faint tingling passed through the flesh of the shepherd. He could hardly believe what he had heard.

"Aw, come on, Ed," said the bartender, still peace-making, "you wouldn't be saying that Tommy, here, would be going around bumping off people like Visconti, would you?"

"Any rat can bite, when it's got into a corner," said the deputy sheriff more sourly than ever. "Why not this one? He owed money to Visconti. By thunder, I think that he's changin' color, right now." He strode towards Fernald, pointing with extended arm.

And the latter shrugged his shoulders. "Who you trying to cover up, Ed?" he asked. "What's happened to some friend of yours, that you want to stick the blame of Visconti on me?"

The face of Walters, never very pleasant, now became positively black. His lips twisted, and his brow contorted. "You've picked up some lip, have you, since you been around here last?" he demanded. "You've got fresh, have you?"

"You've just been calling me a murderer, Ed," said Fernald. "You don't expect me to swallow that, do you?"

"Maybe you'll swallow worse than that, before I'm through with you," said Walters. "I don't like the look of you."

"Hold on, Ed," said the bartender. "What's the matter with you? You been drinkin' too much, or something. I don't want you to be talkin' like that in here."

Ed Walters did not retreat, however, but fixed upon Fernald a steady glare, until the latter shrugged his shoulders again, and stepped back from the bar.

"I'll see what's going on in the back room," he said to the barkeep. "Ed seems to want trouble, and you all know that I'm not a fighting man."

He saw the dark sneer curl the wolfish upper lip of Walters. He heard the barkeep grunt with disgust, but he minded neither of these expressions of contempt. What was fixed in his mind was the sense of his real power, and the knowledge that he would mask it from all the world as long as possible. In the back room, Joe Bane himself would be running a gambling game of some sort, and he determined to look on.

VIII

He was right. The roulette wheel was spinning busily, and around the table were half a dozen fellows, most of them unknown to young Fernald. They played for big stakes with a carelessness that amazed him; he would have laid a large bet himself that their money was not honest.

But that was nothing in the life of Joe Bane. Pale, grim, emotionless, his eyes almost as faded and colorless as his sandy hair, Bane stood behind the wheel and spun it. His game was an honest one. He used to say that the percentage of the house was big enough to break anybody who was fool enough to play against the wheel, no matter with what a system. But fools were more or less plentiful in the town of Griffon, and Joe's roulette wheel, or faro outfit, constantly brought him in a sizeable revenue. For the rest, he was one of the most respected and one of the most feared men in the town. He was respected because he was behind every movement for the betterment of the place.

"I want drinkers, not drunkards," he used to say, and he meant it. His honesty was absolute; his word was as good as his bond; his friendship was a thing rarely given, and then given forever.

He was feared, on the other hand, because he was one of those rare men who avoid trouble but never run from it. Joe Bane had fought only four times in his life, but he had left four dead men behind him. His skill with a gun was proverbial as his unwillingness to use one. In short, Joe Bane was one of those fellows whose capacities and peculiarities are sufficient to make him be called a character.

Fernald watched a few turns of the wheel, and then he ventured $5 on a single number. It was the seven, which had not turned up recently, but he could hardly believe his eyes when the wheel stopped and seven won. Suddenly his $5 had altered to a $175.

That was very little to a man who had almost half a million. But his rôle, he knew, called now for astonishment, and for greedy delight. He expressed both, scooping in the stack of winnings with a gasp. Even the emotionless Joe Bane looked up at him with a faint smile that was his nearest approach to cordiality.

"Maybe this is your lucky day, Tommy," he said.

"Yeah, maybe it is," said Tommy Fernald. "I'm going to play it that way, anyway."

Bane risked one word of advice. "It takes a long run of luck to beat the wheel, Tom. You better pull out with your winnings. I won't call you a quitter."

"Thanks, Joe," said Fernald. "But I'm going to try my hand again."

The others grinned. They laid their own bets, with an eye upon Fernald. He covered the black with $100, straightway, and the black—won!

He hardly considered the money that he took in. Here was a manner in which he could pile up enough winnings to catch the public eye. And, once the winnings were made, he could treble them out of his own stores of wealth. Could he not open a bank account and tell the cashier that the basis of it was "big winnings" at Joe Bane's? It would go hard if he did not make the winning of $500 a sufficient reason for expending $1,500.

All of this was in his mind as the game went on. He won $1,000, $1,100—dropped to $400—rose to $1,500—it was hard for them to keep track of him, now, how much he had either won or lost. For thousands of dollars were washing across the roulette table as the other gamblers plunged, winning or losing in turn. Who was to say how many dollars he was ahead—or behind.

For now he began to dip deeper into the paper money which he had brought in with him. From the packet that contained most of it, he took out fifties and hundreds. A cold glow of excitement seized upon him. His winning or losing were nothing to him.

He began to see that he could make this game the excuse for the establishment of credit in the bank not of $1,500 but of $5,000, say. In short, he would establish himself at a stroke as a real man of luck and fortune. After that, people would be envious, no doubt, but not suspicious. That $5,000 he would turn into $50,000, before many months passed, and no one would doubt that he had made the sum by honest speculation.

So a great content passed through the body and the mind of Fernald. It was shortening the period during which he would have had to exercise patience. He was making it a tenth as long as it might well have been.

Once or twice, he felt the impassive eye of Joe Bane fixed very steadily upon him. There was no comment in that eye, but Fernald could guess at the astonishment of the gambler in this speculation on the part of the shepherd.

"It's my lucky day, Joe," he said not once, but many times. "I feel the luck in me, and it's got to come out."

Into the middle of the afternoon he played. Three of the strangers were broke, and three were winners. The three who had failed fell back and watched unconcernedly while their companions staked higher and faster than ever.

And young Fernald staked with them. His winnings, he judged, were only $2,000 or $3,000, but he was shoving across the board, in addition to this, everything that he had in his pocket. Every penny of his original stake had not been at least once through the hands of Joe Bane, and some of the paper came back to him, mixed with others.

At last, he judged that time had come to withdraw. He could safely bank $5,000 now. So he waved to Joe Bane. "I'm gonna quit while I'm rich, Joe," he said.

Joe Bane made no response. But his cold eye was still felt by Fernald as he turned away from the room.

In the barroom, he found that Walters was still leaning against the bar silently, gloomily. He turned his head and favored Fernald with a silent, wolfish sneer, and the latter was glad to escape out into the brilliant, cutting force of the sunshine.

He went straight to the bank, and shoved across the counter of the receiving teller of the Mining and Merchants' Bank a stack of big bills and small. The teller gaped.

"Have you sold out, Tom?" he asked.

"I struck it lucky," said Fernald. "I had my lucky day. I took five dollars to Joe Bane's roulette wheel, and I turned it into five thousand. Ever hear of luck as big as that?" And he gripped the edge of the counter, and leaned back his head, and laughed wildly.

The teller grinned with sympathetic envy. "Aye, that's luck," he said. "That's a thousand for one. But look out that you don't lose the five thousand for five again."

"Not me," said Fernald. "When I lose the first five, I'm

finished. If it's going to grow, let it grow. If it's going to dwindle, let it sink. That's all right. They'll never catch me out more than five or ten dollars at roulette."

"A bad day for Joe Bane," said the teller.

"No. He's raked in the coin. Some fellows there were playing big. And they were losing more than they won."

He got his receipt for his money. The news of what had happened slipped quietly through the air. The president came out from his den, a fat man, with a rosy face, and a fat, foolish smile that could not altogether discredit a pair of gray, keen eyes, like the eyes of a hawk.

Fernald had felt for him, always, a great deal of awe. The whole town admired and feared this financial genius under whose thumb were so many ranchers, so many miners. He gave life; he gave death.

"Tommy," said the great man, "I'm glad that you've had some luck. But luck is not as good as work. You've worked hard all your life. That's what success is founded on. Luck is only hard work turned into cash. That's all. Don't forget that."

"No, sir," said Tom Fernald.

But he looked through the glimmering spectacles of this fat-faced hawk, and saw, he thought, that the fellow was a mere sham, a rascal, a pirate. How simple are the good. He, Tom Fernald, had been simple, and therefore he had been a fool. The rest of the town men were fools, too. He made up his mind that he never would put trust in this smiling calculating machine.

Said the president of the Mining and Merchants' Bank: "I have faith in you, Tom Fernald. I know your industry. I know your honesty. I shall be surprised if you don't build on that foundation a great success, one of these days. When you want to spread your elbows at the board and finance a larger tract of land, let me know. I can help you, perhaps. With advice, at least. With the capital, perhaps."

He went back into his den with the swagger of one who has given money to the poor, and Fernald stepped out into the brightness of the hot street before he permitted himself to smile. He kept on smiling when he saw Joe Bane approaching.

"I had a great run, Joe, eh?" he said. "I never had such a lucky day before in my life. I hope they didn't clean you out . . . the rest of 'em?"

"No, I took their money," said Bane, without exultation. He took out a $100 bill.

"Where did you get that, Tommy?" he asked.

"That?" said Fernald with a strange pinching of his heart—was it fear? "I dunno. Did I have it? I got it out of the game, I guess. I didn't have that much money on me when I went into the place."

Bane pocketed the $100 dollar bill again.

"So long, Joe," Fernald said, and stepped by him.

"Wait a minute," spoke the quiet voice of Bane.

Fernald turned slowly, reluctantly. He felt those cold eyes upon him, and he met them fairly. If he did not meet them, he felt that he could not be responsible for the expression of his face. Guilt or fear might creep into it.

"That hundred-dollar bill . . . ," said Bane, "you got it from Sid Belcher, didn't you?"

"From Sid Belcher?" exclaimed Fernald, relief pouring warmly through him. "Why not, old-timer. You don't forget that Sid Belcher's been dead for about a couple of months?"

"I'm not forgetting. That's why I'm asking," said Joe Bane. "Sid Belcher was my best friend on earth till he was murdered, and that hundred-dollar bill wears his mark."

IX

Dizzily into the mind of Fernald recurred the picture of Belcher, a big, handsome young fellow, found shot through the heart on the mountain road, only two miles out of Griffon. Yes, it was true that he and Joe Bane had been friends; it was true, furthermore, that friendships never were forgotten or taken lightly by the saloonkeeper and gambler.

"I don't know anything about Belcher, if that's what you mean, Joe," said Fernald.

Bane smiled—that faint, cold smile. "Think it over, Tommy," he said. "You don't have hundred-dollar bills coming in every day of your life, do you?"

"Why, no."

"Then where did you get this one?"

"Out of your game, Joe. That's where I got it, of course. That's where I got all my money, today, bar a few dollars."

"You didn't get that hundred dollar bill out of my game," said Joe Bane. "I saw it when you first laid it. I would see Sid's mark a mile away, I know it so well. Nobody else put that money across the table to me. You did it. Now you tell me where you got it."

"I don't know what you mean," said Fernald.

Joe Bane was silent for a moment, and the air was suddenly shot with electric energy of suspense. A weight was in it, a weight of all manner of possibilities.

"I want you to think back," said the gambler. "I'm not rushing you, Tommy. I don't want to make trouble with you. I simply want you to tell me where you got that bill. It's too big a slip of money to come to you and be forgotten. I know how much you make a year and how you have to count the pennies. Now come clean with me. Tell me where you stand. Where did you get that hundred-dollar bill?"

Fernald saw that he was neatly trapped. He looked wildly into his mind, but could find no escape. "You think I killed Belcher?" he asked.

The faint smile reappeared upon the lips of Joe Bane. "No, I don't think that," he said. "I don't think that you killed Sid Belcher. That's not what I'm asking you, either. But through you, perhaps I can get on the trail. And, God, how I want to find that trail."

Emotion swelled his voice for the instant, then vanished from it. He was as calm as ever before.

"It beats me," said Fernald. He went on, feeling that there was only one thing for him to do, and this was to fly into an honest passion: "You're trying to corner me, Bane. And I won't be cornered. You can't talk about murder to me and. . . ."

"Stop it," said Bane. "Now you're bluffing, and you can't bluff with me, Tommy. I've had men try to bluff me, and they've never managed to win out."

So Bane, too, had failed to see that there was a new spirit, a new soul in the skin of Tommy Fernald?

The latter smiled as faintly and coldly as ever the gambler could have done.

Said Joe Bane: "I've tried to use kindness with you, Fernald. I don't want to harm you. I know that you didn't kill Belcher, though now here's a look in your eye that I don't like. And . . . step in here with me." He turned his back and led the way into Petersen's saloon, his rival in the town, although there were still good relations between them both.

Behind him, Fernald hesitated, but not for long. Something made him follow—the very confidence with which Bane had turned his back, perhaps. But then, everyone knew that Joe Bane was not a man to be treated lightly—that to avoid him for one day was not to escape from him forever. Fernald went in behind him.

He followed through the barroom, where Al Ginnis and Harry Gregg were at the bar, shaking poker dice, laughing with loud, foolish, half-drunken voices. On he went into the card room at the back of the place, laid out in exact imitation of Bane's own bar. A profitable arrangement, indeed, for a pushing saloonkeeper. There they took a corner table. No one else was in the room. It was half shuttered, dim as twilight to keep out the heat of the westering sun.

Across the table the two faced one another, and, as they sat, Joe Bane said, without lifting his voice: "Now, Fernald, make up your mind that you'll never leave this room till I have the truth out of you. D'you understand that?"

How foolish the man was, thought Fernald, *to take so much for granted . . . as though he were playing with pawns on a board, not dealing with a living human being.* He shrugged his shoulders that looked, he knew, so soft and plump.

Of all the world, only a dead man and Bill Ransome knew that he had power to bend iron bars in his hands. Well, it was better that the secret should be preserved against future emergencies. And yet, where and when would a greater emergency than this arise?

There were not two like Joe Bane in the world.

"I hear what you say, Joe," he said, "but you're all wrong. I didn't kill Belcher."

"If you say that again," said Bane, "I'll lose my temper. I never accused you of killing a man like Belcher. No . . . you would rather have faced. . . ."

He checked himself sharply, and Fernald noticed with amusement the tardy courtesy that kept the last half of that speech unuttered.

"But the other question, that's what I want you to tell me," said Joe Bane.

Suddenly Fernald answered, his back against a wall: "I'll tell you this, Joe. You'll never find out from me."

The pale, steady eyes dwelt upon him. "Never is a long time, Tom," he said.

"That is the time I mean, too."

"Then," said Bane, "it seems that I'll have to. . . ." Something flashed in his hand, as he spoke—but, ah, how slow it seemed to Fernald, that famous, lightning draw of the gambler. For his own eye had been delving into the profoundest depths of the soul of Bane, and it seemed to him that a shadowy tenth of a second before, he already had seen the move pictured. Hardly was the gun drawn clear when, with his left hand, he grasped the wrist of the other.

And it was like other human limbs—it crumpled, so to speak, in his grasp.

"Hey, Joe . . . what you . . . ?" thundered a voice out of the doorway behind them where the bartender had by chance seen the flash of steel.

But the right hand of Fernald had finished what his left had begun. He saw Bane jerk up an arm to block the coming blow, but he let it drive confidently. His fist struck the muscular arm, and the arm struck the head, knocking it violently back against the sides of the wall. Joe Bane sank limply in his chair, and Fernald picked the fallen revolver from the table as the barkeep ran up.

He was shouting advice, protest, his voice rising higher and higher in almost feminine excitement.

But Fernald paid no heed to the voice and the excitement of Petersen. He simply leaned forward, and, reaching inside the coat flap of the unconscious form, he removed the second revolver from its clip spring that held it beneath the pit of the right arm. Then, straightening, he put these weapons into his own pockets. A heavy weight they made, dragging down against his cost, pulling at his shoulders.

Petersen tugged at his sleeve. "What in the name of God's

happened?" he said. "What did Joe Bane . . . you . . . you . . . ?"

He threw up his arms, aghast. Into the doorway crowded the two dice-throwers from the barroom. They were agape, also.

Fernald could have ground his teeth to powder, seeing that so much of his hand had been revealed against his will. There was no keeping back from the rest of the world, now, that he was a changed man. Or would they consider it a change? Might they not feel that the same possibilities had always been in him, masked and hidden for secret purposes of his own? He had never been with the others. He had been a sheep away from the flock. And therefore he might readily be looked upon as a wolf, always a wolf, although hitherto disguised.

Now the mask was torn from him.

That was the thing that bewildered Petersen. He still gaped down at Joe Bane, sitting there unconscious. If it had been any person other than Joe—but the invincible Bane, the sure hand, the lightning artist with a revolver—there he sat, helpless, and he had been conquered by the bare hands of the despised outcast, the keeper of sheep, Tom Fernald. It was mystery beyond reckoning.

Petersen said: "What happened? I seen Joe Bane move for his gun . . . I seen the gun . . . but. . . ." He stopped. His face was pale. He looked at Fernald as though he were seeing a ghost.

"Joe had a wrong idea," said Fernald. "Throw some cold water on him. He'll be all right in a minute."

But that very moment Bane stirred, groaned a little, and straightened in his chair, raising one hand to his head. Then, seeing Fernald, the cloud lifted from his eyes, and he was himself once more. He understood. So, rising, he said to Petersen: "Back up and leave us alone for a minute, will you? No, there'll be no trouble."

Petersen protested.

"Do as I say," ordered Bane coldly. "Only half a minute is all

I want alone with . . . this. . . ." He paused at the end of the sentence, and the cold hatred of his eyes, fixed upon Fernald, completed the meaning of his words.

So Petersen left them, and for a long moment the two men remained silent, staring at one another.

"After all, it was you, eh?" said Joe Bane. "Nobody else who I suspected . . . not Ransome, not any of the other ruffians in the town . . . but the sneaking hypocrite, Tom Fernald, eh?" He rubbed his bruised wrists, as he spoke, adding: "I couldn't leave you before I'd told you that I understood, and that one of us will have to die for it, sooner or later. Is that clear?"

X

Fernald nodded. "I understand the way you feel about it, Joe," he said. "But when is there apt to be a better time than now? There's one of your own guns. I have the other one. They're your guns. You know them better than I do. Fill your hand, and we'll go to it."

As he spoke, he laid down the long-barreled six-shooter. The other remained in his pocket. He saw a flash of fire come into the eye of the gambler immediately followed, however, by a look of care and caution.

He was amazed to see Bane actually shake his head, saying: "My right hand is no good for a day or two. You put a curse on it with your trick grip. But when it's better, I'll meet you, and fill my hand fast enough. Don't think that I'm afraid of you, Fernald."

"No, not now," said Fernald, astonished to hear his own words, astonished, too, by the sense of cold power that was rising in him. "You're not afraid now, but you'll be frightened enough later on. You'll learn to be afraid, Joe. When you think this thing over, you'll begin to seem smaller, and I'll begin to seem bigger. I don't think that the day will ever come when you get your courage together for a real showdown. So long. If you won't fight, here's your other gun. I borrowed it because my clothes were empty. They won't be the next time we meet."

As he said this, he put down the second six-shooter, turned away, and walked to the door. While he approached it, he heard footsteps passing softly away from it, a sure sign that the men in the barroom had been listening to what passed between him and Joe Bane. He was glad of it; it would be useful, perhaps, to the purpose which he now had in mind.

In the barroom, he ordered a drink and treated Petersen. He said: "Petersen, Joe Bane has made up his mind to kill me. He's going to shoot me on sight. That's what he's threatened to do. Now we'll see if there's any law in this town."

He saw Petersen looking stunned, expectant, blinking like a sleepy chicken when a light is flashed in its eyes.

"It's a funny thing," was all that Petersen could say. "I dunno what to make of it . . . I seen Joe Bane pull a gun. I sure seen that, but. . . ." He gaped upon Fernald again.

The latter finished his drink slowly. He listened for the footfall of Bane, heard it come out from the back room, and then he deliberately turned about and stared at the gambler. And Joe stared back. Their eyes locked against each other as Bane walked slowly through the room and out to the street, and then Fernald permitted himself the same sort of a faint smile that he had seen more than once on the face of Bane. The gambler was not smiling any more on this day, at least.

Back to the street went Fernald in turn. He could see that the men in the saloon were too amazed by what they had seen to speak. They would talk the thing over. They would try to understand that Joe Bane really had been met and mastered by the town boob, Fernald. Well, let them talk. Now that the mask was stripped from him, let them magnify him as much as they pleased. It was all the better for his purpose.

He went straight to Dick Harnett's store and was hailed by old Harnett in person.

"What's this that I hear about you and Joe Bane having trouble?" said Harnett.

"Me and Joe? Oh, it's nothing much. He says he's going to kill me."

"You look out or he'll do it."

Fernald smiled in the very manner of Joe Bane.

"I tell you, look out for Joe Bane," Harnett repeated. "He's mighty dangerous. He's the most dangerous man in this here town, when he gets all roused up to it."

"All right," said Fernald. "I want a pair of guns. That's all."

Harnett stared at him, hard and long. "You've gone and growed up, Tommy," he said, "and you've growed up mighty surprising tall. But you take care that you don't go and stumble. Because the longer you are, the harder you drop. What sort of guns do you want?"

"Colts."

"You can handle 'em over there. Here's a pair extra special balanced, to my taste . . . if you like pearl handles."

"I like pearl handles because they slip pretty well," said the boy. "I want a pair of good spring holsters that'll fit under the pits of my arms, too."

Harnett scratched his head. "D'you aim to stay here in town and fight it out with Joe Bane?" he asked.

"I aim to have the guns," said Fernald, "but Joe Bane won't fight it out."

"Hey! Hold on! What makes you think that Bane won't fight it out?"

"I'm not here to make a speech," said Fernald. "Yes, this pair will do fine."

"You mean you think that Bane has had enough?"

"I don't mean anything, Mister Harnett. Except that I'd like these guns better with the sights filed off and the trigger gone, too."

"Hullo!" exclaimed Harnett. "You fan a gun, Tommy? Can you fan a gun, really? Is that straight?"

Fernald permitted himself to smile again. He could not fan a revolver. That complicated art was one which he knew little about—although he intended to learn. But he was quietly assured, in his heart of hearts, that the only way for him to keep alive was to throw such a bluff that even the great Joe Bane would be impressed. Hand to hand, he could depend upon his mysterious, his overmastering strength. But at any distance, he knew that Joe could shoot him dead with no trouble at all.

His smile was his only answer to Harnett, who muttered: "Well, I'm learnin' some things about you, Tommy. I guess you been keepin' quite a lot of yourself under your hat. Here, gimme them guns and I'll put 'em in the vise, back here, and do the filin' for you."

Fernald went back and overlooked the process. He saw the sights taken off smoothly. He saw the work on the trigger completed.

"There you are," said Harnett, looking up suddenly and gravely from the work, and holding out the weapons, butt first. "I hope these guns never let you down, Tommy. And I hope that you never do a killing with 'em."

"I hope not," said Fernald. He took the guns into his hands as though he loved them. Then he remarked: "This is Joe Bane's work. You know that I haven't been carrying revolvers until today. Not for a long time. But Joe wants trouble so badly that he'll have to have it."

Harnett nodded, gravely impressed. "There's gonna be a lot of trouble coming out of this, but they say that you handled yourself fine in Petersen's place. I'm proud of you, Tommy.

Only, you be mighty careful of yourself, will you? You don't make any wrong play, or get an idea that Joe Bane ain't a dangerous man, will you?"

Fernald permitted himself, once more, that same faint smile, as of inner knowledge, amusement. "I have to wear guns, just in case," he said. "But he won't fight. You write that down. Joe Bane won't fight."

Harnett was so excited that he followed him out to the street, up which Fernald passed, weighted not only by the guns but by a heavy burden of ammunition. He had need for it. He would require it badly before the next month was out, if all of his premises worked out.

His plan took him next to the house of Deputy Sheriff Walters, who he found seated on the front steps of an unpainted shack, a toothpick in his mouth, a newspaper in his hands, and the usual look of resolution on his face. Ed Walters loved only one thing in the world: a fight.

"Ed," said Fernald, "I want to tell you something."

Walters looked up with his scowl, but it was plain that he had heard something—there was gloomy respect in his eye.

"You're the law in town, mostly. Joe Bane wants to have trouble, he says. And I'll have to give him what he wants. If he means what he says. You tell Joe, if you're his friend, that I'm going to be gone from town for a month. A month from today I'm coming back. I don't think that I'll find him in Griffon. But if I do, I'll expect to find him in front of the hotel, at three o'clock sharp. You tell him that I won't be in before that time, but if he wants trouble, I'll meet him there, one month from today."

"Yeah?" said the deputy. "What's the meanin' of all this? D'you think that I'm gonna stand around the town and let the law be broke?"

"I've taken a lot of talk from you today, Walters," said Fernald. "I don't want to take any more. I say . . . tell Joe Bane what I told you. I'll meet him a month from today, and may the best man win . . . if he has the nerve to stay in town."

"Nerve?" shouted the deputy sheriff, pausing at this part of the speech and overlooking the threatening words applied to himself. "Nerve? Joe Bane'll eat you, you fool! He'll. . . ."

"You tell him what I said, that's all," said Fernald.

Then he left the house where tall Ed Walters stood gaping and staring after him, a man entranced.

He had accomplished what he wished. Joe Bane would now feel honor bound to wait in Griffon for the coming of his enemy. The aspersions upon his courage would be repeated to him by everyone who had heard them from the mouth of Fernald, and the result was sure to be that, a month from this day, Joe Bane would be waiting in front of the hotel. And a strained and shaken Joe it would be, no matter how cold and cool his nerve. A month of steady and deadly expectation would be his share.

Otherwise, not two days, Fernald knew, could have passed before the gambler rode out to the sheep ranch, with his guns, bent on avenging the death of Belcher. What Fernald had gained was a month of grace, and he intended to spend that time in constant practice with his weapons.

A month was not a long time, in one sense. But he intended to expend it like a miser, making every pennyworth of time tell for him.

So he mounted his pinto and rode quietly, slowly out on the road toward his house. As he went by, he heard Jack Service call to his wife from the front porch. She came to a window and stared. Fernald knew that he had this day reached the stature of a man in the eyes of the townsfolk.

Well, it was worthwhile, even if he had to die for it in another month.

XI

Thirty days of grace. Well, there was a chance for close computation, and he made it. A fellow like Joe Bane, expert as he was, might spend half an hour a day keeping his hand in with rifle or revolver, never knowing when his life depended upon his skill. 150 hours in a year. 750 in five years. So computed Fernald, reckoning roughly. And he himself would spend twenty-four hours a day with his weapons. Not handling them and shooting them, always, but at least with them on his person. He must grow accustomed to the weight and the swing of them under the pits of his arms, to the very manner in which he now had to carry those arms, swinging a little free from the sides of his body.

He slept with the weapons still in place; they would grow into his consciousness. If he attempted to turn to either side in his sleep, he would very quickly be wakened by the grinding of the iron into his flesh and against his bones.

So he spent his month, exactly as he had planned. He paid a little attention to the sheep, just enough to keep them going, and they were little care to him.

For the rest, even when he cooked his meals, he would be thumbing the hammer of an unloaded gun; he was fingering it while he ate; it was in his hand when he was out walking.

He did not attempt actual ambidexterity, such as a few men have claimed. The second weapon was merely a reserve, in case something went wrong with the first. He practiced drawing both at once, to be sure, whipping his hands under his loosely worn coat, and jerking out the two with the speed of light. But it was with the right hand that he fired. The left held the reserve gun, which could be flung into the fight as soon as the five bullets his right-hand gun contained were discharged.

For there were never more than five bullets in the chambers.

With such hair-triggers as he handled, he dared not have the hammer resting upon a loaded cartridge. The least jolt or jump would be too apt to throw a bullet into his own body.

The actual firing occupied him three hours a day. He worked in the early morning, at noon, and in the golden blaze of the late afternoon. He worked facing the sun, with his back to it, or with it over either shoulder. He must not become accustomed to shooting with only a given light.

Neither would he use a given target. A stump was easier to hit, for some reason, than a rock of even greater size. But still he must familiarize himself with both. He drew ten inch circles, lightly, on the face of trees and on rocks. He did not want little targets. They might sharpen the eye, to be sure, but he would not have to be a lynx in order to see Joe Bane, a month hence. Then he strove to pour ten shots into the center of the circles. He scattered bullets all about, at first, but he would not shoot slowly. Lightning speed. That was the first necessity; accuracy would increase slowly.

When he drew the gun, it was with an incredibly swift motion, the hand flying up under the flap of the coat and snatching the Colt from the spring that held it. It sounded easy. It was a simple thing, for instance, to see the liquid ease with which the gambler, Bane, produced his weapons. But it was not so simple as it sounded. A fold of the cloth of the coat could easily interpose between stiffly reaching fingers and the handles of the guns. Or else he caught the butts wrongly, so that his grip had to be shifted after the gun was exposed.

Then, again, sometimes he pulled out so strongly that the sway of his arm pulled the gun well to the side away from the right line. Or often it was too weak and did not throw the weapon into the right position, which was exactly before him, at half arm distance. Held in this manner, by the partly flexed arm, the Colt would be about on a level with the middle of his body. He did not sight along the barrel, although at first the temptation to do so was vast. But he knew that an expert like Joe Bane would never do that. Rather, he would elect to throw in half a dozen shots in swift succession, some of them a little high, a little low, a little wide of the mark. But always, at a reasonable distance, the first bullet was likely to knock the other fellow down, or stun, or disable him. And the second or third would be reasonably sure to hit the mortal spot.

That was the system—to fling a group of bullets into space and trust that one of them would hit the right mark. Not to aim every slug, but to shoot by direction, merely by pointing. Some of the great masters were so accurate that they could keep a pair of tin cans rolling before them, as they walked along behind, driving the bullets into the ground so close that the spray of dust kept the can spinning. Others could shoot apples out of the air. There was a story that Joe Bane could throw up a playing card, edge on, and destroy it with a shot, two times out of three.

To such skill as this, uncanny as it was, Fernald could not pretend to attain in the course of a single month. But he would come as near to it as possible. He would not have a long shot, and he would not be shooting at a playing card. For the street passed around a gradual bend just above the hotel, and he would probably be within ten or twenty yards of his mark before he saw the great Joe Bane. He would be in motion, too, coming suddenly to a halt as he pulled his weapon.

So that was his procedure, fifty times a day, picking out a target, walking toward it, suddenly halting and throwing in his group of five slugs. Yes, very sad shooting, in the beginning. In the first place, he could not fan the hammer without pulling the guns out of line to the side, or jerking the muzzles up. But gradually he learned the correct grip, and gave his thumb the necessary adroitness, until it seemed almost as though there were an added joint in the finger.

He practiced for almost endless hours on the thumb work alone. At last, he would work with an empty gun, flicking the hammer so rapidly that it sounded like a rattling of cards flicked under the hand. And while the thumb worked, the barrel of the revolver remained as steady as a rock. Of course, there was a great difference between the work with an unloaded and with a loaded revolver, but the empty practice helped him a great deal.

The first ten days were vastly discouraging. He could hit nothing, it seemed, except by a random shot. His muscles were sore in the heel of his palm. His nerves were jumpy and unsure. But after that came a period of gradual, smooth improvement. He had off days, when everything went wrong, but those days became fewer and fewer.

First of all, his fingers no longer stumbled on their way inside the coat to the handles of the guns. In the second place, the weapons were flung out to exactly the right place and distance before him. In the third place, the bullets flew faster. Finally, and above all, they began to hit closer to the mark.

He was an excellent marksman with a rifle, always. Now he was converting much that he already had gained in closeness of vision and accuracy of touch into revolver practice. The field was not absolutely new to him. He would be shooting, finally, at a human target. But already he had brought down game in the field.

He tried squirrels, with no success at all. But now and then he scared up a rabbit on his walks about the place. No less than three of these he tumbled over. One dropped at his first shot. He considered that very largely the effect of luck. But the other two were hit later in the fusillade, each time. And that he considered vastly important.

However, to shoot at a moving target was not so very important. Doubtless Joe Bane would be standing, and still.

Otherwise, the duel was hardly conceivable. Joe Bane was a man never reproached for fear. Joe Bane would not be likely to try sudden movements. He would depend simply on his skill with weapons.

And how could Fernald hope in a single month to match the science of Bane with a Colt? He did not really hope to match it. He simply wished to give himself every possible chance. Joe Bane would be faster on the draw, but he would only be a thousandth part of a second faster. Joe Bane would shoot closer to the mark, but the heart of a living man is not the smallest target in the world. In addition to the rest, Fernald felt certain that he would be able to shake the nerve of his enemy somewhat before the fight took place. In the meantime, he had become a man of mark, as he learned by two incidents.

In the first place, Jerry Hampton, his rancher neighbor who had shown nothing but disdain for the wretched shepherd until this day, now dropped over for a friendly call. Very friendly he made his talk, although, when he first came, there was rather a haunted expression in the eyes of Jerry, as though he felt that he might not be altogether safe in the presence of Fernald.

But they chatted cheerfully and quietly for some time. Yes, Mr. Hampton would be glad to sell off part of his rocky ground to increase the sheep walk. And, on a day, he had plenty of bottom land to sell, if ever the rising shepherd wished to enter a gentleman's business, the raising of cattle.

"You're a little wrong about sheep, Fernald," he said. "You make your steady profits, I know. But along comes a blight, and that's the finish of your flock. You gamble higher with beef . . . but you gamble for bigger returns. It's worth the game."

Fernald agreed. He would take up the business, one day. It was his hope. Then, when Jerry Hampton left, the rancher remarked that he would have to try to shoot a rabbit to take home with him; they had used up their chickens, and his wife was ill. As he spoke, a young cottontail jumped up from among the rocks, and a tempting devil made Fernald jerk out a revolver and shoot at the darting target. That was the first rabbit he killed, and, as has been said, he got it with the first bullet from his gun. He could not believe his eyes when he saw the little animal tumble head over heels. The big, heavy revolver bullet had simply telescoped it; it was smashed from end to end.

As for Fernald, he had to look down to keep the wild surprise and exultation from shining out at his eyes, but the rancher ran and picked up the kill. He looked down at it as though he never had seen a rabbit before in all his days, and then he turned somewhat grimly to Fernald.

"God help Joe Bane," he said.

XII

Fernald knew very well that even a Joe Bane could barely expect to knock over a rabbit every time at thirty yards with a snap shot fanned out of a revolver held hardly more than hip-high; he knew, also, that in his case the striking of the target had been nine-tenths accident. But, nevertheless, he was delighted that the thing had happened.

It was something to break down the morale of Joe Bane, waiting off there in Griffon for the passage of the thirty days that composed the long suspense of this month. Almost immediately after this, Jerry Hampton rode off back to his ranch house, and Fernald was left alone for another period.

It was just before the date when he was due in Griffon that he received the second intimation of the seriousness with which the townsfolk now took the fellow who had formerly been their laughingstock, and this intimation came from no less a person that Deputy Sheriff Ed Walters.

Ed Walters rode all the way out from Griffon, and threw the

reins of his horse, and waited for an hour or so, until his host came in from the fields. It was one of those bleak, unseasonable spring days when the winter comes back for a moment, and whirs and beats at windowpanes, and moans about the roofs of houses. The whistling of that wind, Fernald hoped, might have drowned the barking of his revolver, for he had been walking through the dark weather with his gun, not so far away.

But the deputy sheriff said nothing about that. He'd made himself at home and kindled a fire in the stove, and put on some coffee, which he was drinking when Fernald came in.

Now he stared fixedly at his involuntary host, for a moment, and then burst out with the business that had brought him: "Fernald, was it bluff or earnest? Are you going to ride into Griffon the day after tomorrow to meet Joe Bane?"

"Yes," said Fernald, "that's what I intend to do."

The deputy sheriff groaned, and threw up his hands. "I dunno what to do," he declared. "Most of the people, they say that I oughta be out of town, or else right there to enforce the peace. But if two fellows like you and Bane wanna shoot things out, I dunno why you shouldn't do it."

"I'll tell you what," said Fernald. "I'd rather have you there, not looking after the peace, but looking after the fair play."

"Hey! What?" said Walters.

"That's what I mean," went on Fernald. "Joe Bane has a lot of friends in that town, and a lot of them who would be pretty glad to drop any enemy of his with a shot from the side. Well, I'd like to have you there to see that things go off fair and square."

"Whatcha talkin' about?" thundered Walters. "I'm hired to be a peace officer. An officer of the law. What kind of law is there in two men meetin' in the street of the town and havin' a damn' duel?"

"Not the kind of law that's in the books," said Fernald, "but it's law which everybody in Griffon will understand. It's law that they'll appreciate. If two men wanna shoot it out, why should the law go and waste it's time to stop 'em? You be there to umpire, and you'll get enough votes to be made the sheriff at the next election. People will like seeing you take things in hand. It'll show that you have an imagination. Everybody knows that if Bane and me wanna have our fight out, the law can't prevent it. But the day after tomorrow, the law can make it an honest fight."

Big Ed Walters got up from his chair with his coffee only half drunk. He grasped the hand of Fernald with an enormous grip, and then he almost shouted: "I can see the light, now! I ain't gonna dodge the fight. I'm gonna welcome it. And the fools that don't vote for me at the next election . . . they can go and hang themselves, for all that I care. Everybody with any sense will know that I'm right."

He hurried out of the house. Fernald followed him to the door, and paused there to watch the long-legged deputy swing into the saddle. It was rather a step than a jump.

When he was mounted, Walters reined the mustang closer to the door. "You're a white man, boy!" he shouted. "And I'm gonna see that Griffon treats you like a white man, too. Some of the boys has just got an idea that you're a snake, but I'm gonna work that idea out of their heads."

Then off he dashed, and the drifts of the falling rain soon blotted him out from the following eyes of Fernald.

Hardly did Ed Walters stop spurring all the way to Griffon, and, when he arrived, he dismounted under the shed near the Petersen saloon, and went inside, and stood streaming water, till it gathered in a pool about his feet.

"Say, Ed," said Petersen, "you decided, yet, what you're gonna do about the fight?"

Walters hesitated long enough to invite comment from a lounger at the bar, who remarked: "There won't be any fight. That fellow Tommy Fernald, he won't fight. He don't know what fighting is."

"Don't he?" said Petersen. "I'd like to've had you in here, son, when he put Joe Bane in a corner."

"He'll be here," Walters said heavily. "I know that he'll be here, the day after tomorrow."

"And then what'll you do?" asked Petersen eagerly.

"I'll be right on hand," said Walters, "to see that that fight goes off fair and square, and the man that tries any crooked tricks, I'm gonna shoot him down. I been and told Fernald that, all the way out in the country, and now I'm gonna go and tell Joe Bane." He swallowed his drink, and strode, sopping and dripping, out of the barroom.

Straight to Bane's saloon he went, entered, and found Bane behind the bar, an unusual thing. But no one was at the gambling tables this particular evening, and Joe was giving the glory of his presence to the drinkers.

"Joe," said Walters, the instant that he had his drink before him, "I've heard that you and Fernald are gonna have a little argument in front of the hotel the day after tomorrow?"

"I'll tell you how it is," said Bane. "I've been invited to be there in front of the hotel at half past three. Not that I think that Tommy Fernald will be there. But he's invited me to step around, and I mean to do it. Why?"

"That's all right," said Ed Walters. "And don't you have any doubt about it. He'll be there. Fernald will sure be on hand."

"I don't think so," said Bane, with a sneer as faint as his usual smile.

"You don't think so?" said the deputy. "I'll bet you a thousand dollars that he is!" The moment that Walters had shouted out this remark, he regretted it bitterly, for he could not help being aware that he was dealing with a professional gambler, one who was ready to take all sorts of sums of money, at all sorts of odds.

However, Bane did not speak at once. He remained behind the bar with one hand resting lightly on the surface of it, and his pale gaze riveted upon the deputy sheriff. "What makes you so sure?" he said. "You never used to be such a friend to Tommy Fernald."

"I never was because I never knew him. He's deep, that's what he is. Compared to the rest of us, around this town, he's as deep as the ocean. I never knew him before, but I know him now, and, I tell you, he's sure to be on hand. I'll bet you a thousand dollars that he'll be on hand," he added again more confidently.

Bane shook his head. "If I bet you a thousand," he said, "you could split the bet, and I suppose that Tommy Fernald would jump off a cliff for five hundred dollars."

There was a certain sting in this remark; it was repeated many times afterwards, but not always to the advantage of Joe Bane.

Joe went on: "But what do you aim to do, Ed? Be on hand to serve warrants on all of us to keep the peace?"

"Peace?" cried Ed Walters. "Ain't it peace when honest men meet in the open street to fight things out? Ain't that better than murder in the dark? To me, it's peace when gents step out in the open, where other gents can watch them, and settle things up like gentlemen. Maybe that ain't the law. But it's my law, and it's the kind of law that I wanna see in this here town of Griffon. I'm gonna be on hand, there, the day after tomorrow, but all I'm gonna do is to see that there ain't any crooked work. If you wanna go there and fight a gentleman, why, step right out and welcome to you. But if you try any crooked work, Bane, I'll shoot you dead as hell. The same thing goes for Fernald, and

I've rode all the way into the country today to tell him so."

XIII

The announcement of the deputy sheriff was enough finally to put the crown upon the excitement of Griffon. There had been enough talk about the challenge long before this, of course, but men and women had been more or less noncommittal about the subject. Some said that it was mere talk. There were old-timers who pointed out a few similar occurrences in the days when the border was young in history; they swore that men lacked the altitude of soul necessary for such exploits today. And, when the two little newspapers took up the argument, the *Clarion* declared that Joe Bane, a well-known and popular fellow townsman, had been insulted by a drunken shepherd, who attempted to bluff him out—in vain. The *Express,* simply because it never could agree with the *Clarion* about anything, declared with almost equal violence that Joe Bane, a shadowy character and saloonkeeper, had insulted an honest shepherd of the community, and was to be publicly taken to task for it.

But after the announcement at the lips of the deputy sheriff, the newspapers advanced the item to the front page, and covered most of the sheet with great headlines. There was to be a fight, after all. The deputy sheriff, in person, would give countenance to it. Everyone in the county would be on hand to see that most unusual event—a revolver duel dated, well known, and sanctioned by the law. As for editorial opinion, of course the two newspaper differed violently.

The *Clarion* vowed that the incident was an outrage, and that a man like Ed Walters was not worthy of the high office that he held. He was plunging the community back into the terrors of the Dark Ages. Trial by battle would commence again. Griffon would become the laughingstock of the world. Murder would hound honest citizens up and down the streets. Mr. Tom Fernald, who had delivered the challenge in the first place, ought to be jailed at once, and never permitted to get out until he had given bonds for his good conduct.

The *Express*, in the beginning, had had little or no feeling about Mr. Fernald and Mr. Bane. But after its first article, it was amazed to find that its edition was sold out rapidly, and that men talked up and down the streets in praise of the editor and his romantic stand in favor of the shepherd.

Therefore, the *Express* jumped into the fight with both feet. All that the war-like editor ever wanted was an opportunity to find a battle; the side he took was a matter of no importance. But he loved to shed ink like blood upon the staring pages of his journal. Now he advocated Fernald in headlines on the first page, and on the second page he advocated the system of duels. He himself was a little man with glasses who had never fired even a revolver in his entire life. But his enthusiasm was immense.

He declared that the early days of chivalry were returning. He swore that now the courts of law would almost fall into disuse. Honorable men would back their opinions gun in hand, and, on matters not worth a killing, they would gladly compromise. Manners would improve; foul language would disappear. Once more, men would discover a native dignity of deportment. The golden age of courtesy would return.

And all due to the originality of Mr. Thomas Fernald, and the insight and profound wisdom of Deputy Sheriff Edward Walters, of whom the entire town was justly proud.

When the ball was started rolling in this manner, the rest of the town could not help taking everything very seriously indeed. All of Griffon divided into two camps. But there was this peculiarity about the camps. All the women were in one; all the men were in the other.

The circulation of the *Clarion* increased the faster; the advertisements in the *Express* climbed far above those in its competitor. For the women followed the dictates of more timid natures. And the men who did not believe in duels were simply afraid to say so. Belief in duels, for the once, became an almost religious creed in the town of Griffon.

The day before the fight was to occur, already the trails and the roads around Griffon were thick with outlying inhabitants moving in upon the town. They came steadily, with keen, expectant eyes. They filled both hotels, particularly "the" hotel, that was Griffon's newest and best.

Bets were offered.

Everyone seemed to favor Joe Bane, at first.

But behind Thomas Fernald, at first, were only the gamblers who always looked for long odds, then those who were willing to back Fernald because of the character of the others who were supporting him. The skill of Bane was known, but the whole character of Mr. Fernald had become a mystery. People love mysteries, particularly in the Far West.

Eventually, on the morning of that day when the affray was to take place, the odds drew to evens. Then the fortune of Fernald rose. Suddenly a tip went around that he was a sure winner. The rancher, Jerry Hampton, a man of integrity, was in the town telling everyone that he with his own eyes had seen Fernald knock over a rabbit with a snap shot. At fifty yards!

That was what made people gasp. Luck with a revolver does not exist at fifty yards, and Hampton was quite unaware that he had practically doubled the actual distance of the shooting. A semi-hysterical excitement had carried him away. He said only what he sincerely believed now. He was ready to fight to prove his point.

But there was no fighting among the excited bettors in the town. Strange to say, the talk about the duel had interested everyone immensely to the extent of laying bets. But the impending fight did not rouse imitation. The gentlemen of the county treated one another with a strange patience and courtesy. It seemed, really, as though the predictions of the editor of the *Express* were already coming to pass. Voices were quieter. Swearing was less. Even footfalls seemed more discreet. Something was in the air, something solemn and heroic. Bullies who would have been glad to brawl and wrangle, even with guns, when half drunk, were appalled at the thought of a battle dated a month ahead and fought with the grimness of a legal engagement.

So that final day arrived. The morning passed. At noon, both newspapers brought out extras. They each reported rumors— quite baseless—that the governor of the state had been apprized of the coming fight and had forbidden it in the strongest language.

No, the governor had not been heard from—simply because he had not yet learned that the meeting was dated for this day. And there was no authority in Griffon to prevent the battle except Deputy Sheriff Ed Walters, who seemed in line to be elected practically unanimously for office on the strength of the strange position that he had taken up.

Lunch was a rapid meal on this day. People hurried through with it in order that they might have a chance to secure the best positions at windows, at upper doors, and along the verandahs of the hotel and the stores across the street.

Men occupied the first ranks, everywhere, but women and children were there, also. The women crowded the windows, and there were adventurous boys seated on the scorching roofs of all the nearest buildings.

As the hour approached, the first of the three important figures of the occasion made his appearance.

It was Deputy Sheriff Ed Walters. Ed was not a showman, but he could not resist making something of an entrance on this day. He dressed himself not gaudily, but in his best. He had a cold in the throat and high in his chest. That was his excuse for wrapping his throat in a white cloth that looked like an old-fashioned stock and gave a touch of dignity to his whole outfit. He was mounted upon his finest horse, that beautiful black five-year-old that he had bought the autumn before, and trained until it was already one of the best horses on the range. Down the street came the black, tiptoeing, dancing, aware of all the crowd, and pretending to be nervous about such a host of spectators. Sometimes it mouthed the bit, sometimes it almost halted. Again it made a little feint at a shy, but the deputy sheriff knew very well that he was as safe in the saddle as though he were seated on a rock. Not until he gave a command by voice or hand would the gelding really break into rapid motion.

As a scepter, Ed Walters carried a fine new Winchester rifle, which he balanced across the pommel of his saddle after the fashion of a hunter on the open range. His finest, his newest, his blackest hat was on his head. His boots had received a careful polishing. He was at every point the ideal type of the Western rider.

The instant that the others saw that he filled their eyes, he was received with a murmur of applause. Even the mutterers, the women who had set their hearts against this sort of a trial by battle, now had to admit that the gravity of Ed Walters lent the occasion a sort of judicial solemnity. After all, why not in this manner? If men were intent on killing one another, why should they not meet in public, rather then brawl drunkenly in the dark of a dim saloon corner? Only—this took nerve—and how much nerve it required. To ride down that open street, to be the focus of so many eyes, and to know that a deadly enemy was there, or about to be there—that was the test of a man's true heart of hearts.

Ed Walters did not dismount. He took his place in front of

the store and drifted his black gelding back and forth in front of the verandah. Two or three people spoke to him, and he answered them with a mute salute in each instance.

Then the little editor of the *Express* came running out with a pad of paper under his elbow. "Mister Walters," he said, "the press would like to have a final statement from you before the event takes place. You know that you have been supported by this newspaper from the very beginning of the argument."

Ed Walters hesitated. He saw that it was a big moment. He wanted to damn the *Express* and its editor for springing such a question on him, unprepared. But, as a man in public position, he had to say something.

Finally he answered: "I'm for freedom for every man. And I'm for the law, but I'm not for lawyers. That's all I have to say." To end the interview, he reined his horse away at the conclusion of his words, but he was not pursued. He had said enough.

The editor felt that he would be a poor man, a man of little wit and invention, indeed, if he could not expand that brief comment into a thrilling column, or more. He tucked his pad into his pocket. He only hoped that his courage would remain high, so that he would be able to ask for final statements from each of the antagonists before the bullets began to fly.

Ed Walters could not help seeing that his statement had made a great impression. It appeared to everyone that the deputy sheriff, after all, was not merely following the dictates of a brutal fancy, but that he really was bent on putting through into action a profound personal conviction. People nodded and whispered together; they followed Ed Walters with such approving eyes that it was all he could do to prevent a smile from appearing on his naturally sour face, and so ruining everything. For he knew himself well in the glass. He knew that in grimness lay his strength and in smiling was his weakness.

But now, just as his glory was reaching its height, there was a gasp and a murmur from everyone, and Walters knew that one of the two main characters had already appeared.

He turned, and now he was aware of Joe Bane, who had come suddenly out of the mouth of the alley that ran along beside the new hotel. He stood at the corner of this alley and the main street and cast his glance up and down the road. Then he shrugged his shoulders and the faint smile was seen again on his face.

It was plain to everyone, from this gesture, that Joe Bane did not think that his opponent would really appear at all.

XIV

After Bane had surveyed the street, up and down, for that moment, he turned up under the arcade of the hotel, where it spanned the distance between the front of the buildings and the long watering troughs that ran in six sections down the street. At that trough, a twelve-span team of one of the big freighters could turn in and drink without unhitching. Two ordinary outfits could pause there comfortably, one behind the other, without any crowding. The hotel, with justice, was proud of that set of fine, tin-lined, brilliantly clean troughs. And the high, shadowy hallway that arched across the verandah and threw shade for half of the day upon the troughs themselves was a resort where a hundred men could stroll back and forth, taking the prevailing mountain winds in the summer. The town children came there to play marbles and throw the horseshoe in corners. It was a center of the life of Griffon.

Through this colonnade sauntered Joe Bane, smoking a cigarette. When he came to the center of the walk, just before the main door of the hotel, he picked a chair off the verandah, and put it down on the ground. There he sat to await developments, his head high and his hat pushed a little back on his forehead, as was his habit when he was deep in thought. So he seemed to be now, brooding deeply upon some problem. Only those who looked closely into his face could see that in his eye there was a quick, hard gleam. A savage and a settled fighting fury was upon Joe Bane. The pressure that had been put upon him during this entire month had made him thinner, paler than usual, but his thinness merely outlined the set of his jaw muscles.

Those who looked calmly down upon him and took note of these things, now changed their minds. The odds that had grown so heavy on young Fernald now switched. Joe Bane was quickly held at two to one, three to one, four to one. And there were no takers. For one thing, men seemed afraid to bet against Bane when the man was there in hearing distance. He listened, his head canted a trifle to one side, and heard the murmur in the distance, and the knowledge of those rising odds in his favor was sweet comfort to him, perhaps, for all the nerve strain that he had endured during the whole of the thirty preceding days.

When he looked up again, he saw the tall form and the mighty shoulders of Bill Ransome. He was not like the once familiar name except in silhouette. His unshaven face was covered with a gray, shaggy beard. His eyes had sunk. His hair, already flowing long towards his shoulders, was so gray as to have a silver sheen. He was now leaning against a wooden pillar—tin sheathed to keep the horses from gnawing at the tender wood—two or three troughs away from the gambler. Deeper than the thought of Joe Bane was that of Bill Ransome.

Presently he said, in a deep, rather hoarse voice: "God has given you a lot of skill with guns, Joe Bane. But has He given you permission to murder poor Tommy Fernald?"

No one smiled, when this remark was made. Griffon might have taken the new convert as a fool and a butt; instead, it had accepted him seriously.

Only Joe Bane was irritated. He said sharply: "Go to the devil with your advice, Ransome. Fernald can take care of himself, according to late reports."

"You've lived with a gun in your hands," said Ransome. "And Fernald has worked in the fields."

Joe Bane turned a bright crimson. Then he locked his jaws, said nothing, and grew as suddenly deathly white. Those who looked on, observed these changes. The excitement that was in the air turned suddenly to a funereal feeling of doom, for many of those who watched the passions of the gambler close by.

But now Bill Ransome was forgotten. A whisper and then a loud call came down the street.

"He's here!"

At least a dozen men looked at their watches. It was exactly half past three when Tom Fernald trotted his pinto down the center of the street. A dust whirl rose behind him and hung there, as high as his head, like a ghost walking behind him. And Fernald himself was slouched in the ragged old saddle.

For, while nearly everyone else had dressed himself for the great occasion, Fernald had on his ordinary working clothes. His coat was fairly green across the shoulders with time. An old pair of overalls, patched and faded and bagging at the knees, clad him downward; the loose brim of a felt hat flopped up and down before his eyes. But stranger than his attire was his attitude. For he was slouched in the most casual manner, as though in the middle of a long, untenanted mountain trail, with no human being within miles of him. His head inclined forward and downward. One hand rested limply on the pommel of his saddle, and the other hand loosely held his reins.

People gaped at this final arrival upon the scene and the attire and the manner of the man. But it was he who had delivered the challenge and set the date and the place. It was verily as though death were a familiar of whose house he needed to have no fear!

When he came opposite the first watering trough, he spoke to the pinto and turned him in toward the water rather with the pressure of his knee and the sway of his body than by a movement of his hand upon the reins. The pinto came to a halt and, thrusting his head down, began to drink noisily around the bit. So still was the scene that people a block away could hear that sound distinctly.

Joe Bane sat forward a little toward the edge of his chair, and waited as a wildcat waits to make a spring.

But Fernald was in no apparent haste. He climbed down from the saddle slowly. He stretched his arms above his head and yawned, not ostentatiously, but as one fatigued by a long ride. Then he undid the saddle end of the lead rope and tied the pinto to the neighboring rack. When he turned from this spot, he would be facing Joe Bane—and the end would come. Yet he did not turn completely or suddenly around. Instead, as he moved gradually away, he saw among the tense bystanders on the hotel verandah, the face and form of old Doc Mahon, sitting with his elbows on his knees, a scowl of grim interest on his face.

"Why, hullo, Doc," said Fernald, pausing. "Haven't seen you for ages. How's things?"

The withered jaws of old Doc parted gradually. He seemed to chomp at the air for an instant before a voice came with which he could make answer. "Things is fair," he said.

"And how's Ma Mahon?" asked Fernald.

"Pretty good, but pretty rheumatic," said Doc. He cleared his throat. "And how's things with yourself, Tommy?" he asked.

"Fine," said Fernald. "Weathers good for the sheep, and that means that it's good for me. The grass is coming along fine . . . and that's about all that I've got to worry about."

Those who studied him—and with how desperate an earnestness did they pore upon the face of this man about to face death, each wondering in his heart of hearts, how he himself would have borne the dreadful moment—saw that his color was normal, and his eye clear and calm, and the conversational smile was steady and easy on his lips. They saw, and they wondered. For they could not read the inmost heart of the boy, who was saying to himself: *Now I've come to the pinch. I've got one chance in five . . . or in three. If his first bullet doesn't kill me dead or jerk me off balance, I may put a slug through him. I've got to remember that I incline to pull to the right. I must aim a little to the left, then. I'll aim at the left rim of his body. But the whole thing is just a gamble, for me. Only . . . the last time that I gambled against Joe Bane, I had the luck.*

These words, almost one by one, were sliding through the mind of Fernald. Furthermore, he had the calm that comes to a man who has made the most perfect possible preparation for a test. He knew that he had done all that was in his power to put himself on edge, to blunt the edge of Joe Bane. Even this last moment pause was calculated by him to rub the nerves of the gambler a little thinner.

But now the moment had at last arrived. He would have to pass from strategy to tactics. He would have to pass from preparation and thought to the final action. Chance, and God Almighty, would be his only helpers now, it seemed.

So he turned, without haste, toward the upper end of the arcade, and there he confronted Joe Bane. It was for this purpose that he had jogged his horse in, so manifestly off guard, as it seemed. For, when he turned the corner of the street and saw the position of Bane, he had done everything else for the sheer purpose of getting to a closer range. At a long distance, the uncanny skill of Bane would end the battle quickly enough. But now they were only fifteen yards apart, and he, Fernald, had a ten times better chance.

Bane had risen, cat-like, to his feet. He was leaning forward a little. He looked like a runner about to leap away from a mark, and with his eye desperately glued upon the distant goal. The death of Fernald was the goal toward which this racer wished to run.

"Hullo, Joe," said Fernald.

Bane did not speak. He seemed to be frozen and brittle with the intensity of his concentration. If he was like a cat, Fernald was rather like a plump, careless, confident dog. Still he was smiling a little. No one knew what that smile was costing him.

"Hullo, Joe," Fernald repeated. "Here we are, and I'm glad that I'm just on time and haven't kept you waiting. I'm ready whenever you want to start. Fill your hand, old son." He had counted on that, long before, the unnerving effect of that offer. Now he saw the mouth of Bane twitch and convulse. A faint snarling sound came from his throat. There was a hitch of his shoulder, a flash of his hand, the glitter of steel as he made his draw.

Ah, with what fluid, what consummate ease did the life-long master perform what the new tyro had labored so hard for a month to perfect. Grim wonder and admiration worked in the calm mind of Fernald as he snatched his own gun. Only half of his thought was for himself. The rest admired his foe man. He saw that he was the vital tenth of a second behind, the interval in which he might receive three of four deaths, when across the line of the guns leaped a dark silhouette.

It was Bill Ransome, his arms flung above his head, shouting: "I forbid . . . !"

The gun of Joe Bane spoke at the same instant. Ransome staggered, like a man who has lost his balance upon a side hill. Then he fell to the ground.

XV

Fernald, with a hoarse cry that was the edge of the roar that went up and down the street, leaped to the fallen body.

But a shrill screech, an animal cry, an animal yell of rage stopped him.

"I ain't been trapped for a month for nothing. Fight your own fight, Fernald, you damned. . . ." A stream of profanity ripped from the mouth of Bane. Joe Bane, the quiet, the well-mannered, the perfect citizen, gambler or no gambler—was it possible that he, of all men in the world, really had forgotten himself so under the very eye of the world?

Aye!

For as Fernald looked up, he saw that the face of the other was convulsed—the face of a madman. It was deathly white, as it had been ever since his first exchange of words with Bill Ransome, but now in his flaming eyes there seemed to Fernald to be an actual stain of red.

Fernald, in that upward glance, understood, understood even as the second bullet of Joe Bane tore the felt hat from his head. It was the true effect of the month of waiting. That was the poison that worked in the veins of the gambler. That was why he was, indeed, a frantic man at this moment. Perhaps his frenzy had caused his second shot to fly wild, by even the margin of an inch, between the hat and the brain of Fernald.

In the thousandth part of a second, Fernald saw and understood these things. Understanding them, he had no particular hatred of Joe Bane. It was simply superior strategy—plus an act of God in the form of Bill Ransome's intervention—that had saved the shepherd. Now let the task be finished.

Still half bent, as he had been when stooping toward the fallen Ransome, Fernald flicked the hammer of his single-action Colt once, twice—the two reports blended, one on the heels of the other. He saw the first shot spin the gambler about and the second one drop him, writhing, to the ground.

For an instant more, standing erect, Fernald with curious coldness of soul looked down at the enemy, seeing that the gun had been knocked out of his gun hand. Apparently the first shot had hit him somewhere near the right shoulder. The second shot had ripped through the hips or the thighs of Bane. He was down. He writhed a little, vainly.

Fernald was being transported by swift memory to another moment when had stood alone in his cabin, and had thought he heard the galloping of horsemen along the trail outside. This moment was surely the blood brother of the other. Or from the former it was bred. Without that grim instant, this one never would have followed.

He had felt, then, as though he had been raised to a great summit from which he could look down upon the world. He was there again, and one of the things that he looked down upon was Joe Bane, gambler and gunfighter.

If they met again, Fernald knew, there would be no need of intervention on the part of another. The next time he, Fernald, would be that vital tenth of a second faster with his gun. He knew it. From the instant that he saw Bane fall, there leaped through his veins a new, a vital fluid, a lightning that had never been a part of him before.

He called now: "Will one of you fellows take charge of Joe and see that he doesn't try for me again? I don't want to murder him . . . the way he's murdered poor Bill Ransome today."

But Deputy Sheriff Ed Walters had now raced across the street on his fine horse, flung himself out of the saddle, and rushed upon Bane, as the latter awkwardly managed to writhe his left hand gun from beneath the right armpit, the right shoulder now running fast with blood. Not a word did Bane say as he saw Walters approaching, but deliberately strove to level his gun and put a bullet through the heart of the man of the law.

Walters could not have suspected such an attempt from a man with Bane's reputation. But perhaps he was to a certain extent forewarned and forearmed by the madness that had contorted the face of the gambler the moment before. Every man in the street seemed to have witnessed that convulsion of the face and to have been shocked by it.

At any rate, Walters managed in the nick of time to swing his boot into the gun hand of the fallen man. The gun spun far away, exploding in the air and sending a bullet through one of the watering troughs.

The next instant, the deputy sheriff had his hand in the collar of the coat of Joe Bane, but the gambler was now disarmed and utterly helpless. The blood from his double wound was draining his strength and he lay back to the ground, with his jaw still set and his eyes hard and glittering. His spirit had not surrendered; it was merely his body that had been overcome.

"Jail me and be damned, Walters," he said. "It wasn't Fernald but luck and that fool of a Ransome that beat me."

Walters, looking down at his captive in a quandary, called out for someone to get a doctor.

But there were already three doctors on the spot nearby. The trouble was that they seemed to think that only one man had been hurt—or rather, only one man who mattered. And that was Bill Ransome. The big man lay still. In his deep-set eyes there was a look of patient resignation, of perfect mastering of pain. But the bullet from the gun of Joe Bane had torn through his vitals. The faces of the doctors pinched with sympathetic suffering when they saw the places where the slug had entered and come out.

It was with difficulty that one of them could be dragged away to attend to Bane.

"That hound needs lynching more than he needs a doctor," said the one who finally declared that he would attend to the wants of the gunman.

"Bill," said another of the two doctors—an old, bent, white-headed man whose word was accepted like gospel in the town of Griffon, "you've got about an hour of life left in you, if that bullet didn't do some dodging after it got inside of you. But if I were you, old man, I'd spend some time making a will, and such things. And tell us first of all what got into your wild head that made you jump right out into the middle of a streak of lightning that way?"

"If I kept that slug from Fernald, I did not more'n my duty," was the strange answer of Ransome. "If a man takes, he has to give." He would not enlarge upon that statement.

They carried Ransome into the hotel, bearing him gently.

Fernald walked beside the body that others carried. When they laid down Ransome on the couch in the lobby of the hotel, to Fernald was given, as of natural right, the place at the right side of the wounded man.

"You're not going to pass out, Bill," Fernald said, looking straight down into the eyes of the other.

Ransome smiled. "Whether we die late or soon, you know, Tommy," he said, "it doesn't make much difference. It's the state of the heart in us that counts the most. If that's right, I'm glad enough to die. If that's wrong, I'm going to hope to hang on until I've made it better. Doctor, I wish that you'd let me have a minute alone with Tommy Fernald, before I pass out."

"Don't make up your mind too quick about dyin'," said the doctor. "You may last it through."

"I feel a sickness and dizziness in me," said Ransome. "I've got an idea that when the dark rises like water and covers my eyes . . . then I'll be through. Well, the first thing I wanna say is that Joe Bane hadn't ought to be lynched the way I've been hearing talk."

A gruff voice among the crowded bystanders, who made a stiff, silent circle close about the couch, remarked: "He's intercedin' for that murderin' Joe Bane. That's too dog-gone Christian to be true."

Said Ransome, his voice fainter, but perfectly steady: "If this was a duel, well then, you boys all approved of it a lot. You wanted the fight to go through. You liked it. You was all on hand to see the turn-up of it. You know that. Well there was no murder in Bane. I just jumped in between as he started his move, and I got what I fished for. You can't harm Bane for what I did."

The silence of the bystanders was grim agreement with this doctrine.

"Then leave me alone with Tommy, will you?" breathed Ransome.

They fell back. They walked silently, on tiptoe, putting down the edge of the boots first, and so stole out of the lobby to the better open air of the street.

XVI

When they were isolated, Bill Ransome said: "Lean over here closer, Fernald."

"Here I am," said Tom Fernald.

"Move over this way a little, so's my eyes can get a better grip on your eyes."

"How's this?"

"That's better. Tommy, I gotta talk fast. I can't raise my voice and do any shouting at you . . . that would let the life out of me the first gulp. But there's life blood in what I'm gonna say to you. Will you listen?"

"I'm going to listen."

"You ain't gonna listen very well, just now," Ransome said. "There's a hard, flat light in your eyes. And I know that, though your face is close to me and your ear is close to me, your heart's a long distance away. I know that well enough. Only, afterwards I've got a hope that you'll be able to remember what I say, and that something good may grow out of it . . . that my words will be like soil, and your own better thought'll grow up out of it into a fine thing."

"Go on, Bill," said Fernald. "I'd rather have you lie still and save your strength for yourself. You need it most. But if you want to talk, I'll memorize every word that you say."

Bitterly, in days long after, was he to regret that promise. But now like a scholar he opened his mind and allowed the voice of the wounded man to flow in upon him.

"You can't get something for nothing, can you?" asked Ransome.

"No," said Fernald.

"What you ain't sowed, you can't reap a crop, can you?"

"No. That's clear. What are you driving at, Bill?"

"What did you do to get the money of old man Visconti? What did you do outside of kill him?"

"I didn't sock him, Bill. My pinto chucked him off right through the door of my cabin. His neck was busted by the fall. But I saw that people would be likely to lay the thing on me. So I buried the body. And then got the money from Visconti's well."

It amazed him to hear his own voice, so glibly and readily pouring forth these words that he had sworn should never be torn from him by wild horses.

Bill Ransome suddenly smiled, and a sort of pleasant fire went upward from his eyes, dim as they were, and through the brain and into the blood of Tom Fernald.

"I been and prayed that something like that might be the

truth of it," said Bill Ransome. "It seemed like to me that there wasn't murder in you, till the day when I tried to rob you the second time. But then . . . I seen it in your eyes. That's why I thought that you had really killed Visconti. But thank God you didn't do it. Now it's his money that I want to talk to you about."

"Go on, Bill," Fernald said coldly.

"What can money get for a man?"

"Money . . . everything!" Fernald said with a burning conviction. "Happiness! That's what money can get you."

Ransome slowly shook his head, smiling at Fernald from out of a strange cloud of knowledge, far removed. Fernald scowled, then cleared his eyes with the expression of one who will wait and endure to the end.

"Money," said Ransome, "can't buy you a father and mother, a sister, a wife, a son or a daughter. You know that?"

Fernald shrugged his shoulders. "Go on, Bill," he said as coldly as ever.

"Money can't but you a friend, either."

"Perhaps not."

"All that money can do is to put your name in newspapers. Is that what you call happiness?"

Fernald was silent. The dropping of these persistent facts upon his mind irritated him.

"No man," said Bill Ransome, "could ever use more money than would buy clothes for his back and food to fill his belly. Aye, or to help others. But that's not what you want the coin for, is it?"

Fernald drew in his breath. "I've been a dog. I've been kicked. Now I want to show them that they've manhandled a lion," he confessed.

Bill Ransome looked upon him calmly, with an infinite understanding. "I know, Tommy," he said. "I've been and wanted to do the same sort of a thing. Yes, money can be a club in your hands and a whole battery of guns. You can scare folks with it, and make 'em bow down with it. If that's happiness to you."

"That's happiness to me," Fernald said, his voice small and hard.

"There ain't enough light in me," Ransome said faintly, "I can't show you how wrong you are. I ain't got the light. And I wish that I could live to try my luck with you again. To go straight, Tommy . . . it ain't exciting, but it's a lot more content-ing, I'd say. I wish . . . wish. . . ." His voice ceased. His eyes glazed. His look fixed upon the ceiling.

Fernald swayed nearer. He could feel no throb of the heart, detect no movement of the breast. So he rose and took off his hat, and went to the door of the lobby.

"Bill Ransome has passed on, boys," he said.

As he saw the others begin to file in, their hats in their hands, he wondered at his own lack of emotion. He must show some concern. Human dignity and the opinion of society demanded this, because Ransome had offered his life for Fernald. But to the latter it seemed that Ransome himself had stated the thing more clearly. He, Bill Ransome, had received a gift of life when he was helpless in the hands of Fernald. This day he returned the gift.

He left the lobby and went into the adjoining small room where Joe Bane had been carried. He only paused to say to the elderly doctor: "You make the final examination of Bill. You tell me when you're ready to make out the death certificate. The funeral . . . all of that . . . of course I'm gonna arrange those things."

The doctor pressed his arm with an old claw-like hand. Sympathy was in his eyes and voice. "Of course, Tommy," he said. "I understand. I know how you feel, too. Once, long ago, I lost a friend almost like Bill . . . with a big heart like Bill's, I mean. And. . . ."

He went on, hurriedly, toward the couch in the lobby, and Fernald continued to the side of Joe Bane.

He was alone. His wounds had been bound up. And then he was deserted. Fernald looked grimly down at him, and Bane looked grimly back.

"It was Ransome that beat me, not you, Tom," he said.

"I know that," answered Fernald. "But the next time, I'm the one who'll win out of hand. I'm your master from now on, Joe."

"You lie," said Bane. "I'll try my hand with you again."

"I think you will, and God help you," said Fernald. "I'm ready for you whenever you're on your feet. But I don't mind telling you again what I told you before . . . I didn't kill Sid Belcher."

Joe Bane looked steadily up at him. "Maybe you didn't," he said, "but you've murdered my life today. Up till now, I've spent my years working up a good reputation. I've been a gambler, but the whole range respected me. Now you've made me seem a hound. I'd rather be dead than have men think that way about me. And you'll pay me the exchange on that idea, Fernald, before I'm through with you."

Fernald smiled, and shrugged his shoulders. He could see that it was true. The high repute of Joe Bane was gone on this day. It was gone, and it probably would never return. As for himself, it seemed to Fernald that he was launched into an upper world, breathing a rarer atmosphere than ordinary men.

It would not be long now before Bill Ransome was under the ground, Bill, the only man in the world who knew the truth about the stolen fortune, and that would leave him free to demonstrate how stolen money could be planted to bring great crops of public esteem, glory, dignity. He would not leave Griffon. He would become a great man in the very community where, so long, he had been less than a Chinamen in the public estimation. They would have to bow to him, the strong-necked fighting men, and the men of power.

He turned from Joe Bane, hearing a whisper, a hum, and then an utter silence in the lobby.

At the door, a man with a frightened face stole to him and caught his shoulder.

"Listen, Tommy! The doc pronounced him dead . . . Ransome, I mean . . . and just now he's opened his eyes and breathed again. He's gone and come back from the dead. Doggone me if it ain't a miracle!"

Fernald, listening, felt a cold wave of dread sweep over him. There was no superstition in him, but he could not help remembering what Ransome had said—that he wished that he could live to try again to show Fernald the right way. With that wish trembling on his lips, he had died—or seemed to die. Now he lived again. Fernald felt as though a hand had reached to him from the dead and held him and all his fortunes in suspense.

★ ★ ★ ★ ★

OUTLAW'S CONSCIENCE

★ ★ ★ ★ ★

I

One year to a day after he shot down Joe Bane, gambler and gunfighter, Tom Fernald rode into town. He had been in a number of times in the interim, but always for brief business visits. Never had a man in that part of the country thriven so rapidly, apparently, as had Fernald. A short year before, he had been a mere keeper of sheep, in a rocky little patch of land among the hills. Now he was a full-fledged rancher. He ran sheep; he ran cattle, too, thousands of them. Cattle speculation—that was the basis of his fortune, people said. It showed what brains could do.

Tom Fernald had remained poor until he was twenty-six years old. But all the while he was accumulating information, and information, properly used, is just another term for money in the bank. Then he began to cash in, swiftly, on his ideas. He bought sheep here and sold them there. The same with cattle. Every deal seemed to be successful, and there were many deals, each larger than the one before. People called him a millionaire. He was about half of that—hardly more. But the Mining & Merchants' Bank would have backed him for twice that sum. The Mining & Merchants' Bank had seen his account grow, knew what he had spent on land and buildings, and was willing to put hard cash, in quantities, behind its trust in him.

Within one year, he had grown from nothing into nearly everything.

One thing he lacked, and that was a certain social standing.

He felt that he probably had this already, but he was not quite sure, and, for that surety, he was willing to take a showdown. He had left the thing in abeyance, while he worked, while he speculated, while he built his ranch house on the spot that was nearest to his heart. But now he was taking one day off to put his foot on a high rung of the social ladder and see what came of the thing. He did not lack confidence. In fact, he was rather amused by the prospect. But his house needed a woman in it.

He was now twenty-seven years old. And he decided, logically, that the time had come for him to marry. In the back of his mind was the need of a house as he rode into Griffon on this day.

There was nothing swagger about his get-up. In his togs he might have passed for any ordinary cowpuncher, a cowpuncher dressed up for a day in town. Like a true cowpuncher, his boots and hat, the extreme ends of his outfit, were the best that money could buy. But in between, his clothes were plain. His horse, too, was not a long-striding thoroughbred, such as he could have afforded to ride. It was the pinto that had been his only mount a year before.

In the hard going just outside of the town, the pinto lost a shoe, so he walked it in the rest of the way and dismounted at the blacksmith's shop to have the damage repaired. Riggs, the owner, came out, puffing through his long mustaches, and nodded and grinned at him.

"Been puttin' up the price of beef again, Tommy?" he asked, wiping the sweat from his forehead and leaving a smudge behind the gesture.

"Not me," said Fernald. "My pinto's gone and lost himself a shoe. Fix him up, will you? Near forehoof. How's things?"

"Iron always stays the same," said Riggs truthfully. "I got nothing to complain of. Not since Bill Ransome got religion and a sledge-hammer." He laughed as he said this. But he had lowered his voice during the last few words. "You'll be wanting to see Bill, I guess," he said. "He's inside there, now, working on a wheel. I'll call him out. But it won't do you no good to offer him an easy job. He's set on blacksmithing and prayers. And nobody couldn't change his mind."

"I'd like to help him," said Fernald. "But you know . . . he won't take help. I owe him something, and I'd like to help him, but he's as stubborn as a mule."

"Yeah, you owe him something," admitted Riggs. "A man's life is something to owe. Still, you didn't ask him to make his play for you that day. You didn't ask him to step out and catch Bane's bullet when it was on the wing. And you've offered him plenty of soft spots ever since, that he wouldn't take. He's kind of strange. I guess he ain't all straight in the head . . . but makes a boss blacksmith, just the same. Hey, Bill! Here's a friend of yours."

"Coming!" roared a deep bass voice from the rear of the shop.

An odd glint of uneasiness came into the cold, steady eyes of Fernald as he heard that voice. "I ought to be getting on downtown," he muttered. "But. . . ."

He waited, however, while the blacksmith remarked, with a nod of understanding: "When a man gets religion hard, the way that Bill done, it's kind of hard on the nerves of a lot of folks. You ain't the only one. Sometimes he throws a chill into me, too."

Bill Ransome came out from the shadowy, smoke-wreathed door of the shop, big, stepping rather heavily. He was thinner than he had been the year before, but iron hard from continual labor. Riggs led in the pinto and left the two together. They shook hands, and Fernald surveyed the big man with a nervous energy.

"Well, Bill," he said, "how's everything?"

103

"Things go along pretty well with me," said Ransome. "I'm busy all day, and I sleep well at night. That's about all that a man can ask from the world, I suppose." He looked steadily, calmly back at Fernald. "And what about you, Tommy?"

Fernald stirred from side to side, and cleared his throat. For a year, now, he had always been uneasy when he was in the presence of Bill Ransome. "Everything's prospering," he said. "I want to tell you again, Bill, that the minute you want the place, there's the best job in the world waiting for you out at my ranch. Foreman, or anything you want. I'll build you a house for yourself, and . . . well, I've offered it all to you before. I just want you to know that I still mean what I said."

Bill Ransome nodded gravely. "But you're not making the offer to me," he said.

"I'm not?" exclaimed Fernald.

"No, it's an offer from a dead man, Tommy. You know that. It's part of Visconti's money that you're offering me. There's no use wanting me to take stolen money."

Fernald flushed. "Is that the line that you take about it?" he said.

"That's the line that I take," said Bill Ransome. There was no venom in his voice, but rather a sad judgment of the younger and smaller man.

"Visconti had no heirs," Fernald reminded, speaking quietly and rapidly. He added: "I'm not robbing anybody by keeping his money."

"You're robbing the state," said Ransome. "I've looked into the thing, all the way 'round. When a man dies and he ain't got no heirs at all, then the state gets the money."

"The state? The state has enough coin already," said Fernald.

Ransome shook his head. "You got about four hundred and fifty thousand out of Visconti, after he was dead," he said. "It's a year ago that you took it. I've let you have a year of grace to use that coin. Well, when are you gonna be ready to pay the state what you owe it?"

Fernald stepped back so that he could study the grimy face of the blacksmith more closely. "You mean that?" he said.

"Yes, I mean that."

"That you'd go to the sheriff and tell what you saw and heard that night?"

"Yes."

Fernald grunted, and the sound was like the growl of a beast. "How could you prove it?" he demanded.

"Likely I couldn't," said Ransome. "But it's my duty, and on that I sure would stick."

"You couldn't make your charge stick in a court," said Fernald. "But what would they think if I accused you of having held me up for two hundred bucks that evening?"

"They'd probably believe you," Ransome said gravely, "though they might wonder a little why you hadn't charged me long before."

Fernald drew in a deep breath. "Listen to me, Bill," he said. "You never could stick me. Never in the world. I can account for the way I've made money in the last year. I've got the bank solidly behind me. If you start telling them a fairy story about how you looked through the window and saw me counting out half a million dollars in paper money on the table in my shack . . . well, who would believe you?"

"I don't know," said Ransome. "I don't think that I care, either. I don't want to harm you. I only want to get the thing off my conscience and tell the law what I know of the case."

"Your conscience!" exclaimed Fernald fiercely.

"Ah, Tommy," said the blacksmith, "there's murder in your eyes now."

"To listen to you," Fernald said, "is enough to make a man want to do murder."

"And one day you will," said the other. "I'm sure of that. I've got to tell Ed Walters what I know. And after I've told him, I'm dead certain that you'll kill me, Tommy. I've had it in mind for months. I always see that end to the thing."

Fernald stepped closer and took the big, rounded, muscular arm of Ransome in his grasp. He shook the arm a little impatiently. "All you'd win by your story," he said, "would be to blacken my name . . . with some of the people that are willing to believe bad things about me. You'd put a smudge on my reputation, but you wouldn't land me in jail."

"It's not you I'm thinking about so much. It's my duty," said Ransome.

"Blast your duty . . . and blast you, too!" said Fernald through his teeth.

"Aye, Tommy," Ransome said rather sadly, "I may be lost, damned. But what about you? If the day comes when you're lying on a deathbed, and you have children to leave your money to, what will you feel, Tommy, thinking that every penny that you leave to them is stolen money? How will you feel about that? It'll darken your last moments of living. It'd be like a curse working in your mind."

Fernald drew back again. He said: "Ransome, if you're wise, you won't go to Walters with that yarn. I don't know what I'll do. I'm not threatening you. Only . . . you and I know that the account's square between us. I've let you live when I might have throttled you . . . and you've jumped between me and a gun. Our account's square. And if you try to knife me in the back, now . . . by all the saints, I'll make you sweat blood for it."

He turned on his heel and walked off down the street.

II

The mind of Fernald was very troubled. During the last few

months, he had almost forgotten Visconti, the source of his fortune. It had been as though he had earned all of that money honestly, or inherited it, at the least. Now the old unease of conscience returned darkly and coldly upon his mind. If the religious fanatic, Bill Ransome, gave testimony against him, who would believe Bill and who would refuse to give credence to what must sound like a fairy tale?

On the whole, Fernald decided that he would be suspected of the murder of Visconti, the instant the rumor was spread abroad. Murder and robbery would both be attributed to him. For his rise to wealth had been too rapid. To be sure, the banker and his admiring business associates were able to offer explanations. They could recite long lists of his deals through which he had made his thousands and his tens of thousands. But the explanation that Bill Ransome had to offer was simpler, more credible; people are always ready to believe that the other fellow has triumphed by crime rather than intelligence and industry.

When he reached the door of the Mining & Merchants' Bank, he had almost reached his decision. Bill Ransome intended to talk, and therefore Bill's mouth must be stopped. Death is the most secure of all gags to fit the teeth and tongue.

There at the door of the bank he paused for a moment, his cold, clear eyes looking far up the street toward the blue outlines of the mountains. He saw them not, but rather his own thoughts, and his thoughts had to do with remembered sayings out of his boyhood and stories of how crime breeds crime.

Now he was the thief of the Visconti money, to be sure, although by taking it he was the robber of the state and not of any individual. But he was planning to secure his gains by murder. After that deed, and the fall of Bill Ransome, tongues would be silenced.

Well, that was what he thought now, but where did the truth lie? What would be uncovered against him, not concerning the robbery of the Visconti treasure, but the killing of Ransome, perhaps? When he had thought of these things, not a muscle of his face changing, he went on into the bank.

President Blair was coming up from the far end of the big room. He was dressed in a working coat of gray alpaca that shimmered like silk. It shook and quivered over the folds of his fat stomach. His whole face quaked, also, in a hearty smile as he saw Fernald and came toward him, hand outstretched. Well, he was a good deal of a bluff and a hypocrite, but, after all, he was still the richest man in the county, and he was the prophet who, just a year before, had declared the coming prosperity of Fernald. Therefore, the latter could smile in return, looking into that fat, gleaming face. He shook the pulpy hand with his own grip of iron and went with Blair into the latter's office.

"I've been wanting to see you for a month," said Blair. "I've had something on my mind. I want you to come in with me. I want you to buy enough stock to give you a good hold on this bank. And then we'll work things out together."

Fernald blinked a little. His mind's eye glanced far back into his past, into his ragged boyhood, his lonely youth, his despised and scoffed-at life. And now President Blair of the bank was asking him into the business.

"You'll be a vice president," said Blair. "Something like that. You won't have to spend too much time here in the town. I know that your interests are out there on your ranch. That's all right. That's your place, and naturally you should be out there. But now and then, when we have an application for a loan secured by land, or cattle or sheep, I want you to look the prospect over. You know, Tommy, that in this part of the world, a man is better security for a loan than the acres of his land or the number of cattle that graze over it. But you know men. You know cattle. You know land. That's why you'd be perfect as a partner to me in this business." He paused, puffing and panting a little. "You're the first man that I've ever wanted to have along with me," he added.

He waited, but still Fernald made no answer. Blair began to talk more blandly and smoothly, extending one hand as though he were making a speech to a crowd. "You have what I want . . . courage, money, and a clear eye. You have money, and I'll show you how to make more money. I've made a lot of money myself. Do you know how much?"

"No," said Fernald.

"About fourteen hundred thousand, if I have to sell out in a pinch, about two millions if I can pick my time for selling . . . and in another few years, five millions, I should say, if things develop the way I expect them to develop. I came out here with fifteen thousand dollars, twenty-odd years ago. I've multiplied what I started with by a hundred. You can do the same thing. So far, you know sheep and cows. Well, there are other games just as good as those. I can uncover some mining ideas that'll make your head spin. I can show you some lumber schemes that ought to be worth millions. But I have to stay here and weight down the center of this machine. And I want a fellow like you to be traveling around on the outside, opening up new terrain. I'll tell you everything that I know. We'll both profit by the combination. Now, you tell me what you think about it?"

"I think it's a great idea," said Fernald. "It's the biggest opportunity that ever came my way. Only . . . I don't gamble, Mister Blair."

"Sure you don't . . . except a little whirl at roulette, now and then. But is that all?" Blair grinned, leaning comfortably back in his chair.

"I don't gamble," insisted Fernald. "When I start into a game, it's because I know that I can win. You talk mining, lumbering, opening up new terrain. That's all right. But I don't gamble."

"What's your main prospect now, Tommy?" asked the banker,

his eyes almost as cold and steady as those of Fernald by this time.

"My main prospect," said Fernald, "is cattle. I buy skinny rats south of the Río. I bring 'em up north this far. I fatten 'em and I market 'em. That's my main idea, just now. I know some districts where I can drive the herds through. I know the right seasons for buying down there and for selling up here. I'll buy 'em big. Five thousand in a herd. It pays when you work stock in a bunch like that. You turn cows into gold, that way."

The banker nodded. He pursed his fat lips and looked straight into the mind of Fernald. "You have a brain. You're going to get on," he said. "But what I offer you is worth looking into, also."

"It is," said Fernald. "I'll tell you what. You line up what you want to talk to me about . . . the new country, the new deals you want to tackle. Then I'll come in, whenever you say, and we'll spend a half day, or a day, and I'll try to see what you're offering. If it looks right to me, you won't have to do any persuading."

The banker nodded, frowning a little, most of his enthusiasm gone, as though he felt that he had opened a door and let in a dangerous wind. Then he muttered: "How far could I interest you in this bank, do you think?"

"Two or three hundred thousand in hard cash," said Fernald.

The fat man blinked. "By thunder, Tommy," he said, "you've certainly grown fast in the last year or so."

Fernald caught and met and mastered the suspicious eye of the fat man. "The cows have been good to me," he said. "And I don't gamble. I play the sure things."

He got up, and Blair went with him to the outer door of the bank. He shook hands, pumping Fernald's arm up and down. An odd feeling came to Fernald—that there was red human blood already on his hand and that there would be more on it before very long. It was as though Blair were trying to wipe the ugly stain away.

He pushed the door open, and the strong light of the outer day rushed on him in a wave against which he had to squint. He saw a buggy stop at the sidewalk and a girl jump down out of it, giving the reins a toss.

"Hey, Julie," called Blair, "you ought to tie up that pony! He's going to run away on you one of these days."

"No loss if he does," said the girl. "How's things, Uncle Alfred?"

"Pretty well, pretty well. Julie, I want you to meet my friend, Tom Fernald."

"Hello, Mister Fernald," said Julie, waving her hand, but not offering it to the stranger. She began to slap her knee with a fringed pair of gauntlet gloves, and still she looked over the boy calmly without enthusiasm. Her uncle did not allow the slight to pass.

"Julie, where were you raised?" he asked. "Don't you shake hands when you're introduced?"

She shrugged her shoulders, in the height of indifferent pride and insolence. "You're the fellow who killed Joe Bane, aren't you?" she asked.

He looked earnestly under and through the wide, deep shadow of her hat brim. She glowed, golden brown. She was luminous as with a light inside her. She reminded him of a high-bred colt in the pasture, full of speed, and courage, and disdain. He smiled faintly at her. "Well, you'll be broken, one day, just like the rest," said Fernald.

"Just what d'you mean by that?" she asked.

"Think it over, and you'll understand later on. As for Bane, I didn't kill him."

"You broke his heart. You killed him in this town. He loved Griffon, and he had to sneak out of it. Oh, you killed Joe Bane, right enough. I suppose that he's not the first one, either, and I'm dead sure that he won't be the last."

"I'm a gunfighter, am I?" said Fernald.

"I don't know," she said.

It was a wonderful thing for Fernald to feel the way she met his glance, unabashed, free, contemptuous.

"Or am I just a plain murderer?" said Fernald.

"That's the sheriff's business," she answered. "Uncle Al, I want to get some money, unless my account's overdrawn."

"Julie!" he exclaimed at her. "Turn around and apologize to Mister Fernald. I never heard. . . ."

"Oh, he can go hang," said Julie. "I won't apologize. I don't like the cut of his jib." And she slid past her uncle and into the shadowy interior of the building.

III

Blair ran after young Fernald and grasped his arm. "You come back in here with me," he said. "I'll make that wild devil of a filly apologize for treating you like that. I'll teach her manners, confound her, insulting a friend of mine . . . a partner of mine!"

Fernald shook his head. "I'll see her again, one of these days," he said. "What she talked about didn't matter to me. You know how it is. When a girl loses her head about a man, she can't help being a little bit hard on his enemies. I suppose she was a little dizzy about Joe Bane. Lots of the girls were."

"You come on back with me," insisted Blair.

"Not a step. I've got some other things to do. Going to the dance tonight?"

Blair made a wry face. "I have to," he said. "I have to stir around among people. I hate it. But I'll have to go. How old I'm getting. But you're sure that you're not hurt by what Julie said?"

"By what she said? Not a bit. Girls have to rattle along. Their chatter never means anything. So long, Blair."

He turned off down the street, feeling that he had come through the thing freely and easily enough; for something told him that, close to the door of the bank and within earshot of everything he said, was young Miss Julie Darden. And what he said would not be any great comfort to her soul. Yet he was not smiling as he walked down the street. She had dared to talk to him as though he were a real land pirate, a man not decent enough to be shaken by the hand. Was it all because of his affair with Joe Bane? No, she seemed to be reading something in his face as she had stood there, calmly facing him, cool, aloof, critical, free. If Bane was the first man, he would not be the last. There were others coming. The shock and strain of the idea made Fernald squint. What the girl thought, others must be thinking. He realized that he never had been very close to the public mind in Griffon, and now, of course, he was further away from it than ever before. He had spent this last year with his cattle business. Nothing but cows and dollars had occupied his mind. Was it common gossip all over Griffon, that he was a red-handed killer?

A little, nervous, white-faced man came up to him, almost running, and clutched at his hand. It was the editor of the *Express*, which by the grace of chance had sided with him on the occasion of his duel with Joe Bane.

"What's the news, Mister Fernald?" he asked. "What's happening? What have you been doing with yourself? Everything that you do is news that our readers like to hear about. Nothing succeeds like success, you know, and the rising young millionaire, he always fills the public eye pretty well!"

"Tell me," said Fernald, "what sort of news they expect about me?"

The editor laughed, his voice breaking shrill and high.

"Anything from discovering a gold mine to a single-handed gunfight against the old scratch on wheels," he said.

"Gunfight?" said Fernald.

The cold tones of his voice made the editor jerk himself a little straighter. He made a gesture with his pencil-soiled notebook. "You know, Fernald," he said, "people have to have a hero. And Griffon has picked on you. You've gotta be Griffon's hero, whether you wanna be or not."

"Griffon's gunfighting hero, eh?" said Fernald. He escaped from the editor as quickly as he could and strolled on. The afternoon light was growing softer, less brilliantly and cuttingly white. It no longer burned his shoulder through the thickness of his coat. It slanted in at such an angle that he felt it now on the back of his brown-black neck, now on the angle of his jaw. The children, who had been fenced in through most of the day by the terrible heat of the sun, began to raise their voices in the vacant lots. Evening was coming. In a little while, men would lay down their work and go home. And among the rest would be Bill Ransome.

For he had decided that this was the time. Bill Ransome had to die, and the quicker the better. The talk with the girl had convinced him of that, for, if such ideas as hers were already afloat in Griffon, every syllable that Ransome informed against him would be believed by Ed Walters and by the whole of Griffon. The words must not be said. That was the end of the matter.

He dropped by the blacksmith shop and got the pinto. Riggs was gone, but Bill Ransome was still there. He came out with his coat over his arm, his face and eyes looking tired from labor of the mind rather than labor of the body. Fernald paid him for the work on the pinto. They said not a word, but he felt the eyes of the other following him as he mounted and rode off down the street. He was thinking that perhaps it would have been as well to do the job there in the blacksmith shop. But, no, that was hardly sensible. Too many people would hear the shot. And Bill Ransome's house was off by the creek bottom, where even a rifle shot would hardly be heard in the town.

It was not the creek road that Fernald took, however. He preferred to follow the windings of the trail that led toward the eastern hills. Half a mile beyond town, he pulled up at the house of Stew Grey. That worthless old reprobate, trapper, hunter, rancher by fits and starts, lazy, inconsequential was sitting on the doorstep, whittling and admiring the sunset that flamed over the big blue western mountains.

"Slide down and throw your reins, Tommy," said Grey, without rising.

"Hello, Stew," said the boy. "Where's Mary? I've only got a minute."

"Hello, Mary. Here's Tommy Fernald," said the father, without turning his head.

A slim girl came into the doorway. She had her sleeves rolled up to her elbows, and she wore a square-cut sailor blouse that left her throat free. She was no golden beauty, no Julie Darden, but she was pretty enough, and she had an honest, quick smile without reserve that lighted both her face and eyes.

"Well, Tommy," she said. "Wait till I shove a pan of biscuits in the oven, and I'll come out."

"Why don't you ask him inside?" said the father, hunching a little to one side on the doorstep, as though to permit the boy to pass.

"Because the house is all hot with cooking," she answered.

Fernald slipped from the saddle to the ground. The pinto began to graze on blades of grass that pricked the ground here and there.

"There's a thrifty hoss," said Stew Grey. "He keeps right on adding one to one till he hits his million."

"Yeah. He gets fat where goats starve to death," said Fernald. "He can live on old rags and a tin-can salad."

"A good desert horse is what he'd be," said the trapper. "He's got plenty of bottom to him. I like to see a hoss with the lines of a flat boat for desert work. Whatcha been doin' with yourself, Tommy, since you went and got yourself famous?"

Fernald frowned. "I've been around," he said, shrugging his shoulders. He saw that the trapper was smiling a little, watching him with a quizzical air of rather detached interest.

Then the girl came out. She shook hands and offered Tom Fernald a seat on one of the several boxes that leaned against the front of the house.

He refused the seat. "I'm only here for a minute. I want to know who's taking you to the dance tonight?"

"Nobody, I'm not going," said the girl.

"Why not?" he asked her.

"I'm just not interested," she said.

"There's twenty fellows who'd be crazy to take you along, Mary," he insisted. "You go and tell me, will you, what's happened?"

"Well, a girl gets tired of dancing her legs off," said Mary Grey.

"You're the first that ever got tired of it, it seems to me," he said. "Look here, Mary, there's another reason."

"What other reason could there be?"

"You haven't got a decent dress to wear. Is that about it?"

"Hey, what kind of rot you talkin'?" demanded old Grey, rising in hostility.

"Sit down, Stew," said Fernald. "Come out with it, Mary. I don't want to hurt your feelings, but isn't that about the trick?"

"Well," she said.

"They've got a lot of dresses showing in the window down there at the Wilder Store," he said. "Would any of them fit you?"

"Of all things," she said. "Are you offering to . . . ?"

"Why not?" he answered. "I want you to go to that dance. You're the only girl in Griffon that I want to be with or dance with. You slide down the hill and. . . ."

"The store's closed," she said.

"Wilder'll open up the store for you," said Fernald. "You go along. How much money will you need?"

"I can't do it. I can't take your money. I. . . ."

"Of course, she can't take your money!" exclaimed the father. "What you think you are around here, Fernald?"

"Here's fifty dollars," said Fernald. "Will that do? That's a dress. Here's another fifty for hat and fixings. I don't know what a girl's togs cost. Will this do?"

"It's three times more than enough," she replied. "But . . . I won't. . . ."

"It's only a loan," Fernald said. "Your father'll pay me back, one of these days."

"Why, lookin' at it from that side," said old Grey, "it's a real friendly offer, Mary. I dunno but what you might accept it."

She did not speak. Fernald had pressed the money into her hand, and her fist gripped the coin hard. She was rigid as a statue, staring at him through the rosy glow of the fading sunset.

"I've got to hurry back to town," he said. "I'll come up here nine o'clock with a rig. So long, everybody!" He mounted and rode rapidly off down the trail.

IV

A man who has just arranged to go to a dance, and has given a girl money to buy an outfit for the affair, is not likely to have gunfighting on his mind. It was for that reason that Fernald had called on Mary Grey. She was to be part of his alibi. She and her father would help him to account for most of his movements during this evening. Yet it would go hard if he could not fit in a visit to the little shack where Bill Ransome lived alone.

Toward that place he was now moving. He left the hill trail and took the rough going that led down to the creek side, and thence along the creek he moved until he was able to see, through the dull light of the evening, the outline of the little squat house of the blacksmith.

In the old days, when Bill had been a gentleman of the road, his quarters, when he had any, were not at all of this sort. He stopped at the best hotels. His money went for the finest of eating and drinking and sleeping. But now he was an altered man.

When Fernald came up, he saw by the absence of a light within the house that Ransome had not yet returned home. So, circling behind the house, he left the pinto tethered in a poplar tangle, and came leisurely toward the shack from the rear. He found that he was walking through a small vegetable garden. He had to pick his way with care among the little paths that checked the surface of the ground. The damp odor of the richly worked soil came up to him, with the sharpness of radishes and a faint, thin fragrance of blossoms that he could not see about his feet. To think of Bill Ransome, road agent, laboring before and after his blacksmithing hours at work such as this. This was not all. Against the house were climbing vines and roses. This had been the most sun-baked little shack in the whole valley. But now it was beginning to be closed over by a bower of green.

Fernald looked curiously about him. In his heart, he wondered how profound the hypocrisy of Bill Ransome might be. For hypocrisy he was sure that it must be. Well, no matter what it was, it would be ended this evening.

He stepped into the house. Underfoot there was a matting. He saw the gleam of the varnished surface of a table. A mirror glinted on the wall. Very strange furniture to be found in the lonely shack of a Western blacksmith. It was all one room, with a shed opening behind, which was stored with provisions of various sorts, and the parts not used in this manner were stacked high and close with corded wood.

All seemed extremely neat and orderly. He could think back to his own days of poverty when such stores as these never had graced his shack on the sheep ranch. Mr. Bill Ransome was lucky enough and providential enough, it appeared.

Fernald made himself comfortable in the storeroom. He had a man-size Colt .45 hanging under the pit of each arm in a clip holster. That was his equipment for conducting the interview with Bill Ransome.

Then, when he heard noises coming up the creek trail, he stood up and took his place near to the open doorway that led into the main part of the house. This was the point of strategic advantage from which he could command the situation. But he did not draw a revolver. His pride prevented him from taking too many advantages.

The sound of the horse scattering the pebbles and gravel of the trail halted abruptly before the house, and a voice sang out: "That you, Ransome?"

"Yeah. This is me," Ransome said in return.

Fernald ground his teeth together in a fury. Two of them! Two of them together! It spoiled everything for him. But he waited, hardly able to move. The shed was pitch dark. He had foolishly failed to locate the rear door of the room. And now the pair was coming in.

He remained quiet, dangerously still, and he noted now, as he had noted before more than once, that the nearness of danger did not quicken his heart or make his nerves jump. A cold and clear-brain calm pervaded him. That was all.

"You don't know me?" the second man was saying in the dark of the front room.

"No," said Ransome, "I don't recollect your voice very good.

119

Wait a minute. I'll have a lantern lighted."

The chimney screeched under his fingers. A match spurted bluish flame. Then the fire licked across the wick of the lantern. Clear and brightly it shone, and the whole of the furnishing of the room spread at once before the eye of Fernald. It was as comfortable a cabin as he ever had seen. It was split into four corners, like four separate rooms—one for the bed, another for the kitchen, another for the dining room, the last one supplied with a small table on which books and papers were stacked, and more books appeared on shelves built strongly up against the wall of that corner. And all was in perfect order and arrangement.

Bill Ransome gave no heed to his surroundings. He was looking intently at the dark-skinned, black-eyed fellow who stood before him in the lantern light. The smoky look of his eyes indicated that he was probably a Mexican. He was a smiling, rather handsome and underbred-looking fellow. There was a big black mole under his left eye, and it gave him the look, from that profile, of one whose eye is crinkling with a continual smile.

"Hullo, Pedro," said Ransome. "It's a long time."

"It's a long time," agreed Pedro. "Such a long time that you don't shake hands with an old friend?"

Ransome nodded. "I don't shake hands with you, Pedro," he said.

"Because you owe me money, eh?" said the Mexican.

"Money? I don't owe you money, I think."

"You do, though. You owe me a hundred and ten dollars. That was my part of what you held out after the Carson job."

Ransome frowned. "I remember now," he said.

"I want that coin," said Pedro.

"I can't give it to you," said Ransome.

"Eh? You can't? You could raise that money in five minutes from any man in Griffon. I know very well that they think that you've reformed, you hypocrite."

"I can't give money to a fellow like you," said Ransome.

"You can't what?"

"I'm sorry," said Bill Ransome, "that I owe you any money, but now I can't give it back to you."

"Why not?"

"Because," said Ransome, "you're a thief, and a liar, and a murderer. There's mighty little charity in you, even for people who've been your friends. I can give you some more reasons, if you want them."

"I'm a thief . . . a liar . . . a murderer, eh?" said Pedro. "You flat-faced dog, what are you?"

"All except the murderer," said Ransome, "and heaven forgive me for it." He pointed to the door. "Go, Pedro," he said. "I can't have you in this place with me. It makes me sick at the stomach to see you and to think about what I know you've done in the world."

"I go?" screamed Pedro, shrieking with hysterical laughter and rage. "I go?"

Ransome had turned and jerked the door open. As he faced about, he was looking into the muzzle of a gun in the hand of Pedro.

"Now, where shall I go?" yelled Pedro, frantic with triumph and with hate.

"I don't care where you go," said Ransome, "as long as you leave this place."

Fernald, from his place of concealment, could look straight into his face, and he was amazed to see that Ransome did not change color. His jaw set a little harder, the muscle bulging at the base of it. He was steady as a rock.

"I'm going to let the light into you!" cried the Mexican. "I'm gonna count to five and let you have it, you sneaking, rotten . . . !"

"Just a minute, Pedro," said Fernald.

The Mexican sagged as though he had been struck from behind. He cast a single wild glance over his shoulder and saw Fernald, stepping into the entrance with a gun at his hip.

"Fernald," said the Mexican in a moaning voice. He staggered back until his shoulders struck against the wall.

"Leave your gun belt, and good bye, Pedro," said Fernald. "You don't need to tiptoe, either. But go fast."

The gun belt was instantly unbuckled, fell to the floor, and Pedro, stepping out of it, raced through the door. They heard him groaning with fear as he ran, expectant each instant of the bullet that must strike him between the shoulder blades. The saddle leather *squeaked* as he threw himself upon his horse and then the hoof beats loudly scattered the gravel of the road.

V

"Perhaps I should have tagged him with a slug," said Fernald. "He's a rat, that fellow. Used to be a partner of yours?"

"I robbed a stage with him," said Bill Ransome. "Yes, and I helped him break into a post office. We got nothing out of the second job, though."

"You kept bad company in the old days," said Fernald. "But that post office business was pretty bad. The fact is they'd sink you in jail for about twenty years for interfering with the mails. That's a thing that people like to do . . . sink you for robbing a post office. But Pedro . . . how did you ever happen to run with a greaser hound like that?"

He spoke carelessly, with a shrug of his shoulders. The other looked upon him with a still, calm eye.

"I was a bad man in those days. Perhaps I'm bad enough now. But when I look back, it seems the worst sort of a dream."

"You've polished up your vocabulary a good deal in the last

year," remarked Fernald.

"Have I? Perhaps. I've been working to that end," said Bill Ransome.

"A polished blacksmith, eh?" said Fernald with a sneer.

Bill Ransome smiled at him without a trace of any answering malice. "As polished as I can make myself," he answered.

"Polish up your wits for a minute, then, Bill, will you?" asked Fernald.

"Yes," said the other. "Do you want to ask me something?"

"I certainly do. I want to offer you a choice."

"Very well," said Ransome.

Fernald produced two guns with a single gesture and held them butt forward toward the other.

"Pick the one that you like best . . . though there's no real choice between 'em," said Fernald.

Ransome looked down at them as though he never had seen such weapons before in his life. Then he shook his head.

"You hear me?" barked Fernald.

"I hear you."

"Then take a gun!"

Ransome shook his head again. "I won't take one of your guns, Tommy," he said.

"Then take one of your own. Blamed if you'll find it half as good and easy to handle as mine." He was amazed to see that Ransome was smiling.

"I never learned how to fan a gun," the blacksmith was saying. He pointed, adding: "And you've filed off the triggers and left it for thumb work, I see."

"Well," Fernald said, scowling, "if you won't have one of these, take your own gun."

"What chance would I have against you, Tommy?" asked Ransome.

"Why not? We're standing here inside the house. It's a question of speed . . . and a bit of luck, that's all."

"You've worked with your revolvers every day for a year," said the blacksmith.

"Who told you that?"

"I'm guessing."

"What of it? You've spent your share of time with revolvers."

"For more than a year, I haven't looked at one."

"The more fool you, then," Fernald said brutally.

"I won't fight you, Tommy," said Ransome.

"You're a coward, then," said Fernald.

"Perhaps."

"A sneaking coward."

Ransome shrugged his shoulders.

"But I'll wake you up," said Fernald, "even if you're the slow-est horse in the team." He made a light step forward and struck the cheek of Ransome with his open hand. Then he was back again, his pace forward and backward as light and swift as the pacing of a wildcat.

But Ransome had not moved. Only the imprint on his cheek was laid in white against the brown, dark skin.

"You yellow dog!" Fernald hissed. "Will nothing make you fight?"

"Nothing," said Ransome, "except to help you, someday, as I pray that I may."

"You?" cried Fernald. "You help me?" Rage and incredulity were in his voice.

Then he checked himself, hearing the other say: "I've owed you my life twice. But, besides that, through you I've had a look at something else."

"You mean your fool change of heart . . . what you'd call your conversion, eh?" Fernald suggested savagely.

"Yes, I mean that."

"When you saw a way to heaven, eh?"

"I saw nothing. But I felt," said the big man reverently. And he actually shifted his glance upward, a little, toward the ceiling.

Fernald, his breast heaving, his whole body trembling, cried out: "Answer me this!"

"Anything I can," said Ransome.

"You say that you owe me something."

"More than I owe to any man in the world. More than I ever owed to my father."

"Then pay me back."

"I wish you'd show me the way."

"I'm showing you now. Keep your mouth shut about what you saw in my cabin."

"The money?" Ransome said.

"Yes. That's what I mean."

Ransome was silent. He seemed greatly moved, and, gripping an edge of the table that was near him, he leaned a good part of his weight upon it, his color having changed. All the nearness of death had not been able to effect such an alteration in his face, and Fernald marveled at it. "I'm trying to think," Ransome said under his breath.

"Let me help you think!" Fernald cried, the words pouring out rapidly. "You know how it is. If you talk, they'll all chatter about me. You think that you can send me to jail that way. But you're wrong. You won't be sending me to jail. You'll only be blackening my character. It won't do me any real harm. It'll just be scratching the surface. It'll make me uncomfortable, and that's all it'll do."

He paused. The other, his head slightly bent, had not changed from his attitude of silent suffering. Fernald, filled with hope, went on: "Gossip. That's what they'll do about me. They'll talk and snarl. But that won't harm me. I'm not the kind of a man to be harmed by talk. It takes bullets to harm me. Ransome, I don't know what's happened to you. You think you're a better man than you used to be. You act in a lot of ways better. But do you think that it's better to act a damned gossip and blackmailer's part by me?"

When he had finished, Ransome lifted his head and looked with hollow eyes at the smaller man. "I've fought it out for the bigger part of a year," he said at last, his voice broken. "But the fight always ends in the same way. I've got to tell the sheriff what I know. I've got to give myself clean hands. I'd rather it were any other man in the world that I had to talk about. But, as it is, I have to talk about you. That's the only way I can see it . . . unless you can show me more light."

"More light?" groaned the other. "Oh, I wish I'd let the greaser let some light into you. Would you be there, stammering and blinking, if I hadn't stopped him?"

"No," said the other. "I'd be a dead man. He meant murder. I could feel the murder in his voice."

"Then . . . what sort of a bargain will you make with me? Will you fight like a man . . . or do I have to shoot you like a dog?" He leveled a revolver, as he spoke, and he swayed a little forward, his glance fixed savagely upon Ransome.

"Don't . . . don't do it," said Ransome. "Not for my sake. I'm ready to die, whenever my day comes. But don't you do it, Tommy. You're not ready. You've got trouble ahead of you. You've got black on your soul, if you do it."

"You . . . you . . . cur," muttered Fernald. He felt a haze of rose and black forming before his eyes. He felt as though his brain were on fire with the passion that was in him. And then, deliberately, with a vast effort of the will, he put up the revolvers. "I ought to shoot you full of holes," he said through his teeth, speaking as one who still argued with himself. "But I can't do it. I'm all the more fool. And you're all the more lucky. I don't think there's another man would let you live. But I can't shoot you like the dog that you are."

Ransome fell upon his knees. He buried his face in his hands, with his face canted somewhat upward and his eyes rolled to the ceiling. Then he began to pray, not for himself, not pouring forth thanks for that life that had just been spared, but thanks to the Almighty because Fernald had not committed a crime.

The latter strode to the open doorway, and there he paused and looked back, his lips twitching like the mouth of a fighting bull terrier.

"You . . . Ransome!" he cried.

Ransome turned his head. "Aye, Tommy," he said.

"Will you tell me when you're going to take your dirty yarn to Ed Walters?"

"Tomorrow, after work. Walters wasn't in his house this evening, or I should have had to tell him then."

"Tomorrow," said Fernald. "I've got a day of grace, then. Afterward, I'm the black sheep of Griffon. May you burn hereafter for an ungrateful coward and traitor, Bill."

He went slowly out to his horse, but, as he walked along, he knew very well that Bill Ransome was not a coward from the way he had faced guns, unfaltering. No, the man had thrice the moral fiber that he had possessed a year before. It was not cowardice that appeared in Ransome. It was a blind devotion to an inhuman thing that he called his duty.

Fernald found his pinto, mounted it, and rode off up the graveled trail, and still his head was down, regardless of the bright stars that now were lifting out of the east and streaming softly across the black arch of the sky toward the west. There were no stars for him that night, other than the angry sparks that flew through his own mind. He could see that he had come to a turning of the ways.

It was strange to him that the two scenes with Ransome, when he had vainly attempted to change the mind of the zealot, were hardly more important to him, seemed hardly more catastrophic, than the scene in which young Julie Darden had denounced him. It was as though two guns, not one, had been held at his head. Well, there were ways of avoiding all sorts of peril.

As for his public position, he could remember, among other things, what had been offered to him today by the banker. Never to another man had Blair made such an offer. So he had said, and so Fernald believed, because the banker had never been known to take in a partner. He played a lone hand, until he met with the full and flowing tide of young Fernald's successes.

He would take up Blair's offer—that is, if the offer were still made when the next day arrived. He would see about that.

Now he jogged on into town and went to the hotel. He put up the pinto in the barn, smoothed his face, and went calmly into the hotel carrying his pack. He had a good, new blue serge suit in it. This he unwrapped, and he had it pressed in a hurry while he took a bath, soaking long and lazily in the hot water. Then he dressed, looked at the dazzling whiteness of the stiff collar against his brown chin, and went out into the street.

VI

He went first to the livery stable. At the door of it, in the poverty of his childhood, he had liked to stand for hours, watching the turnouts come in and rattle out. There he had stood to observe how the wheels of the carriages flashed as they were spun around under the expert hand of the washer, with his big, time-consuming sponges. He, at that time, had aspired to be the attendant in the livery stable. Some of the old awe came back upon him now that he stood again in the doorway. The wood of the driveway, crunched and battered by the passage of ten million iron-rimmed wheels, softened the sound of his heels.

Jeff Bister, the owner, came toward him. He was a big, swollen, red-faced man, who always looked angry. He limped badly. Every bone in his body, men said, had been broken in runaways. He was one of the heroes of Griffon. Not only was he fearless with horses, but, when the Stanley brothers tried to hold up the place ten years before, he, Bister, had routed them, single-handed. He had smoked his pipe calmly afterward, when the doctor cut a .45 caliber slug out of his back.

Of these things, also, young Fernald was thinking when he saw the limping body of the livery-stable man.

"Hello, Jeff," he said. "What've you got?"

"Hello, Tommy," said the other with no pleasure in his expression. "You know the dance, tonight. It ain't left me much. There's been a run."

"Not on the kind of thing that I want," said Fernald.

"No? Well, what you want, Tommy?"

"Let me look, eh?"

"Yeah, you go and look, will you?"

Fernald went back to the rear room. A great deal of the wagon space was empty now, and what remained were chiefly heavy buckboards, such as one would wish to hire for the slogging and slugging of a trip off through the mountains. However, one or two light rigs remained, slim, dainty, their poles or shafts hung by straps from the rafters. They seemed ready to drop over the flanks of sleek horses. Over in the corner was an outfit covered with a great tarpaulin. This tarpaulin Fernald jerked away. Beneath it appeared a little runabout so new, so brilliant in its dark blue, set off with spoke lines and trimmings of red, that Fernald felt a little glow as he looked at the thing. It glowed and gleamed even in the dull light of lanterns that reached this far into the interior.

The wheels were of wire, the tires of rubber. And, for all its lightness, there was a seat for two exactly poised and shaped to the individual comfort of two backs. He took the pole from the strap that supported it, and drew the rig out toward the forward floor. It followed him with a whisper and a light swaying over the bumps—followed almost as though of its own volition.

Then big red-faced Jeff Bister saw. "Hey, hold on!" he said. "You can't have that one!"

"That's all right," Fernald said, unabashed, and he lowered the rubber-tipped end of the pole to the floor gently. Then he went to the harness room, calling one of the helpers to him on the way. The man had on rubber boots, hip high. He had been washing down a horse, and there was a strong smell of liniment about him—a smell as though he had used the liniment outwardly on the horse and inwardly on himself.

"Let's have a look at all this harness," said Fernald.

"It's mostly used up. The slick outfits have all been hired out," said the man.

So it seemed. There were some dim corners where ancient harness were allowed to molder in dust and rust, unnoticed. But most of the pegs, polished with long use, were now empty. In the corner stood what looked to be a small, flat feed box. Fernald opened it. Inside were flannel clothes. He unfolded them, and saw the oily gleam of a light double harness set.

"Hey, you couldn't have that. That's private. That's for the boss," said the helper.

Fernald, unconcerned, was lifting the hames and noting the chased silver mountings. He nodded and appeared satisfied. "This'll do me," he said. "This is just what I want. Now, you show me the horses that belong to this outfit."

"Hey, whacha think?" The helper laughed rather desperately. "He'd fire me, the boss would. He'd fire me in a minute. Them horses are for himself."

"How old is Red Bister?" asked Fernald.

"Him? Oh, coming onto forty-five, I guess. Why you ask?"

"I don't know. I want to see those horses. You take me where they are. Come on." He put his arm under the pit of the other's right arm, and the hired man, apparently surrendering to force and persuasion, went willingly along. He led the way to a pair of box stalls at the end of the long corridor of commoner and open stalls. He held up the lantern that he carried, and Fernald looked over the upper rim of the doors, which stood open, and saw a pair of chestnut beauties with deer-like eyes and slender, iron-hard legs from the knees down, dark and polished as mahogany.

"That's all right," said Fernald. "You get these horses out for me, and slip that set of harness on 'em."

"Me? I wouldn't do that. I'd be fired."

"If you're fired, I'll hire you. I'll pay you more than this red-faced thief pays you. How's that?"

The hired man, amazed, nodded slowly, and gaped after Fernald, who went back to meet Bister.

The latter sat, as usual, near the entrance door, smoking a pipe. His seat was a low stool, padded with a piece of carpet. One of his legs was thrust out before him.

"It's all right, Jeff," said Fernald, "I've found the outfit that I want."

Bister said nothing. His swollen, angry face turned toward Fernald, and he regarded him from head to foot.

"It's a slick-looking span," said Fernald. "Good enough for a wedding. When are you going to get married, Jeff?"

"Aw, shut your mouth," advised Bister. He added: "Who told you I was going to get married?"

"She's a lucky girl, anyway," said Fernald. "How long's she been waiting for you?"

"Well, why wouldn't she wait a while?" said Bister.

"You haven't told me when the wedding comes off," said Fernald.

"Aw, shut up," repeated Bister. "And who in creation's been

shooting off his face to you, anyway? I'm gonna. . . ." He moved as if to rise, but then he settled back on the stool again, and scowled at the younger man. "You got a lot more o' lip than you used to have, Tommy," he observed very darkly.

"I've got a better pair of eyes, and that's all," answered Fernald. "Go on, old son. Tell me if that pair isn't worthy of a marriage present?" He pointed. Out of the shadows came forth the pair. They were mares, fifteen hands and three inches, mated to a hair in color and in size. They moved delicately, their unchecked heads carried high. Upon them the narrow ribbonlike streaks of traces and back pieces were hardly noticeable, only enough to set off the beauty of the bodies that wore them. And silver glinted here and there, especially about the bridles. The light sparkled on it. Neatly stepping, on they came, raising their feet high.

"Oh, they can move," said Fernald.

Bister stood up. "You got a lot of lip," he said, "and you're fresh, too. But you know a horse or even a pair of horses, when you see 'em. Maybe you think that you're going to hire that span into that rig, eh?"

"No?"

"No, you ain't."

"Why are you so dead sure, Jeff?"

"Because I know my own mind. Those horses, they're mine. Nobody else in town could handle 'em. You gotta have a grip and an arm to handle 'em. I wouldn't rent 'em out. They'd smash you up, that's all. They gotta be worked. They gotta be worked down."

"I didn't say anything about renting 'em. I said something about having them for tonight."

"Whacha mean?" Bister looked vaguely at him.

"I'll pay you two thousand for the whole outfit," said Fernald.

"Hey!" Bister cried, startled. He stared at Fernald.

"Two thousand. Talk up," said Fernald. "I want that outfit."

"I paid sixteen hundred for that span, alone," said Bister.

"What?"

"You ain't looked close enough at 'em. And then, you ain't seen the pedigrees, either. They're cheap at eight hundred apiece. That's what they are."

"I'll give you three thousand for the whole outfit," said Fernald.

"Three . . . you're positively drunk, Tommy!"

"Here's the coin, and. . . ."

"Hold on," said Bister. "I didn't know it was that way. You pay me tomorrow, after you've tried 'em, that is, if you're satisfied with 'em. Three thou . . . well, that's enough. Hey, Tucker. Move around, will you? Get Sammy. You fool you . . . tryin' to handle that span all by yourself?" Then he turned to Fernald. "They're half wildcat and half fire. Won't they break you all up?"

"I'll handle 'em," said Fernald.

He held out his hand, but Bister did not take it. Instead, he kneaded the rubbery muscles of his forearm.

"Yeah. . . ." Bister sighed. "I guess you'll handle 'em, all right."

VII

When all was ready, Fernald stepped into the driver's seat and took the reins. The grips were so far down on those reins that it seemed as though one would have to pull the span fairly into the dashboard in grasping them, but Fernald knew the play that there may be in the supple, long necks of high-bred horses.

He settled himself well into the seat, held the reins with one hand, and with the other swept the lap rug across his knees. It was of young wolf skin, a soft, deep fur, and it was lined with chamois. The very touch of it was luxury to Fernald.

"Give 'em their heads!" he called.

The two attendants sprang back from the bridles of the pair, and on a single common impulse the chestnuts leaped into the collars. The floor, always a little damp, slipped under their hoofs. They seemed to be running on a treadmill, and would have fallen except for the powerful pull that Fernald gave them. The attendants yelled advice. Bister told the hired men to shut up, or he'd brain them, and then, suddenly, the horses found their footing and in an instant were in the middle of the street. They swerved. The light wheels cut through the surface dust, casting it out like spray from the bow of a ship, and the tires slid with a shudder over the rough ground beneath.

Then Fernald coolly straightened them out. He knew horses well. He had ridden them, broken them by the score, and he liked to handle them. He had had many a pair of tough, iron-mouthed broncos galloping before him, dragging a rattling buckboard behind. But he never had had such a span as these lean greyhounds. They were all suppleness. All give and yield, as it seemed, and yet ever shooting forward. They did not try to gallop now. They were trotting, but such trotting as he had never dreamed of before in all of his life.

Their names were Bird and Belle. He called to them, soothed them by word of mouth, coaxed them, petted them with gentle terms. In addition, he gave them the strong pull, the strong, pulsing pull that teaches bitted horses that they have found a hand both wise and masterful. The chestnuts were neither nervous nor wicked. But they were as full of spirit as a steam engine under high pressure. By the time they had whipped the buggy over the roads and then over the trail to the house of Stew Grey, Fernald had them well in hand. Now they stood dancing a little, looking eagerly about them into the night as though, bird-like, they were ready to leap off and take wing across the ravine. They looked capable, indeed, of running lightly upon the air.

The heart of Fernald was filled with pride and content.

Old Stew Grey came out with a lantern. "Here's Tommy and his rig!" he called. "Come on out, Mary. He's . . . hey! What do you know . . . he's gone and robbed a bank!" he shouted with amazement. "There never was a rig like this in Griffon before," said Grey. "There never was two horses, so mated up, like this pair, and with the looks of 'em. Look at 'em, Mary, will you? Have you got an eye in your head? Don't that spell money to you?"

The span had begun to prance uneasily. "Don't go too near to them, Dad," said the girl. "They're a nervous pair of witches." She stood in the darkness of the door of the house. There was a smell of cookery in the air—bacon, it seemed. Fernald began to feel that he had reached too far and too blindly into the dark in asking this girl to the dance. Something of the kitchen air was sure to attach to her, it seemed.

All he could make out about her was a wisp of white, a dark cloak over that, and a wide-brimmed hat. *Was she wearing a riding sombrero to the dance,* he wondered, somewhat cast down. Well, he had never noticed clothes of women before tonight. Before today, rather, when he confronted proud young Julie Darden before the door of the bank. He had been a fool, he thought, not to notice them more before this. He took a good grip on the reins and stepped nimbly down to the ground. The lurch of the span almost pulled the wheel against his leg, but not quite.

"You done that pretty good. You're a regular circus driver," said Grey, full of admiration.

"I'm no circus driver, Stew," Fernald said quietly. "Hello, Mary, are you ready?" He had the reins still in one hand, so he could lift his hat to her.

"Yeah. I'm ready," said Mary Grey. She came up to him and then paused when he was about to help her onto the step. It was only a moment of waiting as she looked up into his face. What could she discern through the darkness? At any rate, she slipped back a little—an inch—from him.

"Dad," she said, "you hold the lantern up and let Tommy look over the outfit he's given me, will you?"

"You bet, and it's a beauty." Grey held up the lantern. "Look at her, Tommy . . . all white like a bride, dog-gone me if she ain't."

She was all in white, indeed, and the lantern light flashed softly over her. She looked slimmer than Fernald had remembered her, and her skin darker, her eyes darker, too. The coat was a slimsy bit of dark silk, with a glister in it, and the hat was the thinnest straw, the brim curling a little in the wind.

"Why . . . you look . . . fine!" Fernald said, amazed. "You're great, Mary."

"It cost seventy-two dollars," said Mary Grey. "Everything. There's twenty-two dollars back to you, Tommy, and a heart full of thanks, too. There's a whole year of parties in this dress for me." She put the money into his hand. He helped her into the buggy.

"Good night, Stew," he said, and held out his hand.

Stew Grey held out both. He whipped the money rapidly into a trousers pocket.

"God bless you, Tommy," he said. "You've made my girl happy. You two kids, you have a good time. You'll take care of her, Tommy. I know that. Hey, Mary, I might go over this evenin' and see old Tomlinson about that mule he wants to swap with me."

"All right, Dad," she said. Then, to Fernald, she said: "You pass me the reins, Tommy. I'll hold them while you get into the rig."

"You couldn't hold 'em," said Fernald. "They'd get away."

"I'll hold 'em, all right," she assured him.

"You couldn't hold them," he argued. "They're like quicksilver. They'd slip through your hands."

"Give me the reins," she commanded.

Suddenly he felt ashamed, as though he had been boasting, and he handed the reins to her without a word. Forward surged the span, and back again. She spoke to them in a light, cheerful voice. The chestnuts stood still. And between the wheels, which were as still as stone, he stepped, and was in the driver's place.

"By Jiminy, you're wonderful, Mary," he told her. "You have a trick with horses."

"I have a sort of a trick with them," she agreed. "Here are the reins."

"You drive," he said, feeling like one who puts money on a strange chance. "You'll do it better than I can."

"I'll drive, if you want," she said. "I never had silk like this under the reins. What a pair of mounts. Good bye, Dad!" She took the reins in one hand, and waved to her father. At the gesture, the chestnuts leaped away, but all in an instant, with the alarmed voice of her father ringing after her, she had mastered the span and turned them in an amazingly small circle, and brought them well out on the road.

A pressure relaxed across the forehead of Fernald. He had been frightened, he told himself, for the first time in a year. Now she let the team sweep forward. The reins were taut, yet she was not leaning back to give weight to her pull. With the merest touch she seemed to be keeping them in hand. The stars were rushing into the face of Fernald. He kept his eyes half closed. He was still frightened. He was cold with fear, but an odd delight was mingled with it.

"You can drive," he repeated.

They swept around a narrow curve. A chasm reached for them from the inside of the bend, but the girl regarded it not, apparently. She turned her head and he felt, rather than saw, that she was smiling at him.

"You shouldn't've given Dad that money," she said. "He'll go on a spree."

"I didn't mean you to see," he said.

"No, I know that. You didn't mean me to see. It's all right. He has to have his good times once in a while." She added: "Only I sort of wish that he'd work for 'em."

"You know," Fernald said charitably, "some people hate to work."

She said nothing.

He began to lose all nervousness. It was still a miracle that with so little effort she could swing and slow and handle that splendid sweeping span of horses. The pull on the reins had made him pant, driving up to the house. She was not at all concerned, taking them down toward the town again.

The dark mountains were shifting against the sky. The whole world was moving about them to the pulsing stride of the horses. The soft springs absorbed most of the shocks. They could hear the rubber-shod tires bumping over both rough and smooth places, but to them, in the body of the rig, it was like the motion of a boat across easy waves.

"Look here, Tommy," said the girl suddenly, "what made you do it?"

"Do what?" he asked her.

"You know. Everything for me. You wouldn't have to buy clothes for a girl. Great heavens, they'd make a whole outfit just to get half a smile out of you."

He turned his head about toward her. After a time, studying the dim profile of the girl through the starlight, he said: "Don't talk that way. Don't laugh at me like that, Mary."

"Laugh at you?" she exclaimed. "D'you mean to say you don't realize that you're the rich Thomas Fernald?"

VIII

He considered her again for a time. "You want to make me feel small, Mary?" he asked her.

"No. It's true. It makes you feel pretty good, too, doesn't it?"

"What? Being pretty well off?"

"Yes. And having the girls all ready to shy their hats at you."

"*Humph!*" he said.

"Go on. Talk up," she urged.

Suddenly a desire to confess seized on him. "Yes, it makes me feel pretty good," he admitted. "But it's not true."

"No?"

"No, it's not true."

"Who snubbed you, Tommy?"

"Julie Darden."

It came out rather unexpectedly. He had not wanted to say as much as that—name any names.

"Today, eh?" said the girl.

"What?"

"It was today that she snubbed you?"

"Well, I don't know about that," he murmured, growing hot and confused, glad of the darkness.

"It was today!" She laughed, and went on: "Then you came up to see me."

He was silent. He sat straighter in the seat. He was no longer aware of mountains or stars, only the red sparks of anger that flew incessantly upward in his brain.

"Then you came up to see simple Mary Grey. Go on, Tommy. Confess!"

"I came up to see you, after she snubbed me," he stated, his voice hard and steady.

"That's all right," said Mary Grey. "It doesn't matter . . . with me. I'm just as glad to have the dress. And I'm just as glad to be going out this evening with the catch of the county."

"Oh, quit that, will you?" he declared.

"I'm not hurting your feelings, am I?"

"No. I can stand it."

"You're a baby, Tommy."

He was silent again. His anger increased with every moment and suddenly she laid a hand, lightly, on his shoulder.

"It hurt, didn't it, when that cat of a Julie Darden snubbed you?"

He felt that he was too big to lie about such a thing. He said: "Yes, it hurt like the devil. I wanted to kill her."

"Or marry her, eh, Tommy?"

He started. "What in creation put that in your mind, Mary?"

"You know," she said. "We're all humans. People react about the same way. If I were a man, I'd like to tame Julie Darden. I'd like to marry her."

"Yeah?" he queried. "You don't like her, eh?"

"I didn't say that," she hastened to break in. "Julie's all right, too. Only she was born with a handicap."

"A terrible handicap," he said gloomily. "All that money and the looks she's got."

"Yeah. That's the trouble with her. Every pretty girl has a hard time before the finish. You can bet on that!"

"Why, Mary? Why d'you say that?"

"You know. They get to relying on good looks. They lean an elbow on that. And you can't rest on your face all your life." She laughed at her own remark. "A pretty girl is always careless. She gets proud. She thinks that she's on a throne. Well, someday the throne is yanked from under her. And she comes down with an awful bump."

He nodded. He felt much better. He began to think that Mary Grey was about the most intelligent person he ever had talked with. "You've got a brain in your head, Mary," he said.

"Thanks," she replied. "D'you feel better, now?"

"About what?"

"About Julie."

"Oh, she doesn't matter."

"Yes, she does, to you. Is there less ache in your heart?"

"Why should there be any ache? And why should it be less now?"

"I mean . . . to think of Julie having a fall and a bump."

He laughed in turn. "You're all right, Mary," he said. "You're straight from the shoulder. Yes, I've had an ache inside me. I've been hating the world. I've been wanting to do harm to people. I guess it was all because of Julie's way with me."

"Where was it?"

"Right in the street before the bank. Her uncle introduced us. But she wasn't shaking hands."

"I can just see her . . . lifting her head, the cat," said Mary.

"Yes, she did that."

"But isn't she beautiful?"

"She is," he confirmed. "There's a kind of a glow about her. Like gold."

"That's it," she agreed heartily to his surprise. "And she's other things, too. She's brave. She's a regular horsebreaker. She'll ride anything. She can shoot. She's shot grizzlies . . . all by herself! She's honest, too, and straightforward. But she's too beautiful. Men have made her think that she's a queen. That's the trouble with her."

"You know, Mary, you're not short on looks yourself," he stated.

"Don't you be paying compliments," she answered.

"I'm not. I'm telling you straight. You're mighty pretty. I hardly ever saw a prettier girl than you, tonight, when your father lifted the lantern."

"Thanks," she said.

Then she was silent. So was he. The road began to seem bumpy.

"Well, why stop?" he said. "Have I stepped on your toes?"

"Not a bit. I was just thinking."

"About what?"

"About my face. I know that's been the trouble with me, too."

"What, your face?"

"Yes. I'm blessed with good looks, too. Not like Julie. I'm no beauty. But the boys know when I'm around. A girl can tell. Any fool of a girl can tell. That's what brought you up to see me, wasn't it? After Julie snubbed you, you thought of faces in town. You thought of my face. And it brought you up the hill. Am I right?"

"Maybe I wanted to have a pretty girl around," he admitted.

"I'll bet that was it. A sort of a comfort to you, eh?"

"Yes, sort of."

"I hope I'll look well at the dance," she said. "I dance pretty well, you know. I'm not a beauty like Julie, but I can dance as well as she can, I think. But you know, old son, if I'd had a stub nose and wider mouth I would have done something for myself. Worked harder. Learned enough to teach school. Learned enough to make my way along, live a decent life, help poor old Dad. The way it is . . . I'm no good for anything. I just cook cornbread and bacon. That's about all I do. That, and wait."

"For what?"

"For a man."

"Hold on, Mary."

"It's true. I'm looking for a husband. I hardly care what sort of a one, so long as he has a little money. I'm not trying to fish a star out of the sky, either. He can be anything under forty-five. That's what he can be. I don't care . . . if he's reasonable, and has some money. I'm tired of living in a shack. Now go on and despise me."

"I don't despise you."

"You do, Tommy. I know you do."

"No, I don't. I've done some . . . bad things for money."

"You have? I've never heard of it."

"I've made a lot of money . . . in a year," he said.

"Well, what of that?"

"It meant driving some sharp bargains. It meant squeezing the dollars pretty hard."

"That's just business," she said.

"What about you?"

"Well?"

"Marrying is your business, I suppose."

"Ah, Tommy," she cried, her voice sinking down, "I hate myself, when I hear you say that. I despise myself, as I know you do, in your heart. I don't want to be a base thing. I don't want to sell my wretched self. But I'm going to! The nice fellows I know . . . they're all too young. They haven't made a start, yet. And I don't want to grind through. I don't want to fight alone and wait for years, until things come right."

He was silent again. He felt an odd pain take hold of him, a sort of world sorrow. Then he sighed.

"I'm a pig!" she cried.

"No, you're not. I don't mind your talking."

"I'm a pig," she repeated.

"No, you're only honest. I couldn't be as honest as you are. If I were, you'd never speak to me again."

"Good old Tommy," she said. "Anyway, here I am with the catch of the county."

"Is that the reason why you laid the cards on the table?" he asked her curiously.

She hesitated. Then she said: "Yes. You were so dog-gone straight and nice. Giving me this outfit was so fine of you. I could take it from you. I couldn't from hardly any other man. It wouldn't have been right. But you're a friend. Well, I had to tell you the truth about myself."

"Thanks," he said. "I appreciate it, too, I'll tell you. You're ace high with me right now."

"Good old Tommy," she repeated, sighing.

"And I'll tell you," he said, his heart warmed and expanding, "I'll help you more. I'll stand by you, Mary. I don't want you to sell yourself to somebody like old Jeff Bister."

"Ah!" she cried with an indrawn breath.

Suddenly the sweat stood out on his forehead. She had spoken of the possibility of marrying a man forty-five years old. Jeff Bister was just that age! All at once, he understood a great deal.

IX

The dance was in the old Carver barn. It came to be built there in rather an odd way that showed something of the wild and careless spirit of the early days. Dean Carver was a giant. Men said that he stood nearly seven feet tall and weighed 300 pounds. He was traveling through the country with ox teams, which were continually falling ill. One of his best spans having died, he fell into an evil temper and began to consult the jug of whiskey while his wife stood by and begged him to get on to the next settlement before dark.

There were plenty of hostile Indians about in those times. Finally, in a half-drunken fury, he told her that he was tired of the journey, and that he would go no farther than he could carry a certain rock that loomed black and massive beside the trail. So he leaped up, hauled at the thing, uprooted it, and carried it, probably on his knees, a little distance from the trail. There he let it fall and dropped upon the stone in a swoon, caused by the immense effort he had made. Blood had gushed from his mouth and nose as he lifted, tradition said. When he recovered from the swoon, Dean Carver remembered his oath, and there he straightway began the erection of a barn for the animals and a house for his family. Right around the great rock he built the foundations of the barn.

Since then the family had prospered a great deal, and the house had grown, and the barn had been much enlarged, but still the Carver Rock, famous in the community, stood in the center of the floor of the barn. Every year at about this season, when the summer supply of hay ran low and the next lot had not been laid in, the Carvers cleaned out their barn and gave a great dance to the community. The heavy wooden floor, polished by the friction of many seasons of hay storage, made a perfect surface, and there was room and to spare for all who came. It was a public occasion, and it was also a sort of permanent advertisement for the greatness of the Carvers to all who saw the great rock and read upon it the inscription, which was painted in white lead, roughly, and in the following words:

> **Pounds sixteen hundred and forty-two,**
> **Dean Carver lifted and carried, too,**
> **For twenty feet, and spilled his blood,**
> **And raised his fortunes from the mud.**
> **In Griffon town he lived and died;**
> **God save us all from sinful pride!**

That the stone did actually weigh "pounds sixteen hundred and forty-two," there was good attesting, for on an occasion when the floor of the barn was overhauled, the stone had been pried up, with labor, and weighed. Then, perhaps because some earth adhered to it, the exact poundage was a little over 1,650.

This was the dance and the occasion to which Fernald was taking Mary Grey.

When they came to the driveway that led from the street down an avenue of big trees to the farmyard of the Carver place, they found that colored lanterns were hanging from all of the trees. In the yard itself there was a great jam of horses and vehicles of all sorts. People came 100 miles to the festival. It was only required that everyone should have been an actual resident within a mile of Griffon for a year of his life. That was as good as a ticket of invitation. No wonder that saddle horses, buckboards, and buggies, phaëtons, heavy carriages, and small-sized ponderous stages were all ranked straggling under the wide-spreading sheds that surrounded the yard.

There were a sufficient number of lanterns hung about to light the entire scene, and, when young Fernald came in the rubber-tired rig, with the flashing span of chestnuts before him and the flushed, happy face of Mary Grey near his shoulder, there was a ripple, a general exclamation, and then someone roared out a cheer for the finest turnout of the evening, not barring the Carvers' own family carriage.

They gave that cheer, those who knew what the shouting was about, and those who were always willing to cheer anyway, out of sheer high spirits and willingness to make a noise.

That roar made the eyes of Mary Grey brighter than ever. "The folks just love you, Tommy!" she exclaimed as they got down from the seat.

He answered with a grim glance into the truth: "They love good luck and a fine span of chestnuts. But that's all right. They certainly yelled for us, Mary. It's surely going to be a great evening."

"Sure, it is," she agreed. She stood by, and presently was swallowed up in a chattering group of youngsters, while Fernald saw to it that the mares were put into stalls and given a feed and blanketed. They had been treated like spoiled children by Jeff Bister, and they would have to be handled in the same manner for some time to come.

When he went back into the yard, youngsters were still swarming about Mary Grey, and her voice sang out in the middle of the group. It was just as he had hoped. She had always been a favorite, and now she was shining like a star among the rest. She was more than pretty—yes, indeed, she was actually radiant.

He went in with her to the barn. The music was sounding, but very few had danced so far, except for a few steps to try the slippery state of the floor, and with the new influx of which Fernald and Mary were a part, the whole festivity came to life. Instantly the rapid dancers were gliding about the floor, and the laughter was tingling up among the rafters and seemed to be making the long streamers of bunting, the twisted, gay-colored pennons, and the fringed lanterns all tremble with the waves of the happy sound.

On the dance floor, Fernald was not at home. Since he began to keep the sheep ranch a good many years before, he had not danced a single time, and now his feet almost forgot the measures. So he kept to the edge of the floor. He seldom turned. He kept his steps short, and concentrated seriously on the time.

"You're thinking too much, Tommy," said the girl. "You're a little red, too. Just give yourself a shake. Nobody cares if you can't dance. You can do other things."

"Like making money, eh?" he said rather bitterly. For it seemed to him that every bit of approbation that he gained because of mere wealth was a poisonous sting. Stolen money was the source of his income. When they praised him for money, they praised him merely for a theft.

But she was saying: "No, there's other things. Like shooting up the gunfighters, you know."

"*Humph!*" he grunted. "Joe Bane? I'd like to forget about him. I'm sorry for him."

"Has he gone all to pieces?"

"Yes, all to pieces, they say. He was a pretty good citizen and a pretty good fellow, too. I'm really very sorry about him."

"Whatever started you and Bane on the warpath?" she asked.

"You know . . . he got a crazy idea. He thought that I'd killed a friend of his by the name of Sid Belcher."

"But you didn't, of course."

"Of course not. It was just an idea . . . a saloon idea . . . a barroom thought, you know."

"Joe Bane wasn't the sort to have crazy ideas. He was cold and keen as a knife," said Mary Grey.

"Yeah?" murmured Fernald. "He was smart. But everybody makes a wrong turn in the road, now and then. You know how it is."

"Yes, I know," she answered.

But he could tell that she hardly meant what she was saying. She had a doubt in her mind; she was thinking of the possible other side of the question; she was wondering if, after all, he had killed Sid Belcher. In the old days, when he had been the butt and the laughingstock of the town, no one would have dreamed of putting a man-size killing at his door. But it was different now. They looked on him as a person capable of any deed of violence. Well, that was all right, too. They might have suspicions about him, but they respected him all the more as a person of force.

"Don't you start getting any wrong ideas about me, Mary," he advised.

"I'd be afraid to get any wrong ideas about you," said the

girl. She laughed a little, but there was a touch of seriousness in her tone.

The dance ended, and he was rather glad of it, although she encouraged him. He was getting better; he only needed to keep on; pretty soon he'd lose his self-consciousness.

They went back and were the center of a swirl of people. Everyone was speaking to Mary Grey. Even the girls beamed at her, without envy of her looks, and the lads were a cluster about her. He was glad of his choice in picking out Mary. A great evening for her. A sort of triumph. Eyes were upon him, also, but covertly, shyly. He saw that Mary was quite able to take care of herself, and then he moved vaguely away.

Jenkins, the cattle dealer, hurried after him. He wanted 1,500 head of cows in thirty days. What part would he, Fernald, deliver? Fernald would deliver them all. The dealer blinked.

"But . . . I know you haven't got 'em now. Where will you . . . ?"

"I'll deliver fifteen hundred head in thirty days," Fernald insisted quietly. He was thinking quickly, accurately, calmly. He knew where he could pick up fifty head, 200 head, seventy-five three-year-olds from the river bottom, 100 miles away, and a good-size herd was drifting over the border, unless he was wrong. Wet cattle, perhaps, but still they would do in a pinch. Yes, he could find 1,500 head.

Jenkins began to laugh loudly, but with relief. "You make cows grow like wheat, Fernald," he said.

Fernald shrugged, and went on. He noticed that few people now called him by his first name. He was Fernald to most of the world, except to his schoolmates. That was as it should be. He was growing into a man's maturity.

He came near the entrance, hearing the swell of voices, and seeing a group of people as they swept through the wide sliding door, with Julie Darden shining like a planet among dimmer stars, and big, handsome, brown-faced Jim Carver at her side, Jim Carver, sole heir to the famous name and the biggest fortune in the county, next to Blair's.

Something pinched the heart of Fernald, but he said as cheerfully as he could: "Hello, Jim."

Jim Carver walked straight past him, almost rubbed shoulders with him, and went on, looking straight before him as though Fernald had been a dream and a voice from a dream.

X

As generally happens when a man has been insulted, Fernald looked hastily around him as though he had been the one who had offered the provocation and hoped that no one had seen it. But it had been seen. Arthur Craig stood just opposite, covertly turning his head with a smile that was more in the eyes than in the mouth. Suddenly Fernald knew that he would have to do something about this affair.

It was the girl's fault, he knew. He had always known Jim, however slightly, and he had always received a word, no matter how careless, from the man of fortune. It was Julie Darden, who must have related the story of how she had slighted him and encouraged her escort to do the same. They were trying to put him down; they were trying to show that the sheepherder, Fernald, could not rub elbows with the better blood of Griffon.

Well, that was all right, too, but the important thing was that he had been insulted, and, therefore, he would have to do something about it. He had been insulted in public to make the matter worse.

He stood by the door, brooding. In his heart there was a cold iron of hatred. He wanted to kill. He wanted to kill not big Jim Carver, perhaps, but Julie Darden. His fingers twitched as he looked after her.

A tag dance started. Vaguely he noted it, the spinning of the couples, and Mary Grey shining like a star in the crowd, constantly swinging from one man to another as her partners were slapped on the arm or shoulder. But even Mary Grey was no longer a star, no more than a star beside the moon, compared with Julie Darden. Golden as a harvest moon she shone. She was dancing around the room with Jim Carver. A hundred youngsters must have yearned to tag him, but awe of his position and awe of the girl prevented them. They made the complete circuit of the place before big Walter Grainger, fifty plus, the color of red mahogany, heavy as a horse, always laughing and cheerful, Grainger, the rancher, tagged Jim Carver, and the girl whirled away in the arms of her new partner, laughing. And Carver looked after them, laughing, too.

Apparently, Grainger would do. He was acceptable, rough and ready as he was. Acceptable, perhaps, because of his broad acres? No, rather because he had been a friend of the girl's father.

Then a thought came to Fernald, and the impact of it caused the blood to fly upward to his brain. The wave of heat receded and left him colder and clearer of mind than ever. He crossed the floor, picking his way through the dancers. He felt a faint smile on his lips, although there was no mirth in his heart. Presently he could tag the fat arm of Grainger. The big man stepped back instantly.

"Here's another partner, Julie," he said.

Before she could speak, she was in the arms of Fernald, and slowly dancing backward through the crowd.

She looked straight into his eyes, with contempt, and with rage. "You puppy!" she said.

He smiled at her with a deliberate satisfaction.

"I'll call out in another moment," she said.

She stood still. He took her by the arm, and she winced under the pressure. He held her more lightly, but made her walk along at his side.

Now that she had been tagged, half a dozen youths swarmed toward them, but he picked them off with quick, keen glances, and the enthusiasm faded out of their faces. They shied away from the pair who walked, and pretended that they had other targets.

They came to the great rock in the center of the hall, big, black, looking like a gigantic caricature of an anvil, with end thrusting out. They paused by the legend, painted in big letters with white lead.

He only saw: GOD KEEP US ALL FROM SINFUL PRIDE! That applied to Julie, he thought.

She was saying: "You're doing a vile thing. You're going to force me to make a scene. Besides, you're bruising my arm. If you don't go away from me, I'll cry out."

"I wish I were bruising your heart," he said. "One day I shall. Tonight, I hope. But you're going to stand here for a minute. It won't take me long to tell you what I want to say." He released her arm. He felt that with his eye alone he could hold her. And, in fact, she stood still. A white patch was on her bare arm where his grasp had lain. She remained there, close to him, but surveying him still with a glance wonderfully calm.

"You're being the big, strong, brutal man, aren't you?" she said. "You'll wind up with a horsewhipping before very long. Do you guess that?"

"You got young Carver to insult me," he said.

She answered nothing. The coolness of her survey heated his blood.

"He never would have done that," went on Fernald, "except for you. You know that, I suppose?"

Still she said nothing. Her lip was curling a little.

"I want to tell you," he went on, "that other people were

standing by. I don't care about you and Carver. You're both no good. Only, I have to tell you that I'm going to make him apologize to me before everybody."

Suddenly she laughed. "You're going to make big Jim apologize to you . . . before everybody?"

"I think I shall," he said.

"I see," said the girl. "If he won't, you'll murder him . . . before everybody. Murder him in self-defense. You don't alarm me. Not a bit. Braggarts never do what they say."

He considered her for a moment. "What a fool you are. What a cruel fool, too. Cruel to Jim Carver, I mean to say."

"Here comes Jim now," said the girl. "You tell him what you've told me, will you?"

He turned a little.

People in their dancing were eying the group by the central rock curiously, but they were verging to the sides farther and farther away. Their eyes were half anxious and half curious. He saw Craig grinning widely, covertly, maliciously, studiously avoiding a glance at the big rock and the people near it. Craig would be a good subject for a killing, too, he decided.

Then Jim Carver came up. He was very big. His wrath made him still bigger.

"You . . . Fernald!" he exclaimed, his voice thick with rage. "What d'you mean by it?" He gripped the arm of Fernald. The other tensed his muscles and felt the iron-hard fingertips of young Carver spill away from the slippery surface.

"Tell Jim Carver what you told me?" said the girl tauntingly.

"I told her," said young Fernald, "that she'd made trouble by getting you to insult me. I told her that I'd make you apologize to me before the entire crowd."

Carver stared at him. Then he broke into abrupt, harsh laughter. "You are a fool. Not drunk with booze, but drunk with pride, eh, you guttersnipe? You think, Fernald, that because you have made a little money with your dirty, tricky cattle deals, that you're as good as the next man, do you? You'll learn that there's a difference. You think, too, that you can work me up to a gunfight? You think that I'll lay myself open to being murdered by an expert mankiller? Not I! I have half a dozen armed men in this room, though, and, if they get a signal from me, they blow you off the face of this earth, Fernald."

Fernald waited for a moment. He could remember a moment in his childhood when he had been struck heavily in the face and tasted his own blood. It was like that now. His very soul was bitter with revolt. And what could he do? He heard the girl laugh a little lightly.

"Now," she said, "why don't you give an answer? Why don't you lift a hand? By heaven, Jim, I'm glad to see the way you've put a ruffian in his place. He almost crushed my arm."

"I'll have him horsewhipped out of the hall!" exclaimed Carver fiercely.

Said Fernald at last: "Jim, will you come out of this place into the dark where I can . . . talk it over with you?"

"To have his throat cut in the dark," the girl said contemptuously. "D'you pretend that you'll face him honestly, hand to hand."

"Aye, he looks big enough to do that, doesn't he?" chuckled Carver.

Fernald sighed. "You think that you're winning, Carver," he said. "But I tell you what . . . I'm going to do what I said."

"What?" snapped Carver.

"He's going to make you apologize," mocked the girl.

"I am," Fernald said, "if I have to tear the words out of your throat with my bare hands." He took a short step forward. A devil was raging in him, stifling his breath. Carver did not shift his ground.

"Don't hit him, Jim," said the girl. "He's out of his mind.

Don't hurt him. But you'd better have some of the boys throw him out."

"Don't try that, Carver," Fernald warned. "I'm begging you not to try that."

Suddenly Mary Grey was beside them, her face pale, and her eyes bigger and darker than ever. The dance had ended. People had gone to the corners of the room. There was a dead silence while all eyes were fixed upon the central group.

The orchestra leader, knowing his business, immediately struck up a brisk tune, but no one danced, and still all eyes were fastened upon the four in the middle of the floor.

"What is it, Tommy?" asked Mary Grey. "What's happened?"

"This . . . woman," Fernald said, picking out his words slowly, "got this . . . man . . . to insult me . . . snub me. Now I tell him that he'll apologize."

"Tommy, you can't make him do that," urged Mary Grey. "What they say doesn't matter, not to anyone who really cares about you. They're being contemptible, that's all. And Julie Darden is trying to play the queen again. But you can't make a scene. Not in here. The whole town is looking at you!"

"I'll tell you what," Jim Carver announced mockingly, "I'll apologize to you before the whole crowd . . . when you pick up Dean Carver's stone and carry it across the room."

Blinding red madness struck across the eyes of Fernald. "I'll take that bet!" he exclaimed, and turned to the great rock.

XI

Mary Grey was still beside him. She was trying to dissuade him, muttering and murmuring at his ear.

He simply said: "Look here, Mary . . . I'm going to do it, or break my back trying. That's all! Stand away from me. Something may crack." Then he leaned, took hold of the projecting end of the stone, and lifted.

His feet sank straight through the floor to the ground just beneath, with a brief, *crunching* sound. No doubt the wood was worn and decayed where the moisture that crawled up the sides of the rock had eaten into the flooring. Still, it was a strange sight to see the apparent height of Fernald shortened by several inches.

With his stance on the ground, he heaved again. His coat ripped up the back—exploded, rather than ripped. But the stone slowly swayed up from the ground and showed the lower surface, weighted down and clotted with great lumps of earth.

A deep-throated, brief shout went up all around the hall.

He could hear the voice of Ed Walters, calling: "Good boy, Tommy!"

Ed Walters was a hound of the law, but Ed Walters was also a friend whose voice at this moment must never be forgotten. It cleared his brain and made him breathe more easily as he rested against the upended stone.

The effort had been like the lifting of a horse, but it was nothing compared to the struggle he would have when he had to get that complete burden up. So far, he had had the advantage of a sort of natural lever. There would be no advantage of that sort when he strove to sway up the entire weight of the burden. And yet the strain of the first lifting made the blood sing in his ears, and his shoulders and arms seemed to have been stretched longer.

Mary Grey, he saw, was on hands and knees, digging the adhering soil away from the bottom of the stone. Mary was a helper, and he would remember her, too.

It seemed to him that he never had lived before this nightmare hour in his life.

Then he heard, very close at hand, but seeming to come to him out of enormously distant space, the voice of Julie Darden, who was saying: "Jim, you ought to stop him, you know. No matter what he is, you most certainly don't want him to break his back."

"I don't care what he tries to do," Jim Carver said. "But, by heavens . . . I've tried to heave up that stone by the same end . . . and . . . and . . . he seemed to manage it like nothing at all."

With a grave and grim pleasure, Fernald listened.

He could hear Mary Grey saying: "Give it up, Tommy. The far end is lodged deep in the ground. It's a terrible thing to try to move it. You can't do it. You mustn't try!"

He made no answer. He was breathing with less trouble now, and, glancing around him, he marked the way to the big side door that opened off the floor. That was the shortest way for him to go, to get the rock out of the room, as he had declared that he would do. Yet the way seemed infinitely long, and every broad, bright-faced board was to him like a mile's journey, merely in prospect.

1,642 pounds—that was the weight of the mass that he was going to handle, if he could. He said this to himself. It was the weight of a horse—no mustang, no long-legged thoroughbred, even, but the weight of a draft horse that works at the wheel in a long team, patiently lugging onto the collar. Such would be the poundage of one of those ponderous animals. And to think of handling it with his naked strength!

He shook his head, and then rocked the stone from side to side, to loosen it at the farther end. Even to rock it was not the easiest thing in the world. But, as a determined and grim man will do, he fixed his mind not upon the difficulty, but upon the ways of overcoming it. There are ways of turning the human body itself into a system of leverages and supports. A small man may be able to handle 250 pound bales of hay all day long by pulling one end over the knees and then heaving up with the entire body.

He knew about those systems of handling great weights. He knew that a lightweight could manage immense bulks by care, and he was no lightweight. Every ounce of his body was an ounce of strength, now surcharged with electric determination.

So he set about taking hold on the big rock as he would have taken hold upon a great, hard sack or a bale of hay. He lowered the higher, longer end across his knees, stooping to make a platform that would receive it. As the thrust of the burden came down, it seemed to grind through his flesh to the bone. But presently he reached over, got a good finger hold on a rough projection at the lower end of the stone, and then heaved, letting his might flow into the effort slowly, increasing his pressure, like the flow of water out of a reservoir, and swaying back a little on his heels. Balance would have to be kept, or else his back would certainly break. And if not his back, what of other bones?

In all his life, since his childhood, he had never put forth his full strength. No, his full might had not been enlisted even on the day when he bent the iron bar in the presence of Visconti, the money-lender. But now it was enlisted, and he himself wondered at what seemed the exhaustless reserves upon which he could draw.

But at the points of the shoulders, it seemed as though the tendons were snapping. His thighs shook crazily. A shooting pain ran through the back of his neck. Between his shoulder blades he could swear that his body was dividing, as a biscuit divides when hands break it open. It was as though he had to use a separate strength, a set of muscles never before used to offset that inwardly disintegrating force of his own lifting.

He swayed. He told himself that he had reached the limit of his power. He could see no more—his eyes were veiled with darkness. It was as though hands were pressing outward, behind those eyes, trying to push them out of his head. His cheeks were swelling as though he were blowing his breath into them fiercely. And a roaring filled his ears.

"It's horrible!" he heard a voice crying. That voice was not that of a bird screaming on a far-off wind. It was Julie Darden, close at hand. "It's horrible! He's killing himself. Stop him, Jim!"

"Well, let the stupid brute kill himself, if he's bound to do it," answered Jim Carver.

"A hundred to ten that he ain't gonna lift it clear of the floor!" called some man from the side of the room.

There was only a laugh in answer. "We've seen that he can't," came back another.

A laugh rose in the throat of Fernald. He could not utter it. It merely helped, more than half, to strangle him. But there was a despairing force in that laughter that ran down to his fingertips.

"A hundred to one against!" yelled the same voice.

And then a wild screech of scores and scores of half-hysterical people smote the ears of Fernald.

He could not imagine why that should be. There was only one oddity about his present position, and that was that he was swaying back more than he seemed to need to balance himself. There was less pain across his back, also, less sense of something drawn out to the snapping point.

Then he made out the cry of Mary Grey through the blind darkness that surrounded him: "Tommy, Tommy! You've done enough, lifting it. Let it drop again! D'you hear? Let it drop again!"

He forced his eyes open. It was true. He had lifted the stone clear of the floor. That floor trembled about him—for men and women were leaping, shouting, and clapping their hands. He could see them only dimly, through veils of black and of red. His eyes were mere slits. Then he realized why. The electric frenzy of his effort had made his lips grin widely back, and so the cheeks pressed up higher against the eyes. He forced that grotesque stretching of the mouth to relax, also. There must be no wasted effort. So, out of his terrible glazed eyes, he looked toward the door and strove to move his feet. Yes—a fraction of an inch, and no more, he could succeed in thrusting his feet forward.

Julie Darden was crying out, in a wilder voice than ever: "Jim Carver, if you're half a man, tell that boy to stop! Tell Fernald to stop it! I don't care how many men he's killed . . . he's killing himself now with his own hands!"

Mary Grey was close beside. She had clawed away the last adhering bit of the earth that clung to the heavier and bigger end of the stone. He felt no difference in the apparent poundage because of her thoughtful care, but he could guess that he was being assisted.

"Thanks, Mary," he said. He saw her jump as though he had struck her, and he was not surprised, for it did not seem his own voice that uttered the words, but the grinding of immense, brazen hinges under the weight of a monstrous gate. So did those groaning words come out of his throat, shaking his whole body with the vibration.

"A hundred to ten that he don't get it all the way to the door!" shouted somebody.

The loud voice of Ed Walters beat in: "I'll take that bet! I'll lay you another ten at the same odds. Twenty to hundred that he makes it to the door."

Others began to shout. The whole crowd had flowed toward the door, so that he went down a path bordered with closely packed humanity. He could see his own dreadful effort faintly reflected in the faces that were packed about him. Men and women actually groaned aloud in sympathy with him.

But, inch by inch, he was taking his burden forward, and the thick planks groaned beneath him, like the people, from the weight that they had to bear. A good floor, a strong floor. But one projecting nail upset him. Against it he stubbed his foot and, instantly losing his balance, toppled forward and heard the rock fall, with a booming thunder.

XII

Many a time, when he thought afterward of that moment, it was to Fernald as to one who remembers, dimly, the delirium of a fever.

He fell with the rock before him, of course, and his body toppled limply across it. There he lay extended, helpless, breathing with an odd rattling in his throat. He had no feeling in his body for a few seconds. Then queer, twisting pains began in his knees, his ankles, and his shoulders, as though the tendons were shrinking and shortening to their ordinary length.

Every one was packing closely around.

Above him, he heard the authoritative voice of Blair, the banker, saying: "There's been enough of this. He's probably ruined himself for life. Here, some of you, get him out of the place. We'll take him over to my place. Somebody call Doctor McPherson."

Mary Grey's hands were grasping one of his. She was on her knees before him, saying: "Tommy, Tommy, how'd you feel? Is something broken in you?"

He could see her more clearly now, and, when he spoke, his voice was no longer that sound of grinding metal upon metal. "I'm all right," he said. "You're a good girl, Mary. You've helped me a lot. Did the rock smash through the floor?"

"It fell on a cross beam, I guess," she said in answer. "It's only smashed in the top of the planking. That's all."

"Good," he said. And suddenly he arose lightly. All mist was gone from his eyes. All pain left him. Instead, a nervous ecstasy of resolve was leaping through his body. A sense filled him as of the rushing of a spring flood through an echoing cañon.

"Tom, you come home with me," said Blair. "We've had about enough of this Hercules business, I think."

He smiled at the banker. "I'm all right," he said. "I'll just see what I can do with this little old stone once more, and then. . . ."

Suddenly, as though he wished to surprise the terrible bulk of the thing, he leaned, gripped the lever end, and upended the great rock. Then, as before, he brought it down across his knees, stooped, laid hold with the right hand once more and, behold, it was easily swayed up from the floor. Aye, easily, but at a price!

Whatever frenzy had nerved him with a greater might than before, now something gave way in him under the incredible pressure that the lifting put on every part of his body. Blood gushed from his nose and his mouth and streamed down over the stone, and, streaked with crimson, the proud inscription that commemorated the exploit of Dean Carver long ago.

The spectacle was too much for many of the onlookers. Even men turned away; women screamed out in horror. But a needle sharpness of agony was in the voice that pierced the ears of Fernald.

"It's on your head, Jim, if he dies from it. Stop him! Stop him!"

That was Julie Darden, proud and fair and scornful. That was Julie Darden, begging for his life! A brief smile twitched at his lips. But he was going on.

The planks passed groaning behind him, one by one. The door was closer. A peculiarity was now that he could not breathe. There seemed to be no air in the room. He was a swimmer, immersed in water, unable to take a breath except one that would end his life. And the place was a furnace. Burning heat consumed him. His body became drenched in a few seconds with perspiration.

Other things were happening. His coat burst across the still-swelling muscles of his shoulders as already it had burst down the length of his back. With the snapping of the cloth he felt a little relief, at the first, and then a greater weight than ever. The strength of the fabric had resisted the pulling weight that threatened to tear out his arms at the shoulder blades. Slower and more slowly, the planks passed behind him.

"Jim," he heard that wild, appealing voice of Julie Darden crying, "tell him that he's won. That's the only way!"

"I'll see that gunfighting, murdering ruffian dead first," Jim Carver hissed.

It was a hasty speech and made before people who were not ready to listen to it. The ringing, rather nasal voice of Ed Waters came in with hasty protest: "You say a thing like that and I'll run you in, Jim, and I don't care if you're ten times a Carver. You ain't God Almighty!"

Dark were the looks apportioned to poor Jim Carver now. But the welcome blackness outside the open doorway was now reaching, as it were, for the feet of Fernald. He wondered if his eyes would burst from his head as he crossed the final plank, or if his arms would be torn out bodily by the sockets.

Then he heard Mary saying: "Let it drop. It'll roll out now. You've won!"

Others were shouting. The voices seemed glad, amazed, triumphant, and horrified, all at once.

But he could only make out the words of Mary as he answered: "I don't know how to drop it. It's tearing my arms out."

Suddenly it tore its way from his fingertips, struck the floor, jarred heavily, and then it toppled slowly off the final plank and *thumped* with a shuddering force upon the ground outside and beneath.

Fernald felt, then, as though all his body were pulling together, the individual tendons straining back, striving to react after the immense strain they had been under. And there was lightness in him. He seemed to be hitched to a balloon that was dragging him upward. He staggered.

Ed Walters caught him on one side, and Mary Grey on the other. "Steady," said Walters. "Steady, Tom. Lean on me. I'll take care of you. Pull yourself together. That . . . that bleeding will stop in a minute or two, I guess."

"I don't need to lean on anything," said Fernald. "Where's Craig?" He rested his hand upon the shoulder of Walters and, with a handkerchief, wiped the blood from his face, but still it was trickling from mouth and nose. He could breathe more easily, gasping in the air with a harsh sound, a rattling intake that sounded like the shaking of pebbles in a wooden box. His whole body was trembling, only a trifle at first, but increasing more and more. That same tremor was in the voice with which he asked for Craig.

"I'm here," said the latter, after a moment.

Even then, perhaps, he would not have spoken, but men caught him and thrust him forward. He was frightened. He looked desperately about him.

"I ain't done a thing," he protested.

"You heard me speak to Jim Carver, and you saw him pass me by?" asked Fernald.

"Yes, I saw that," agreed Craig. "You bet I saw it, and I was surprised. I thought. . . ."

"Now you're going to hear Jim Carver apologize to me in front of the whole crowd. He wouldn't use guns with me . . . he wouldn't fight with me . . . and he said he'd apologize as soon as this here rock was carried off the barn floor. Where's Jim Carver?"

There was a rustling and a stir as everyone turned from side to side. But no Jim Carver was to be seen. His big form was no longer head-high above the throng.

"Jim Carver's gone," said someone.

"He can't be gone," said Fernald. "He wouldn't be such a sneak." He looked grimly around him. "I'll find him," he said, and started to leave.

Ed Walters, the big deputy sheriff, tugged to keep him back, and suddenly the girl was there in front of him—Julie Darden. Then he stopped, swaying more and more unsteadily. He was like a thing thrown off balance and bound to fall.

"Jim Carver's gone," she said. "I saw him go. He slipped away rather than make a scene."

"You talked to Jim and set him against me. You stirred his pride up to make a fool of him and to insult me. You've started the trouble, and you can collect the result of it. It's your credit. I want people to know what you are."

He saw her flinch. Yet, he saw the horror widening her eyes, as she looked item by item, as it were, upon the features of his distress—upon the ripped coat, hanging in shreds almost, the shirt burst open at the throat, the collar thrusting up like horns about his ears, the blood on his face, still running, and the blood on his hands, too, where the rough points of the heavy stone had pricked through the skin. Bit by bit, she marked him down.

Yet, although she flinched and her color waned, she did not shrink away. A man with a noble head, covered with short-cropped, silver hair that made his sun-darkened skin seem almost the brown of a Mexican's, broke from the bystanders and caught the arm of Julie Darden.

"Julie, come out of this with me," he said.

"No," said the girl. "No, I'm going to stay here. He's right. I started all the trouble. I'm going to see what comes of it."

Fernald saw this from the corner of his eye as he stepped

past her and toward the darkness that lay outside the side door of the barn. His mind was only half with him. He was like one who has just risen from a profound, feverish sleep. Half of his wits were gone, and only a fixed purpose remained in him. That purpose was, somehow, to get to Jim Carver. Even if he had to tear down stone walls, he must find a way to the side of Jim Carver, and so bring him back to the dance hall to do the thing that he had promised.

Ed Walters was still holding him, arguing rapidly. He picked the hands of Walters away and brushed the deputy sheriff back. The pleading voice of Mary Grey he closed from his ears by stepping into the dark and jerking the heavy sliding door shut behind him. There was a staple and a latch. In a moment he had secured the door so that he could not be pursued for a few seconds. He had a little interval and leeway, and he hurried to make use of it.

XIII

The Carver house was set well back from the barn, perhaps fifty yards, and there were trees filling the interval, big, round-headed trees that had been planted there by Dean Carver, the giant. Fernald began to run forward beneath the trees. Lanterns were everywhere, casting a sort of moonlight and mottling the ground with the patterns of leaves and the broad, black shadows cast by the branches themselves. Those heavy shadows seemed to be striking at him as he ran. He ducked and swerved and dodged from the blows. His wits were wandering more and more. The rage and the malice had left him. But a great ocean was roaring at his ears, and he knew only that he must find Jim Carver and take him back to the barn.

He reached the front steps of the house and ran up them. There was a bell pull and a knocker, too, but he used neither.

He laid his hand on the doorknob, turned at it, and found that it was latched. So he freshened his grip and pulled back hard. With a ringing snap the bolt burst, and he walked on into the hallway. It was big, dim, solemn. A lamp with a good circular burner hung by three chains from the ceiling, and, by the light of this, he saw a bloodstained, ragged, nightmare object standing opposite him. He walked straight up to it and laid his hand on the bloody face. His fingers touched glass. He had simply been marching toward his own reflection in the hall mirror.

"I'm not seeing very good," muttered Tom Fernald to himself. "There's something wrong with me." Then he stood for a moment, and listened to the sound of his breathing, which was steadier and less gasping, now, and with less of a rattle deep in the throat.

Where was Jim Carver? A groan sounded behind him. He turned and saw the big buck Negro who worked in the house. The black man was paralyzed with fear of this horror in the dimness of the hallway.

"Where's Jim, George?" asked Fernald. "Show me where to find Jim, will you?"

"Right up in his room, I reckon, sir," said the Negro, trembling. "Is this Mister Fernald, sir?"

"I want Jim. I gotta see Jim," he repeated. "You show me the way." He gripped the arm of George.

"Oh, lawzee, sir, you're crushin' the bones in my arm," said the servant. "I'm gonna show you right quick. I hope that you ain't come to no terrible harm tonight, sir. I hope that they ain't gone and shot you. . . ."

They were at the head of the stairs by this time. Outside, there was a sound of many footfalls running toward the house. Voices called, too.

He'll hear that, and he'll know that I'm coming, thought Fernald.

But he hardly cared. The delirious longing to see Jim Carver was all that possessed his brain. "Here's the door, sir," said George.

"This one?"

"Yes, sir. I'll knock."

"Never mind. I'll surprise him, if I can." He laughed silently in the dull light of the hall, and the Negro stared and shrank from him. A caricature of fright was the face of George, with his rolling eyes. "I'll surprise him," whispered Fernald again.

He could hear footfalls pounding on the front steps of the house, and there was a faint, rushing sound that was much nearer to him, coming up the stairs in the front of the house. He tried the doorknob. It was locked. He laid his left hand against the wall, tightened the grip of the right, and drew back with all his incredible might. There was not a sign of yielding. He relaxed and jerked; something cracked, but the lock still did not give.

"Who's there?" called the voice of young Jim Carver.

"Tom Fernald's out here and wanting to see you pretty bad," said Fernald.

"You murdering hound," Jim Carver said, his voice running high up the scale, "if you try to get into this room, I'll fill you full of buckshot, d'you hear?"

Fernald laughed. He thought of buckshot, as he often had bought them, the big black beads of lead. To his mind, there was no harm in such a thing. As for his own revolvers, he had even forgotten that he had them on. For the only picture that obsessed his mind was that of himself carrying or dragging Jim Carver back to the barn dance floor, where he would have to make his apology before all the people. Therefore, standing in the hall, he laughed.

The Negro, overmastered with panic, was running down the hall, screaming over his shoulder as he ran: "Save yourself,

Mister Jim! Climb out of the window, because Mister Fernald's a devil that will claw his way through your door!"

Fernald stepped back across the hall, ran three short, driving steps forward, and struck the door with the big, rubbery muscle that padded his shoulder. The door crashed and Fernald pitched headlong into the bedroom beyond.

"Take it, then, damn you!" screamed the voice of Jim Carver, inhumanly harsh and high. As the door fell, he fired both barrels of his shotgun.

One slug ripped the heel from the right shoe of Fernald, but that was the only part of the charge that struck him. He had literally gone down like a ninepin, and, for the split part of a second, his heels were higher than his head. He got to his knees.

Down the hallway, the Negro had stopped running and was screaming steadily, like the ceaseless shrieking of a maniac who seems never to need to pause for breath. Many heavy feet were running through the house, beating, as it were, in the very brain of Fernald.

He looked up, as he rose, and saw Jim Carver still staggered off balance from the heavy recoil of the shotgun. Fernald did not wait to get cleanly to his feet. He jumped from all fours at the throat of the bigger man. He saw Carver drop the shotgun and pull out a revolver. That is to say, the gun was more than half out of its sheath when the hands of Fernald reached Carver. He struck big Jim on the side of the jaw. His head dropped loosely to his side upon his shoulder; his knees sagged; his mouth opened. He remained standing, but the wits were out of him. Fernald took the revolver and hurled it through the window. It crashed a great, jagged black hole in the gleaming face of the pane.

"You come with me, Jim," Fernald said, and took Carver firmly in hand, holding him under the pit of the left arm.

Blindly, helplessly the stunned man sagged, without protest, and as Fernald turned, he saw Julie Darden standing in the doorway, leaning there, rather.

She was in exactly the attitude of Jim Carver, it seemed to Fernald, except that he was supporting Jim and the side of the doorway was upholding the girl. But in the same nerveless, stricken manner she leaned there and seemed to be seeing a horror enacted before her eyes.

In a vaguely troubled way, he was sorry for her. "I won't hurt him," he said. "I'm not going to kill him. I haven't even thought about killing him. I just want him to do what he promised. I won't hurt him. I guess he means a lot to you. But I won't hurt him."

He had the staggering form of Carver across the room by this time. Now the hall behind the girl filled with people, and wildly excited faces gleamed there, and terrible, frightened eyes.

"Nobody's hurt," said Julie Darden. "Oh, thank God, there's nobody. . . ."

How had she managed to get ahead of the crowd of running men, he wondered. Then he asked her: "What got you here first?"

"The dread of what you'd do," said the girl. "It showed me the quickest way out of the barn."

Fernald strode past her into the hallway, dragging and propping the still semiconscious body of tall Jim Carver along.

The people separated. Even Ed Walters, agape, stepped back to let him pass with his prisoner. Even Mary Grey said not a word, but shrank aside. Yet Julie Darden did not leave him. As he got to the landing of the front stairs, she slipped in front of them and put her hands against the breast of Fernald.

"What are you going to do?"

"I'm taking him back to the barn," said Fernald.

"You're out of your wits," she said. "You're not thinking straight. If you humiliate him any further, you'll have to kill him afterward. He won't be able to live without fighting you with guns. The way it is, he'll have to leave the country for a long while. Isn't that enough revenge for you?"

"Don't try to stop me," said Fernald. "He's got to do what he promised."

Big Jim Carver, his consciousness slowly returning, began to struggle feebly.

"If you do that," Fernald warned, looking curiously up into the face of the taller man, "I'll kill you, Jim. I'm beginning to sort of want to kill you. You . . . Julie Darden . . . stand out of my way. Bah! You can't stop me." He took her by the chin, between the thumb and forefinger of his left hand, and so pushed up her face a little and studied her gravely. Twenty people, massed on the stairs above and below, watched them breathlessly.

"Julie!" called her father suddenly from below. His voice, wild with anxiety, pierced needle-like into the dimness of Fernald's brain.

"I'm all right," answered the girl. She went on, speaking to Fernald: "I'm trying to talk to you for your own sake. Nobody in the world could do what you've done tonight. But if you keep on, you're going to make a horrible scene. You're going to shame Jim Carver so that his life will be wrecked . . . or else he'll fight you tomorrow, and you'll have to kill him. If he insulted you, it was my fault. I ought to be killed for it."

He still had her chin imprisoned as she spoke. Her head moved and trembled in his grasp. Then it seemed to Fernald that a great weariness overcame him. He was somewhere between a sigh and a yawn, as it were. No matter how he gathered himself, he could not find words or an idea. He found himself swaying.

"You started it," he said. "Maybe you'd better finish it. You've had to beg his life for him. So let him have it. I don't care. Take him." He loosed his hold on big Jim Carver and went on slowly down the stairs.

Someone came like a rush of wind behind him. It was Mary Grey.

"You're a good girl, Mary," he said, "you stood by. And. . . ." He interrupted himself to look back, and he saw, above him, that Julie Darden was carefully taking the reeling Jim Carver by the arm and leading him, coaxing him, up the stairs to his room.

"You come outside into the air," Mary Grey advised.

"Julie Darden . . . she's kind of a surprise," he commented. "Look how she stood by Carver. Look how she loves him."

"Loves?" cried the girl as they came to the front door, and more people gave way before the awful figure of Tom Fernald. "She hates him like a snake. Only, she's made of the right steel. You look sick. I'm going to take you home, and Dad will take care of you. He's been a grand doctor . . . he's learned a lot from Indians . . . and you'll be all right tomorrow. The only wonder is that you didn't burst your heart in pieces."

XIV

He did not go with Mary Grey. Instead, he stopped at the hotel and sent out a man to drive her home. She left him with a lingering and anxious farewell.

"You're a good girl, Mary," he told her. "You're the best sort in the world. You didn't back up once. I'll never forget it." Then he went up to the best room he could get.

His head was still spinning in clouds of darkness. There was still, when he breathed deeply, a very thin spray of blood from his nostrils. He stood for a time inside the door of his room, balanced, thinking. He needed a doctor. He must be brought to his full senses immediately. After that, he would have to devise a way of keeping Bill Ransome from telling the story of the Visconti money. Some people might not be willing to believe that story, but a good lot of them were sure to be glad to. Bill Ransome had to be stopped, with persuasion or with a bullet.

But a wave of darkness deepened upon his mind. He decided that he would lie down and rest for a few moments before getting a doctor, and, reaching the bed, he swayed forward. All strength went out of him. He pitched forward and lay still, face down, feet sticking out from the top of the spread.

It was about midnight when he lost consciousness. It was nine in the morning when he wakened.

He was on fire, inside and out. His face was swollen and hot to his touch, and his hands were dry. He got up and looked at himself in the mirror. There were still streaks and hardened, black ridges of blood upon his face. His collar still thrust up around his ears like a pair of horns. His coat was ripped and broken across. One might have said that steers had stampeded across his body. He looked to himself like a dead man. Even in his open, bloodshot eyes there was no life.

He looked at the watch and saw that it was nine o'clock. He had seven hours to stop Bill Ransome. Seven hours or eight. Perhaps Bill had said that he would not spread his news until five o'clock in the afternoon. Well, eight hours should be enough. First, he had to allay the burning heat that consumed his body.

He filled the adjoining bathtub with cold water and soaked his body in that until a hand of ice gripped his vitals and set him shuddering. Suddenly he was so weak that he could barely lift his body from the tub and walk back to the bedroom. There, in a mirror, he saw that his flesh was blue and purple.

He dried himself hastily, wrapped himself in a blanket, and fell on the bed again. Waves of numbness were beginning to start at his feet and pass on up to his head. They broke upon his brain in fire-streaked clouds of darkness. Then he slept.

When he recovered consciousness, his brain was clear, his body was strong, and his eye was bright. But there were two things urgently worth noting. One was that the sun that came through the window was golden in color and slanting from the west. The other was that a hand was thumping vigorously at his door.

He sat up and looked at his watch. It was 5:45! Then he understood. Out there in the hall was the forefront of the curious world, waiting to question him.

"Hello!" he called. "Wait a minute, will you?"

The bumping against the door ceased. He stepped into underwear, and, opening the door a crack, he looked out upon Ed Walters.

"Hullo, Ed," he said to the deputy sheriff. "I'm just dressing. Come in while I get my togs on, will you?"

Ed Walters did not smile. He had a curiously keen and business-like air about him, and how could Fernald forget that the business of Walters was that of arresting criminals and enforcing the law? The shock stripped from the wits of Fernald the last effects of the terrible effort that, until now, had worked upon him like a fever. Merely to be in the presence of this danger made him lighter and sure of himself.

So he began dressing. He put on his regular riding togs, because the blue serge was a bloodstained tattered wreck forever. In the meantime, he chattered with Walters.

"How's things?"

"Fair," said Walters. "You look knocked out."

"I'm sort of knocked out."

"Pull something loose in yourself?"

"Feels like I'd pulled something loose in my brain."

"I remember," recalled Walters, "there was a time when a fool of a one-eyed bronco fell on me and laid still, and the heaving and the straining that I done to get out from under, it put me in bed for a week. I looked at you last night, and I thought that you was going to bust . . . your face and your whole body swelled up so much."

"I didn't bust, then. But I nearly busted when I got back to the hotel." He pulled on his boots, and then stood up to wriggle into his shirt. When he had worked it down over his head, he saw that Walters had drawn a Colt revolver and was aiming it at him.

"What's the idea, Ed?" he asked.

"I might wanna arrest you, son. If I do, will you go along peaceable?"

The thinking of Fernald was lightning-fast. If he objected to that, if he asked questions, he would appear to be guilty. "Of course, I'll go."

Walters put up the gun. "That's all right, then. You know that I don't want any trouble or any part of any trouble with you, Tommy."

"Thanks," said Fernald. "But what's this funny story that you're telling me?"

"It's not funny. It's about you and the Visconti money."

Fernald looked up to the ceiling. He puckered his brows. "That's right," he said. "I owe him some money. And I'm ready to pay it."

"About five hundred thousand dollars? You ready to pay that?"

"Five hundred thou . . . ! What you talking about, Ed?"

"Half a million. That's what I'm talking about. You swiped it from Visconti. You killed Visconti. Why not come clean with it all, Tommy? We've got the story straight already."

"I killed Visconti? I got his money?"

"That's why you got rich so sudden. A year ago, you were poor."

"I can show you a list of my deals. I've made some money by cattle deals."

"It's a pretty sudden growth. You can't get away with that. The state wants you, Tommy."

"All right. The state can have me. I'm not going to go outlaw for nothing. I won't be bluffed out, Ed."

"I'm not bluffing."

"Yes, you are. You're trying to throw a scare into me."

Walters laughed, sudden and short. "Nobody is fool enough to try to bluff you, old son," he said. "Nobody's fool enough to try to throw a scare into you, either."

"Between you and me, Ed," demanded Fernald, "what's the meaning of all this chatter about me and Visconti?"

The long, lean face of Walters wrinkled and brightened with pleasure. "You're a cool one, old son," he said. "But that's all right. I like to see you as cool as all that. I expected that you would be. I didn't really hope to scare any confession out of you. You come over and see the judge with me, will you?"

Fernald nodded. "I'll come," he said. He ran some water and washed his hands. His shoulders ached and his fingers throbbed wickedly. That was the only sign of the vast effort he had made the night before. He was almost glad of this new crisis, which took his mind from the other thing.

"You tore up your hands, all right," Walters said, partly in admiration and partly in horror.

"Yeah, I tore 'em up a little."

"That was the most mannest-sized thing that I ever seen in my life!" exclaimed Walters, glowing with admiration.

"Aw, go on. I made a show of myself. That was all."

"You pried that fathead . . . that Jim Carver . . . off his high horse. That's what you did. And finally he had to let a girl beg him off from trouble. That's what he had to do."

"He was sort of stopped and puzzled," Fernald commented.

"He didn't want to make an apology before that whole crowd. Neither would you or I. But me . . . I made a fool of myself. I made a holy show of myself, and I know it."

Walters grunted and shook his head. "I'm glad that I seen that show," he said. "It's something that I'm going to remember, and don't you forget it. That time when you dropped the stone, my heart jumped into my mouth. I thought you were a goner."

"Maybe you had some money on me, eh?" asked Fernald.

"I had about five hundred dollars, by that time, and pretty good odds, too. But I thought that coin was blown. But when you picked that stone up like nothing at all, again . . . well, that was more than I could take in with one pair of eyes. You seemed to me to swell, Tommy. You seemed about twice your regular size, if you foller my drift."

"Oh, forget about that," Fernald said. "But I'm glad that you picked up a little coin on me. What about the judge now? Who in the world could hang anything on me? Me and Visconti?" He allowed his voice to swell with a virtuous rage.

Walters, his eyes narrowing a little, like those of a man who is prying into the far distance, thrust his head out and looked hard at the other. "By rights I oughtn't to tell you, but you'll pretty soon find out. It's Bill Ransome that told."

"Hold on!" Fernald cried, agape. "It couldn't be Bill Ransome."

"Why couldn't it?"

"Because Bill Ransome has got religion. He wouldn't go around and tell lies like that."

"You talk like you meant it," the deputy said, much impressed.

"Bill Ransome? But Bill's a friend of mine. He pretty near died for me once."

"And you haven't had a falling out since?"

"Falling out? I should say not. It can't be Bill Ransome."

"You put your money on it. It's Bill Ransome, all right," said Walters.

XV

They went down to the street and, even in entering the lobby, Fernald saw that his world had been altered since he went to bed the night before. The clerk looked from behind the desk with an air both frightened and curious. Two or three men put down their newspapers, and, when the pair started out for the long verandah, they got up noiselessly and followed after. He had become, he saw, notorious. Yesterday he had been a celebrity and a respected one.

Walters was willing to pause at the Jenkins' outdoor lunch counter, while his prisoner ate scrambled eggs and drank some coffee.

"Twenty-four hours since I've eaten," Fernald said. "And you know . . . I'd like to buy one more meal before the state begins to put up for me."

Jenkins was scrambling the eggs, blowing away the smoke and steam like a blacksmith to look at his work. "What's all this talk in the street?" asked Jenkins. "I mean about you socking Visconti and getting away with his spondulics?"

"Hello," said the boy. "Has it got around like this?"

"Yeah. Everybody's talking about it."

"Kind of envying me, Jenkins, aren't they?" asked Fernald.

Jenkins turned and blinked. He met a steady grin from Fernald. "Well," said Jenkins, nodding and balancing his long cooking fork, "I kind of felt that you hadn't done it. You got too much sense to do a murder, I always thought. Try these here eggs."

Fernald ate them slowly and sipped the coffee, and he watched the people sauntering up and down the street. When they saw him, each one halted, made a sudden half step, and then went on more slowly. Nearly all of them, after a few paces, turned and looked back. Those who spoke to him did so with startling eyes and unnatural voices.

A spanking pair of grays came down the street, whipping a light runabout behind their streaming tails. In the driver's seat was Jeff Bister and Mary Grey sat beside him.

"How long's that been going on?" he asked of Walters. "Mary Grey and Bister, I mean."

"Oh, I dunno. Jeff has made enough money to want a wife, I guess. I hope that Mary ain't gonna go and chuck herself away."

The outfit pulled up.

"Hey, Tommy! Come over here!" called Bister.

Fernald finished his coffee and went, but, as he approached, his glance was not for Bister, but for the face of the girl. She was flushed, sitting, stiff and straight, in her place, and her eyes were very wide and startled as she looked back at him.

She believes that I'm a crook, Fernald thought to himself. He came up to the hub of the runabout, tipping his hat to Mary.

"Look here," said Bister, "now that you're gone and socked yourself with so much trouble, you won't wanna have that team of chestnuts, of course. And I'll tell you what, I'll take 'em right back and make no charge for the hire of last night, even. What say to that, Tommy?"

Fernald shrugged his shoulders. It was the girl's attitude that impressed him. "Mary," he said, "you think that the yarn is true?"

"Bill Ransome couldn't lie," she stated. "You know that, Tom."

"You think that I murdered Visconti?" he asked.

She leaned a little toward him. "Listen to me, Tommy. I'm still fond of you, anyway. You know I'm fond of you. But I know that you're the only man on the range who was strong enough and man enough to handle Pete Visconti."

"I don't want you to be staying here talking to a murderer, then," Fernald declared bitterly. He stepped back and tipped his hat again, adding almost as an aside to Bister: "I like the chestnuts, and I'll keep 'em . . . till I get out of prison." He went back to Walters, noting gratefully that the latter had not followed his movements like a watchdog. "She don't believe in me, either," said Fernald. "Nobody believes in me, if she's turned me down, because she's true blue."

"You bet she's true blue," said the deputy sheriff. "But I'll tell you how it is . . . a fellow never knows his friends till he's down and out."

"If they'd do a little thinking," Fernald said in angry answer, "they'd see that I'm not down yet, and that I'm not out."

They went on toward the house of Judge Henry Rush.

"You see how it is," said Ed Walters. "The judge is a white man. You don't have to talk to him private, like this, unless you want to. Only, he wants to sit down kind of social and talk things over."

"That's what I want, too," Fernald said.

They came to the little staggering house. It looked hardly better than a Negro shanty of the far South, with the same sort of a leaning length of stovepipe above the roof line. The judge, in the last sun of the day, swayed back and forth in a rocker that rumbled like a wagon over a bridge upon the warped and uneven boards of the front porch. He was not reading a newspaper, but smiling with a sort of fat content upon the world in general. For he was a bulky man, much broken by time and his adventures. His pale eyes were so nearsighted that he did not recognize the pair until they were halfway up the path to the house. Then he heaved himself up with a deep groan, and shook hands with them both.

"You go inside and get me a couple of chairs, will you, Eddie?" he asked. "Fernald, I'm glad that you've come to see me. It's a personal tribute, I feel, and I want to justify your confidence."

The chairs were brought and the three sat down, while the judge went on: "Perhaps you'd rather go inside the house?"

"No," Fernald said. "Perhaps half the town will see me here talking with you, and I'd like that."

"I thought so, too, and now we can try to get at justice and the truth," said the judge. "Truth, you know, in my conviction, is no man's enemy. Not even the enemy of the criminal. It's better to get the truth out into the open. It stops the aching of the heart or the wretched callusing of the spirit. I don't want to take grounds that are too high, or to seem to be talking just to hear myself, but, after all, we have to take a viewpoint. I want you to know that my viewpoint is not against you, Fernald. It's on the side of truth that I want to be, and I always pray that I'm going to be able to find every accused man innocent."

"Thanks," said Fernald. "I'm glad to hear you talk like this."

"You know what you're accused of?"

"Bill Ransome says that I've killed Visconti and stolen his money."

"Eddie," said the judge, "you need not have specified Ransome." His rocking chair began to make soft thunder upon the boards of the rickety porch once more.

"The whole town knows all about it," said Walters. "Ransome . . . he went and told the newspapers, too. The yarn will be selling on the street before many minutes."

The judge turned directly to Fernald. "Did you kill Visconti?"

"No."

"Think twice. Don't answer so quickly. I was told by a man who is not likely to lie. And he told me in the manner of one who is broken-hearted at having to speak. He said that he was going to tell the newspapers, too. He felt it was his duty. And I never saw a man with a sicker face. I never listened to a man who was more convincing."

"Look at me," Fernald said.

The judge looked. He leaned a little in his chair the better to see.

Fernald raised his right hand. "I swear that I didn't murder Visconti," he said.

At the sound of these words, the judge seemed to wilt. He sank back deeply into the chair once more. Ed Walters, on the other hand, started up with an exclamation, and slowly sank down again into his place.

"He's telling the truth, Judge," he said.

The judge sighed. "He's as convincing as Bill Ransome," he said.

There was a pause. A thousand words came to the lips of Fernald, but he shut them away. He kept a steady silence.

"Listen to me," said the judge. "There are other ways of going about the matter. We can make inquiry into your books . . . if you have them. You've become, suddenly, a man of a good deal of money, and that is one reason that we've listened and believed when Bill Ransome told of looking through the window and seeing you at work counting those stacks and stacks of greenbacks. Will you let me see your books?"

"I'll show you every record that I have," Fernald stated, frowning as though in thought, for he realized that he had come to a difficult moment in his defense. "I'll show you everything. But you know how it is. I'm my own clerk, like 'most any other rancher. I've got some scraps of paper with figures jotted down on 'em. That's about all that I can show you. But I can remember a lot of other deals. I can remember most of 'em, I think. And I can get witnesses for every deal that I remember."

His confidence grew as he spoke. Now he would reap the

benefit from his long campaign, his skillful deliberation in investing the stolen money. He never had allowed it to appear in great sums at any point. But gradually rolling it up, his deals had simply become larger and larger. A wise men, a genius able to look through the dark, would be needed to separate his crooked from his honest gains. So he was able to look steadily, confidently back at the judge, and the latter suddenly struck his fist upon his knee.

"By thunder, there's such a thing as religious hallucination, and Bill Ransome is pretty close to a religious freak. Fernald, d'you know of any reason why Bill should want to do you out?"

"He stepped between me and a bullet once," Fernald reminded. "And he's never let me do anything in return for that. I've wanted to set him up. But he never would listen. He's been pretty stubborn about that. But maybe he's begun to hold a grudge against me, in spite of everything. Matter of fact, I don't know Bill very well lately. I knew him when we were kids together. But the last year or so, he's changed."

"He told me," said the judge, "that what changed him was a moment when his life was in your hands. He felt that God sent down his power to change your mind and let Ransome live."

"That his life was in my hands?" Fernald said. "Well, I don't make anything of that."

The judge made a sweeping gesture. "I'm not going to let this charge come to court, Fernald," he said. "No matter what people say about it, I'm not going to waste the county's money on a hard trial in which the state has only one witness, and not one scruple of solid proof in hand to show, besides his naked testimony. After all, the lives of our citizens cannot be talked away, or their property, either, otherwise government and law would be a joke. Fernald, you're free. But if we learn more, later on, that may change my attitude. In the meantime, I wish that you'd get your accounts together as well as you can, and bring them in to me one of these days. That's all, Fernald. I know you'll be wanting to stir about and let people know that you're not even to come to trial."

He smiled, shook hands heartily, and Fernald found himself suddenly alone again, in the street, a little bewildered and with a savage sense of triumph. He had escaped. He felt rather like the cunning fox than the fighting wolf, but he vowed in secret bitterness of heart that big Bill Ransome would feel his teeth.

Ed Walters had remained alone, behind him; slowly he went on down the street and passed the doors of the bank, the front windows blazing with sunset gold, as Blair came out and locked the door behind him. Fernald waited, and saw the older man start with a shock.

"Tommy," Blair said, recovering himself, "I'm the sorriest man in Griffon to have heard the story that's in the air. And. . . ."

"Yesterday," said Fernald, "you wanted me in the bank. That doesn't go now, I suppose?"

"Ah, Tom," said Blair, "a man's brilliance can never make up for a certain lack of public confidence."

"Blast the public confidence," said Fernald. "Judge Henry Rush has talked to me, and he's not even bringing Bill Ransome's pipe dream into court."

XVI

The astonishment in the face of Blair was sweet to the eye of Fernald, but he did not wait to let the banker utter the change that had evidently come again over his mind. By a theft he had made himself rich; by a lie he had defended himself. A deep disgust with himself and with Blair, also, made him turn on his heel and stride away. Blair called after him once, but he hurried on, head down and chin thrust out.

When he found Bill Ransome!

A dainty, wire-wheeled sulky with a dancing black between the shafts darted around the next corner, then drew up suddenly close to the sidewalk, close to him.

Julie Darden, more golden glowing to his eye than the western color in the sky. High-headed, flushing, she looked down at him for all the world like Mary Grey. He took off his hat and waited. All the rest had discarded him. It would be rather amusing to have her do the same. Only, it was wonderful that she had even paused to speak to him.

Far off, he heard voices like the crowing of roosters—boys out selling extras for the newspapers, and the crowing sounds, thin and high, dissolved and developed into:

"Fernald accused of murder!"

"All about the big killing!"

"Visconti mystery!"

"Have all the rats left you, Tom Fernald?" she asked him.

"Mostly all," he responded.

"I haven't left you," said the girl. "Not if you'll have my friendship. I know that you're innocent."

He stepped out closer and laid a hand upon the rubber-mounted shaft; the hot side of the horse pulsed against his knuckles. "Why do you know that I'm innocent?" he asked her.

Suddenly, if she was glorious before, she was a radiant star now.

"Because I saw you last night," she said. "No one except a hero could have done what you did. No one but a good hero could have kept from killing Jim Carver. But you didn't. You held yourself in hand. I watched you, and I couldn't believe. I was awake all night . . . building up my imagination until it could grasp a man like you, Tom Fernald . . . but I'd never dreamed of such a person before."

"You don't think that I killed Visconti?"

"Killed him? I don't know. Never except in a fair fight. Never murdered him."

He nodded. "And never stole his money?"

At this, she laughed with a fling of her head that tossed the query to the winds.

"Could anything as cheap and low as stolen money be near you? I scorn such an idea. There's no counterfeit about you. You looked me in the eye and told me the truth the other day. I was a proud, silly fool. I only stopped tonight to tell you that you were right and that I believe in you through thick and thin. You can't be wrong."

Suddenly she seemed overwhelmed with confusion. She spoke to the horse, called farewell to Fernald, and was gone down the street in whirling dust.

Fernald looked after her grimly, but with a hot swelling of the heart.

Her heart's been opened. I could marry that girl tomorrow, he told himself. *And why not? The rest have dodged me. The black marks are on me. I'll never have the real trust of the world again. So why shouldn't I make a fair exchange, and have her? And blast Bill Ransome for a traitor. If I've lied and robbed . . . well, in my time I've been lied about and robbed, too. I'll call it square. This is justice.*

So, concluding, he turned up the street again, but, as he walked, the face of the judge arose before his eyes, the kindly, peering eyes that strove dimly to find the truth. Fernald knew that they would follow him through his guilty life.

★ ★ ★ ★ ★

CLEAN COURAGE

★ ★ ★ ★ ★

I

Through an iron country, empty of everything except the voice of the wind, rode Tom Fernald, traveling fast, as was his custom. He had with him a very light pack, but two horses. One was a half-bred gelding, mean as a devil and enduring as a devil, also. The other was the pinto that had been his only mount when he saw Pete Visconti die and gathered the miser's half million of hidden dollars.

He had two horses not because he expected booty or intended to transport provisions when he came to them, but rather because every two hours he changed saddle from one horse to the other. In this manner, he was able to add long leagues to his journey every day, and he did so with the greater pleasure for two reasons. The first was that time was always money to him; the second was that he was crossing Indian country, a reservation ground where the tribes wandered as wild as beasts of prey and where scalps were taken and boasted of as in the old days of the red man's glory.

It was a desperately naked and abandoned waste through which Fernald was passing. There were no trees. There was little grass. For two days he had not seen a sign of a single head of game. Another than he might have turned back to a longer and easier route. However, he was accustomed to living on parched corn, alkali water, and hope while he was making one of his forced marches, and, therefore, he persisted now from long and powerful habit.

He could cut off two or even three days by holding to his present line of march, and, although by so doing he was in some danger of starving one of his horses, or of being picked off by a red scalp hunter, seeing that he was on the land without a permit, the saving of time was worth more danger than this to him.

He was not at all surprised when a wasping *hum* darted past his ear, followed instantly by the *snap* of a rifle shot. The instant he heard the brief wicked, buzzing noise, he did not hesitate. Instead, he checked the pinto, which he happened to be riding, and then he gave an imitation of a wounded man toppling out of the saddle toward the ground.

With one arm he grasped at the mane of the horse, which seemed to be halting as a good horse will when it feels the rider losing balance and grip in the saddle. The other hand flung out vainly into the thin air for support. And so he twisted deliberately over to the side, and, as the pinto came to an easy trot, he dropped to the ground. The fall was still of enough force to have broken the neck of another man, but Fernald knew how to do it, and he received the shock of the impact on the thick, rubbery cushions of muscles across the back of his shoulders.

He lay now, with his left arm flung wide, his right across his breast, his head turned a little toward the side from which the sound of the rifle shot had come. Now that he was flat on the ground, he half felt that he was a fool. It seemed more natural and right to have galloped swiftly ahead on the horse and taken chances. This regret was the impulse of panic, he was sure. On the other hand, he remembered the infinite numbers of safe coverts in the broken rock, to the right and the left, and how close to his head the first bullet had whizzed. It was not likely that such a marksman would miss a second shot. So he reasoned himself into a feeling that, after all, he probably had done the proper thing.

He was very sure of that when, a moment later, he saw a solitary Indian come out from the rocks on his right hand and move toward him with a peculiarly shambling run. Such was the eagerness of the fellow that he dropped his rifle; he threw from his shoulders a ragged skin robe that had covered them and came on clad only in a breechclout, with a naked knife in his hand.

Never had Fernald, looking through the veil of his lowered eyelashes, seen a man who looked closer to starvation. Every rib stood out, marked by shadows above and below. And the face was the face of a maniac, overhung with thin strands of black hair, like the scant mane of a high-blooded horse. Running so, knife in hand, the red man might have stood for famine, rushing to cut the throat and drink the blood of a human victim.

When he was within ten yards, Fernald sat up and brought a revolver from beneath the pit of his arm. The Indian ran almost upon it before his desperate, bloodshot eyes were able to recognize the death that waited for him. Then he stopped, and the effort of checking himself made him stagger heavily. He stood swaying from side to side.

"Drop the knife," said Fernald.

The other hesitated. The knife was gathered for an instant close in his fingers.

"You know that a bullet is as fast as a thought at this distance, friend," Fernald advised.

The red man dropped the knife to the ground. Fernald stood up and at his whistle the pinto turned and came obediently back to him, bringing along the unwilling half-breed at the length of its lead rope.

"What's your name?" asked Fernald.

"John."

"John what?"

"Oh, anything you want. I'm a Comanche. Just John is

enough for me."

"Where did you learn to speak English like this?"

"Clear back in Omaha. I went to school there. They had a good idea there."

"What was the good idea?"

"Give red men white words and you'll give them a white soul, too, before the finish."

"But they couldn't whiten you, John, eh?"

The other shrugged his shoulders. His reddened eyes were veiled with a profoundly patient resignation.

"Part of your tribe's on this ground," suggested Fernald.

"Yes."

"Far away?"

"Three miles."

"They haven't driven you out?"

"No."

"Then why are you half starved?"

"I'm not half starved," said the other. "I'm two-thirds starved."

"And they haven't driven you out? Are the others the same way?"

"Yes, a lot of 'em. Those that aren't dead."

"Dead, eh?"

"Yes, dead."

"You mean that your people are here dying of starvation?"

"Yes, partly."

"Why don't they get out for provisions?"

"They've been hunting for provisions pretty hard."

"And no luck?"

"Yes. Some field mice."

Fernald shuddered. "Why didn't you send out a horseman to take word to a town? Food would have been sent to you."

"We had no horses. They were stolen . . . by some whites."

"Tough luck," said Fernald. "But why not have sent a runner for help?"

"Because the medicine man said that we'd better help ourselves this time."

"So you've just starved to death, waiting here?"

"No, not only starving. There was something else that killed us faster."

"What?"

"Smallpox."

Fernald felt the sudden shock of fear, and a sickening falling of the heart. He knew the sudden virulence with which the disease might attack a tribe and wipe out whole hundreds in a few days or weeks.

"And no doctors?" he asked. "Nothing but your accursed medicine men?"

"That's all," said John the Comanche. "Except a white man, and he's not really a doctor, either."

"A squawman, eh?" Fernald muttered with contempt in his face. "And so, John, you came out here to find meat, and you wanted to make sure of me with your knife before you drove the horses into camp and made yourself a great man with the tribe."

"I wanted your scalp," said John with astonishing calm. "I didn't think that I would need to cut your throat, because I was sure that my slug had gone right through your brain."

"You really wanted my scalp, eh?" Fernald murmured, his eyes narrowing.

"Yes. I don't like the whites."

"They've been good to you, though," said Fernald. "They've taken the trouble to educate you."

"That's one reason that I hate them," said John. "You people educate us up to give us thinner skins. We feel the cold more, when we're educated. We can't live on one meal a day any longer. An educated Indian is neither white nor red. He's simply a puzzle and a trouble to both sides."

Fernald considered the mingled bitterness and truth of this remark with a good deal of care. "There's a lot in what you say, John," he said at last.

"Yes," said the Indian. "Anybody but a fool or a missionary could see that I'm saying what is true."

Fernald chuckled. "You go to that saddlebag," he said. "There's a bag of parched corn hanging there. About four pounds. You help yourself to that and take the rest back to your people."

The Indian, without a word, went to the horse and took the saddlebag. He returned to the spot where he had dropped his blanket, poured the contents of the bag into the hollow he made in the tattered robe, and replaced the saddlebag on the saddle.

"You look hungry enough," said Fernald. "Why don't you eat?"

"I am waiting," said the other with a frown.

"But tell me why?"

"Because I have made a vow that the white man in our village should eat before I eat," said the Comanche.

"He's your friend, eh?"

"He's the friend of all men."

"Red men?"

"Color makes no difference to him."

Fernald leaped into his saddle. "Smallpox or not," he announced, "I'm going to see that man. Get onto that other horse and I'll take you home."

II

The Comanche still hesitated.

"What's the matter?" asked Fernald.

"You know that my people may murder you for the sake of

the horse meat."

"No, they won't murder me. Comanches always understand a good turn. They'd rather kill each other than kill me," answered Fernald.

He saw the other straighten, and realized that John, after all, was hardly more than a boy.

"You have eyes out of which you can see," John said, and wriggled up the side of the lead horse. Then they started for the village.

It was in a good spot. There were no trees, but there was brush enough for fuel, and there was a thin trickle of water that ran down the hillside as though starting for the sea, but wound up by sinking into the ground.

The only fault that could be found with the situation was the lack of good forage for livestock, for, all around, the hills were the color of gray iron, with only a sparse prickling of dead grass. In the center of the hollow stood a circle of lodges. They seemed to Fernald, perhaps because he had heard the story from John, to be huddling together as though in fear, and he noted that no smoke arose above any of the clusters of lodge poles.

Down to the hollow within 100 feet of the village he came, and from that point he sent the Indian in with the corn and with a message that he wanted to see the white man. So John went with shuffling haste, but weak-kneed even on this pleasanter errand. He disappeared.

Afterward, there stumbled from the doors of the tents several emaciated, bowed forms. They did not attempt to advance toward the white stranger, but remained shadowing their eyes against the sun and studying him.

He winced a little. The horses had meant lifeblood to those starving people.

And then, slowly, out came the white man.

He looked like a giant to Fernald, and perhaps this was

caused by his gauntness, perhaps by the rough beard that climbed from his breast to his eyes. He was clad in tatters, wrapped in a worn robe like any other squawman, and Fernald awaited his approach with a certain amount of disgust, mingled with pity. The red man had said that this fellow was good, and, therefore, there must be something in him.

He came nearer with a long stride, irregular with weakness, but when he was close, he halted suddenly.

"Sure enough, it's Tom Fernald!" he exclaimed.

Fernald squinted at the other, but could make out no resemblance to anyone of his acquaintance. Neither could he place the hoarse voice.

Said the bearded man: "I've prayed to God for help and He has sent me out of the whole world . . . Tom Fernald!"

"You'd rather that I were any other man, eh?" Fernald asked sharply.

"Yes," said the stranger. "I had rather see the face of any other human being."

"Why?" demanded Fernald. "Because I can't recognize you, partner."

"Because," said the other, "in order to serve God I have had to injure you as no other person in the world has injured you. I have eaten the heart of your reputation, Tom. I've cast a shadow in front of your feet. Can you recognize me now?"

A dark red flushed the face of Fernald. "By your talk," he answered at last with a hard ring in his voice, "you're the king of sneaks and hypocrites in the world. You're Bill Ransome."

"I am that unhappy man," said the other.

"And what else do you deserve?" asked Fernald. "If they threw you out of Griffon, because you'd spread your yarns about me and couldn't back them up, what else did you deserve?"

"I told the truth," the big man stated calmly.

"Tell the truth and hang your brother. That seems to be your idea," said Fernald.

"If my brother stands between me and the truth, my brother must die," Bill Ransome said sadly.

"Well," Fernald said with an acid satisfaction, "you have almost as much as I could wish you to have. You're out here starving just like a dog."

"And then God sent you to help these people," Bill Ransome stated.

"Sent me?" exclaimed Fernald.

"Yes. You can't refuse them help. You have horses under you strong enough to take you out of the hills to the first settlement in half a day. From there, you will send back beef cattle to feed them, and other things, also. I know your heart, Tom Fernald."

"I'm a fool and a soft fool," said Fernald. "I'd rather help any man in the world than you, but I can't refuse to do something for those poor, starving devils. How many are there?"

"Fifty-seven now, living."

"How many with the smallpox?"

"More than twenty."

"Are you nursing the lot of 'em?"

"I do what I can. Most of the others are too busy wailing or asking the medicine man for new riddles. Another score of them have died."

Fernald shuddered. "What brought you to this gang?"

"I heard a rumor of a lost tribe among these hills. I followed my thought and found them," said Ransome.

"And started in to make a martyr of yourself, eh?"

Ransome smiled gently, as though from the deeps of a greater understanding.

"I am doing what I can," he said. "I have only two hands. If you can find a doctor and tell him about our plague, here, and beg him to send the right medicines. . . ."

Fernald nodded as the other paused. "I have to do it," he

said. "But not on your account, Ransome. I want you to know that. If the smallpox started eating you today, I'd be laughing tomorrow."

Ransome nodded. "Because I saw the stolen money of Visconti and had to tell the world, at last, how you had become a rich man. God forced the truth through my set teeth, Tom. I couldn't hold it back," Ransome said with deep emotion.

"You and your truth may go to hell," said Fernald. "I've this to remind you. You saw the stolen money. You didn't see the dead body of Visconti, and yet you've made a lot of people believe that I murdered him for his coin."

"Was it only accident that Visconti disappeared and that you got his money?" asked Ransome.

"Why should I answer you?" Fernald asked. "But I'll tell you this . . . Visconti was killed by a fall from a horse. And I had nothing at all to do with it. Believe that or not."

"I do believe it," said Ransome, "and I'm sorry if a few people are persuaded that you may have killed Visconti."

"A few?" Fernald said bitterly. "Seven people out of ten think so. They always will. I've been too successful. The fellows who are full of envy have to have some poisonous way of explaining my success."

"I haven't seen you for months," said Ransome. "Not since the people of Griffon invited me to leave town as a scandalmonger. Are you still successful?"

"They drove you out," Fernald said, "but they've never forgotten the scandals that you started about me. And the more successful I am, the more they talk and whisper behind their hands. They don't dare to say the things out loud that they think in secret to themselves."

Ransome nodded. "I wish you profoundest happiness," he said, "but only after you have washed your soul clean."

"You rotten hypocrite!" snarled Fernald. "But I'll tell you this in addition to what you know, Ransome . . . for the last few months, everything I've touched has turned to gold. It was four hundred and fifty thousand that I got from Visconti, the miser. It took me a year to get that money invested without arousing suspicion, and to boost the capital to a little over half a million. But since you left Griffon, everything has gone with wings. I've cleaned up fifty thousand dollars in three weeks on a timber option alone, and I've got a half interest in a ridge of copper ore that sinks as deep as the roots of the mountains. I wouldn't sell out for a million in cash this minute, Ransome. Put that in your blasted malicious pipe and smoke it!" He panted with rage as he spoke.

Ransome said nothing, but watched with a calm, almost a pitying eye.

"And," went on Fernald, as though infuriated to find that his story of success had not stung the other to more impatience and to some jealous expression, "no matter who the knockers may be, I'm going to put a crown on my success, Ransome. I'm going to marry Julie Darden."

At this, Ransome started violently.

"That finds the quick, does it?" Fernald said, sneering as he peered eagerly into the face of the big man.

"Julie Darden!" gasped Bill Ransome.

"I'm building the house for her now," Fernald said, drawling out the words with an infinite satisfaction.

Ransome sighed. Then he shook his head. "God won't let her marry a thief," he said.

An oath rushed out of the throat of Fernald. "If I hear you use that word again, I'll . . . I'll throttle you, Ransome! You hear me?"

"I won't use it," Ransome said gently. "I won't tempt you to murder, Tom. God bless you for whatever you can do for these poor people. They are ready to die." So saying, he raised his hand in a dignified salute, then turned and moved with that long, uncertain step of weakness back toward the lodges.

It was plain that he brought good news for, as Fernald turned his horse, he heard a screaming of joy rise from many throats. But there was no sympathetic pleasure in his own heart. He was cursing savagely as he drove the pinto on across the gray, barren hills.

III

Twenty beeves Fernald sent to the stricken tribesmen, and with them he sent a big wagon loaded with all that six horses could draw of foods of other kinds, and medicine for the sick. But the provision of all of this charity was to him a thing of no gratification whatever. He got much praise for dispatching the caravan of mercy, but he listened sourly to the words. Bill Ransome was still in the back of his mind.

Afterward, to be sure, he began to understand that his action had called for much comment that was too important to be overlooked. Public opinion helps to make business good, and now he knew that public opinion was saying: "They tell stories about how Fernald got his start. But I'll tell you what he did. There were forty, fifty Comanches starving and dying of the smallpox and he sent. . . ."

Well, a story like that was of capital value to him, and Fernald had become such a businessman that he was not unaware of every stroke that increased his prosperity.

This special journey had been made in speed in order to reach a great cattle sale where, as he understood, the cows of a district tormented with a water famine would be auctioned off for whatever they would bring. He determined that he would see what the prospects were of picking up cattle that might possibly have strength enough to last out a drive to the first hope of water.

He reached the auction the night before the sale began. There were many grim-faced men ready to sell. There were a few like himself, cold and calm of mind, ready to buy. And there were thousands of weakly milling cows waiting for death to come.

For two days, with wonderful skill and precision, Fernald went through the herds, picking the animals he thought could stand the drive he had in mind. Others would take their cattle north. But he would take this herd straight south toward his home country, for he knew of two water holes that he had found fairly full on his way up. He picked cattle for apparent strength and straightness of leg, and some for their viciousness, and some for the spirit that shone in their eyes. They cost him little more than their hides and hoofs and horns would have been worth, and he lost only twenty percent of them on the southern drive.

That bit of work cost him six weeks of terrible, constant watchfulness and labor. But he brought through over 4,000 head and he felt that nothing could rob him of a profit of $100,000 or $150,000. And that could not be called stolen money!

When he split up the herd and put it to pasture on his lands near Griffon, he rode on into the town, not to rest and luxuriate in his achievement, but to look over the field for fresh opportunities—and to see Julie Darden, incidentally.

He looked like the commonest cowpuncher on the range when he tied his horse to the Darden hitching rack and swung down to the ground. But when old James Darden, her father, looking like a composite picture of all the Kentucky colonels, saw his guest, he took him warmly by the hand.

"That was a fine thing . . . about the Comanches," he said. "We don't spend much compassion, to say nothing of dollars, on the Indians. Come in, Tom. Julie'll be the happiest girl in the county when she knows you're here. We half expected you last night. We heard that you'd completed the big drive."

"I had to split the herd up," Fernald said shortly. "Where's Julie?"

She came down a moment later, and Fernald looked at her with his head back, his eyes half closed, like a famine-stricken traveler who sees green trees and blue water in the white-hot middle of the day. Afterward, they sat on the big, cool verandah that ran down the north side of the house. A breeze came through the cottonwoods and touched pleasantly upon the face of Fernald.

"You're not talking," she told him.

"Being near you is all I want," he said.

"You were thinking about money," she answered.

"I?"

"Yes, about money. I can tell."

"How?"

"By the set of your jaw and the hawk look."

He looked squarely at her. "I don't like that, Julie," he said.

"I know you don't," she answered.

"What's upset you? Why are you picking a fight like this?" he asked.

"Because we have to get used to each other before we marry, Tom. I'm not going to have either of us walk in blindly. To get at you . . . well, that's too much for me, usually. But today I had a peep through the shutters, and you might as well know it."

"What did you see?" he asked her. He was alarmed, but like a good poker player he kept the alarm out of his eyes.

"I saw a miser, Tom," she said.

"That's not true," he answered, unimpressed. "I don't mind spending money."

"Not as long as you can pile up more of it. You'll spend a

little . . . to please me. But I call you a miser not because you're close with money, but because you love it more than anything else."

"You're being pretty hard," he said.

"I don't think so. I'm telling you the truth as I see it."

"Who's been talking to you?"

"Nobody. I don't have to be told everything by other people."

"Julie, you're making an issue out of this."

"Yes, I think I am."

"If you want me to protest how much more I like you than my business, you're mistaken. I won't do it. It may be as true as the stars, but I'm not going to protest to you and flatter you."

"I don't expect that, either," said the girl. "It's not words but truth that I'm hunting for."

He watched her for a moment. There was always that quality of iron about her. In their first meeting, when she had insulted him so grossly, it had seemed to him that he could tell the ring of steel on steel. Even after he had captured her admiration and her affection, it was always the same—from time to time there was a ringing of swords when they talked together.

"You want trouble, not the truth," he said. "You're like a bull terrier. You're never happy unless you're having a fight."

She did not answer at once. The calmness of her eyes, at such moments as this, was most dangerous, he knew. But he would make no concessions. He felt as hard as a stone wall, and as impenetrable. No relenting showed in his face.

Then she stood up. "Well," she said, "I see that I've gone far enough."

"It's just that you like to fight, Julie," he told her.

"Perhaps I do," she said. "But I'm always beaten . . . by you. I may want to fight to get at what you really are. But I'm always shut away."

He was standing. "This is a grand homecoming," he said.

"Tell me, Julie, what's really the matter with you?"

"Because there's no past about you," she said.

"I'm not of an old family. That's true," he admitted.

"You know that's not what I mean. But the moment that a thing has happened, you forget it. You've never mentioned the Carver Stone, since the day you lifted it."

"I made a public fool out of myself."

"Other people don't think so. Now you've gone on this trip, and you come back having done a pretty fine thing. We've all heard about that, but you won't talk about it, even to me."

"Want me to toot my horn?"

"You could talk to me without praising yourself. You could tell me how those poor fellows looked, and what the place was like, and about the Indian who took the shot at you that. . . ."

He started. "Who told you that?" he said.

"I don't know. It's around in the air. Everyone knows how you played 'possum and caught the Indian."

"It's a strange thing," he muttered. "I haven't told a soul about that, and wouldn't expect John to chatter about it very much."

"Are you ashamed of it, Tom?" she asked him, her voice sharp.

"No. Why should I be ashamed of it? I didn't shoot him, as I might have done."

She sighed.

"Go on, Julie, tell me what you want to say," he urged.

She looked at him, then, more golden, more beautiful than ever before. She seemed wiser, colder, more removed and remote from him. For the thousandth time, he told himself that this woman never really could be his wife. Was it love that he felt for her, or was he simply wishing to add another priceless treasure to his possessions, and so arouse the envy of other men?

"I'll tell you, then," she said. "If you'll have patience and not answer me till tomorrow."

"Yes, I'll wait till tomorrow."

"Then," she went on, "I think that the reason you never talk about your past is because somewhere, down the years, there's a thing that you want to cover up. So you fix your mind on today and tomorrow, and never chatter about yesterday."

"You think that there's something in my past?" he repeated. And he felt a slowly stealing, cold sense of dread.

"Yes, I think that."

"You think," he suggested, "that what Ransome said about me was the truth?"

She paused, and looked at the ceiling of the verandah.

"Go on, Julie. Tell me," he said. "You think that I murdered Visconti, and then stole his money?"

"Yes," she said. "I've always thought so."

His teeth *clicked*. Then he remembered his promise. He picked up his hat and turned to go.

"I'm going back to town," he said. "We'll have another friendly little chat tomorrow."

So he left her, but his heart was dead in him. He could feel the shadow out of the past beginning to lengthen before him down the way of his life.

IV

He saw James Darden on his way from the house, and the older man looked at the grim, set face of the boy before he said: "Something wrong, Tom?"

"Julie," the other said briefly. "She still believes the yarns that Bill Ransome told about me. Do you?"

Darden smiled. "What girls think doesn't matter. What they do is the important thing," he said.

Fernald hesitated for an instant, his heart dark, then he went on: "It's never too late to change. You tell Julie that. I won't hold her to any promise."

"Don't be a baby, like Julie," said Darden.

Fernald stared at him a moment, and then shrugged his shoulders and left.

He did not feel that he had been a baby, but that something definitely had to be done. He was being crowded against a wall, and it was Bill Ransome whose knowledge of the past crushed him. He had had the life of Ransome in his hands more than once. He wondered, now, why he had refrained. Everything would have been simple with that man out of the way. But now Ransome was safe from him. If anything happened to the big man, the first question that would be asked would be about Fernald. For the harm the latter had sustained from the talk of Ransome was too well known. The bitterness of Fernald increased as he rode on into Griffon from the house of Darden. The savor of his last financial achievement was ruined for him. His whole future was darkened. And gloomy was the mind of Fernald as he jogged his horse through the dusty streets of the town.

The place looked smaller to him than ever, more wind and weather worn, more battered, unpainted, sunburned. He had wanted to be a great man in Griffon. Well, he was a great man now. And what of it?

He went past President Blair of the Mining and Merchants' Bank; he had his reasons for not noticing the banker, as the latter stepped out of the Clovelly Store, but Blair hailed him loudly. So he reined his horse in and turned it to the sidewalk.

It seemed to him that Blair was not so rosy as usual, not so smiling and fat. His jowls hung in great folds, and his eyes were buried under a frown.

"Hello," Fernald greeted. "You look as though you had the grippe."

Blair did not answer the flippant greeting. He jerked his thumb over his shoulder. "Come into the bank," he said.

Fernald shook his head. "I'm not doing any banking today," he answered.

Blair's frown deepened. "You come into my office to talk to me," he commanded, and, turning on his heel, disappeared through the door of the bank.

Fernald did not hesitate long now. In the air and the manner of the banker there was something that did not brook delay. He tethered his horse in front of the Mining and Merchants' rack, and went inside.

The paying teller saw him and leaned his face against the steel bars of his cage to smile and nod a welcome. Fernald saluted him with a wave of the hand and went into Blair's office without knocking at the door. He had reasons enough for treating Blair with a rather scant courtesy.

He found the latter standing before the window, his hands clasped behind him under the skirts of his long-tailed coat. He was the only man in Griffon who wore such a garment. He wore a wing collar, too, and a black four-in-hand tie, spotted with little gray flowers. Griffon was as proud of the outfit in which its banker dressed as other towns are proud of public buildings.

"I'm glad you came in, Tom," Blair said, without turning. "Sit down. Find some cigars in the top left-hand drawer of my desk. Help yourself. I'm getting my ideas in order."

Fernald did not help himself to a cigar. He made a cigarette instead, and took a chair in the corner of the room. For two years, he had grown to prefer corner seats, where he would have the solid strength of walls fencing him in on two sides, at the least.

At last Blair turned about. "I'm going to offer you a bargain," he said.

"Go on." Fernald nodded. "I'm a trader."

"I'm going to offer you a quarter of a million dollars' worth of information," Blair stated.

Fernald smiled. "Thanks," he said. "I'm not buying that many words."

"There aren't many words," said Blair, "but they really mean something."

"To me?"

"Yes."

"What?"

"Your life," said Blair.

"Do I pay you first?" Fernald asked sardonically. "Advance payment or installments?"

Blair waved a hand that brushed this flippancy aside. "Don't treat me as though I'm a fool," he requested.

"All right," said Fernald. "I won't."

"You're holding an old grouch against me," said Blair. "There was a time when I wanted you as a partner in this bank. Then the Visconti scandal broke, and I no longer wanted you. You've never forgiven me for that."

"No," Fernald confirmed frankly. "I never have."

"You've got to put that behind you," suggested Blair.

Fernald shrugged his shoulders.

"I mean what I say," said Blair. "I want you as a partner again. And you can buy in for a quarter of a million. Spot cash."

"Thanks," said Fernald.

Blair stood over him, shaking a forefinger down at his guest. "I need a quarter of a million," he said, "or I'm going smash before the end of the week."

"You're worth a million and a quarter," said Fernald. "I know that much about you."

"I'm worth more than two millions," said the banker, "in spite of losses the last year or so. But everything I have is tied up. I could raise a hundred thousand or so, but not as much as I need. You're the fellow to finance me, and I let you in on an even basis. The stock you get will be worth half a million. You understand? You'll have an equal say in the running of the bank. Whether I remain president or not will be at your disposal."

A cold gleam came into the eyes of Fernald. "Go on," he said. "You interest me a lot."

"I knew that I only needed to show you how to cut my throat," said Blair. "Well, I'm showing you the way now."

"What's happened to your bank?" said Fernald. "I'm to take your word that it's really sound, but just pinched for the moment?"

"If you'll spend forty-eight hours with me, I'll prove the thing to you. But you'd better take my word for it. I'm a hard man. But I'm not a liar."

"No, you're not a liar," Fernald agreed. "But I don't like the deal. I'm not putting a quarter of a million into your bank, Blair."

"You will, though," said the other.

"You'll persuade me, eh?"

"I'll buy you with what I'm going to tell you."

"I don't want to hear it," said Fernald. "You say it's life or death to me. Well, I've always been able to take care of myself." He picked up his hat and settled it rudely on his head before leaving the room. "So long, Blair," he said.

The latter let him get as far as the door. Then he said: "Joe Bane!"

Fernald whirled about. One hand instinctively flew to a gun beneath his coat. His glance swept keenly about the room.

Blair smiled. "That touched you, eh?"

"That touched me," admitted Fernald. "If Joe Bane has come

back to town, I'm not dodging a meeting with him. I met him once before."

"You sank a bullet through him the other time," said Blair. "But he's been in practice with guns ever since. He might not be so easy this time."

"If that's your quarter of a million dollars' worth of information," Fernald said, "you can go to the devil with it. I wouldn't give ten cents for it. If Joe Bane is looking for me, he can find me any time of night or day. I won't dodge him and I don't need help against him."

"Jim Carver," said Blair.

Fernald scowled. "What the devil does all this mean?" he demanded.

"Sam Loring," said the banker, and this time he raised a grimly triumphant forefinger.

Certainly he had scored a heavy point, for Fernald slowly came back and stood with his face only inches away from that of Blair. "What has Mister Murderer Loring to do with me?" he asked.

Blair merely smiled. "I wondered if you'd like the list of the names," he said. "Loring, particularly. They say he's killed twenty-two men, and perhaps he wants you for number twenty-three."

"Loring hasn't killed twenty-two men," answered Fernald. "But he's killed enough at that. What's the idea, Blair?"

"There's an idea, too, behind it all," said Blair. "I was wondering whether you'd want to buy a half share in this bank for a quarter of a million. I'm still wondering, and I'm asking you, too."

"We'd better have a little talk," Fernald stated. He took off his hat, threw it into a chair, sat down in his first position, and began to make a cigarette. And, as he studied Blair, he saw that the older man was gleaming with sweat, and that he was breathing heavily, as though he had just passed through a great crisis. "Go on," said Fernald. "What's it all about?"

"Money talks," said Blair.

"Well, I'll buy a half interest in your accursed bank. Go on, Blair. Or do you want me to pay right now?"

Blair sank slowly into a chair and covered his face with his hands. His whole body shook. "I've been a hound," he groaned. "I'm still a hound. But thank God that I've pulled through this."

V

Fernald said grimly: "Don't you be so sure that you've pulled through. If you're talking to me about Sam Loring, and Jim Carver, and Joe Bane, they'll have your heart out in slices if they find out that you've given me a warning."

"They'd do anything that they could," said the banker. "But they're not to know. There's no way in which they can find out, unless you choose to tell 'em, Tom."

Fernald went on: "You've given me their names," he said, "but you haven't told me what they have in mind about me."

The banker was half red and half white, as though both fear and joy were raging in him. Now he thrust out his head and grinned at the cattle dealer. "You guess, Tom!"

"I guess that they want my scalp."

"Yes. That's what they want. Of course, that's what they want."

"Tell me," Fernald said, "how you happened to find out what they have in mind."

"In a funny way," said the banker. "You know crooks are pretty simple, sometimes?"

"Yeah. I know that."

"These fellows had heard that I was not a very good friend of yours, not since we sort of fell out a year ago."

"That might be in the air." Fernald nodded, grinning a little. "For a year or so you've been telling people that you believe Bill Ransome's story."

Blair flushed. "I've been wrong about you, Tom," he said.

"Because I can buy a half interest in your bank?" asked Fernald.

Blair shook his head. "Because you've kept on succeeding. A man cannot keep on succeeding on stolen money. You've made money fast and steadily all along. Nobody but an honest man can do that."

Fernald said nothing, but stared straight at the other. The argument was so specious that it was not worth even a smile. "Let's get back to the three, and how you found out what they want," Fernald stated at last.

"Why, the three of them called on me at my place out of town," explained Blair. "And you know what happened? They simply laid their cards on the table. A mighty strange thing, a mighty foolish thing. Even supposing they thought that I didn't like you, what let them dream that I would be ready to plot your murder?"

"It's really murder, then?"

"You'll see for yourself. I was riding down into the bottom land along the creek. My foreman had told me that alkali was beginning to show up in patches, and he was right. Big bald places that freckled the face of the fields. Grass would never grow where that dusty white had once shown itself. It made me feel pretty sick. I cursed a good deal to myself, and I was still cursing, when I looked up and saw three riders coming around the next bend of the creek trail. I recognized them as they came up . . . two of them, but not the pinch-faced, sallow rat who rode in third place. The others were Jim Carver and Joe Bane. I reined up and talked to them. The first sight I had of Carver and of Bane, of course, I thought of you, because you'd driven them both out of town. Then they introduced the third man, and said he was Sam Loring. He grinned and showed me his buck teeth."

"I know," said Fernald. "He's got a half-wit look when he smiles."

"Of course, I recognized the name, and I knew that, if Carver and Bane were with Loring, there was trouble in the air . . . and probably a killing not far in the background of the day."

"Anybody could guess that," murmured Fernald.

"I asked where they were heading, and they said, right out, that they were aiming to put down Tom Fernald, and Jim Carver asked if I'd be interested in that job."

"And you said that you would be?"

"It's more my business to listen than to talk," explained the banker. "People are always coming to me with propositions. I sit tight and listen. Besides, I was rather afraid not to listen to the three of them. They meant business. I sort of thought that if I said no to 'em, they might sink a bullet in me. Anyway, I listened, and encouraged them with nodding. As I said before, they put their cards right on the table. Bane and Carver felt that they couldn't come back to Griffon unless Tom Fernald was out of the way. Everybody would sneer at them, and remember how you had put them down. And that's pretty true, too. They wanted to put you down, and the only way to do that would be really to prove Bill Ransome's story against you, or else to . . . bump you off . . . murder you, Tom." He banged his soft, fat fist on the desk as he said this.

Fernald moved neither his head nor his eyes. He was devouring the perspiring face of Blair.

The latter went on: "They tried to show me where I had an interest in helping to put you out of the way. They pointed out what everybody knows . . . that you've been doing your business for more than a year with the First National Bank over in Gerson. They pointed out that a lot of people around Griffon have followed your lead, not because they were really dissatisfied with the Mining and Merchants', but simply because it was a novelty to do business with the people in Gerson. They said that had hurt me a lot." He paused, frowning.

"And has it?" asked young Fernald.

"It has." Blair nodded gloomily. "And more than I'd care to say. But if your account. . . ." He paused.

"If my account came back from Gerson to the Mining and Merchants', some of the smaller fellows would probably follow my example again. Is that it?"

"Well, that's about it."

"Go on, Blair."

"You see that they were rushing right ahead and unloading on me. I kept on nodding and looking serious. I felt serious, too. I began to wish that I were a long distance from the three of 'em. They were as dangerous as rattlesnakes."

"Yes. I think more so."

"Finally they came to the point. Their idea was that I should ask you to come out to my house to see me about business. And when you got there, or while you were on the way, they would waylay you and shoot you up."

"That's simple." Fernald nodded. "Do you mean to say that Bane and Carver both liked that idea?"

"You'd think that Bane, the gambler, would be the keenest for it. But he wasn't. Carver's the fellow who hates you most. He turned green when he mentioned you. His eyes rolled in his head. He asked me over and over again if it were true that you're engaged to Julie Darden. Yes, he hates your heart. The girl has something to do with the way that he feels about you."

"When were you to ask me out to your house?" Fernald asked.

"Tonight, in fact. This evening . . . for dinner. That would put you on the road in the dusk . . . a good, comfortable time for a murder."

"Yes, that's the best time. Was it decided on the house finally?"

"No, for I wouldn't have that. I insisted that they would have to pick out another place. They hit, finally, on the bridge over the creek. You know there are a lot of poplars growing on both sides of the bridge and that would make a good covert."

"Yes. That's the place where Sid Belcher was killed, wasn't it?"

"The very same. I'd forgotten that."

"Didn't Joe Bane remind you that was the place?" asked Fernald.

"Bane? Now I come to think of it, perhaps he did mention it. My mind was full of a lot of thoughts just then, and I didn't hear everything clearly."

"Well," Fernald said, "I'm glad that you picked my side of the fight."

Blair rubbed his hands; his voice lowered. "Ed Walters is the man to take into your confidence," he said. "Ed will pick up a few real fighting hands and take them along with him. You and he together ought to be able to bag the three beauties. We'll none of us breathe freely and easily, if they slip away."

"You're right," said Fernald. "If they get away, we'll all be in fear of our lives." He stood up.

"You'll see Ed Walters?" asked the other.

"Yes. I'll see Ed, I think."

"Tonight's the time. They'll be there in waiting at about dusk. Don't forget. About dusk." Blair rubbed his fat, trembling hands together again. "For heaven's sake, don't fail to crush out the whole trio, Tom!" he begged. "Otherwise, we're all ruined."

"I'll do my best," Fernald said. "Do you want my check now?"

"I don't want your check now. The stock has to be ready for transfer, and a lot of legal procedure. You drop in here tomorrow morning. I hope everything will be cleaned up then. And you and I can begin to build a new success, a business that will out top anything ever dreamed of in this part of the range."

"It's a fair exchange in this affair, Blair?" suggested Fernald.

"Sure it is. No gratitude necessary anywhere."

"That's good. I like that. You're sure that they won't change their minds? It's the bridge over the creek that they've picked out to nail me?"

"It's that bridge. No mistake about it. I pointed out all of the advantages myself."

Fernald waved his hand. He was standing at the door, and it seemed to the peering eyes of Blair that a flicker of contempt and of pity, combined, darkened the eyes of the younger man. Then Fernald opened the door and passed out.

He stood for a moment on the street, settling his sombrero on his head, making a cigarette with absent-minded fingers. For his thoughts were busy. Blair, he could guess, had probably engineered the entire deal. The shifting of funds to the Gerson Bank had been a mortal blow to him. But, when he saw Fernald in the street, a sudden thunder stroke of policy occurred to him—to betray his associates and capitalize their fall.

Money seemed a dirty thing, and the dirt on it was the red of blood. So strong was the feeling born in Fernald, that he shuddered as he walked down the street at last.

VI

He went to the house of Ed Walters, the deputy sheriff, and found him in the corral behind his shack, snubbing the head of a refractory, wild-caught four-year-old to a post in the center of the yard. It was sweating, dusty work, and Walters was cursing loudly, monotonously.

Fernald leaned on the fence and watched him with a curious interest for some time. "Hey, Ed!" he called at last.

Walters looked around with a scowl darkening his long, lean face. He was red-brown with sun and effort.

"This four-year-old son of damnation and a thunderbolt . . . I wish you would break him for me, Tom," he said.

"You wangle a saddle onto his back, and I'll try him," said Fernald.

"You will?"

"Yeah."

"What's your fee?"

"It's a gift."

Walters grinned, and started for the shed. "You'll have your hands full," he said.

Fernald looked over the shining, sweating body of the colt and agreed. It was an ugly mustang head on as fine a mechanism as ever carried a rider. The little eyes were as red as blood. The ears were pressed back into a shag of mane; the nostrils flared like trumpets.

The heart of Fernald lifted in his breast with light fear, as a cork lifts in water and floats, trembling. However, he was glad to have something to do, some physical task that would occupy him. He hardly cared whether or not the colt bucked him out of the saddle. Even that was going to help rub off his hands and out of his mind the dirty intrigue in which he had plunged this day.

Money, money. That was the curse that was staining him. The more one had of it, the deeper one was committed to vile practices.

Bill Ransome, off there in the iron hills with a tribe cursed by smallpox—he was really enjoying a better life, no matter how he rubbed elbows with death. For the first time, Fernald sighed for the old days when he had worked innocently and happily on the sheep range. It had been hard labor, but his hands had been clean, and he had put unit to unit, saving, planning, scraping, working toward the goal of a little fortune, finally—a little thing that would never free him from the necessity of more and more work.

Walters came out with a saddle and engaged in a twenty-minute struggle. At the end of that time, the horse was blindfolded, saddled, and ready for the rider.

Fernald drew up his belt until it pinched him. Then he threw the gate of the corral wide, propped it open, and entered. When he mounted, the blindfolded mustang did not try to buck. It simply humped its back and lowered its head.

"It's a beauty," said Walters. "It's going to ride you on a thunderbolt, Tom. But are you ready?"

Fernald pressed his feet into the stirrups, freshened his knee grip, and nodded. "Let him go!" he ordered. The blindfold was whipped off, and, like a lighted rocket, the mustang rose into the air with a scream.

It bucked in a circle around the post, as though it felt that its head was still fastened securely. Then it seemed to realize that its head was really free, and it scooted for the corral gate. That bolting saved Fernald. He had lost a stirrup; his head was dizzy; his body was sick with the hammering that he had received. Yes, he was not the man on a horse that he had been in the old days. But when the mustang bolted, he recovered his balance and found the stirrup. Outside the corral gate, the bronco began to pitch again, and in earnest, looking toward the distant hills for which it yearned to race as soon as the horrible human encumbrance was shaken off its back.

For a quarter of an hour—long, endless minutes—it struggled.

But in its first rampage in the corral it had displayed all its tricks. The rider knew them now. He was taking the measure of the bronco every moment more and more. He began to swing his long-lashed quirt and urge the horse to greater efforts. But suddenly the mustang stood still and dropped its head.

"It's done!" called Walters. "You certainly sat that hoss, son!"

Fernald jerked on the bit; the mustang turned slowly and came at a walk back toward the corral.

"It's beaten this day," Fernald admitted, dismounting. "But you look out tomorrow. That's going to be an educated outlaw, or I miss my guess."

"I'll handle him tomorrow," Walters assured him. "When the cream is taken off 'em, I can handle the skimmings all right." He laughed, looking admiringly at his friend. "You ain't forgot how to fork a hoss, Tommy," he said.

Fernald shrugged his shoulders. His head was still spinning; he was a little sick at the stomach. "I've forgotten a lot," he said. "Put that horse up and talk to me, Ed."

Walters turned the bronco into the corral, put the saddle in the shed, and returned to his friend. "I picked that colt up for sixty dollars," he said. "After I got it, the fellow that had caught it gave me the horselaugh. He said that I'd get more than sixty dollars' worth of busted bones out of that devil, and nothing else."

"You go easy with it," murmured Fernald. "He'll buck again tomorrow. Some of 'em keep on learning, from day to day."

Walters whistled thoughtfully, looking at the ugly head of the mustang. Then he asked: "What's up, Tom?"

"Trouble."

"I know. It's always trouble that brings folks to me."

"Bad trouble, this time."

"Aye, and it's always bad trouble that brings folks to me. I hardly got a friend that drops around to see me, unless it's something that I've got to ride down, or somebody to shoot up. A devil of a life I lead, Tom."

"You like it, though," Fernald said.

Walters squinted at the distance. "Yeah. I like it pretty well, I guess," he said. "I'm getting old, though. I'm not going to last at the job very long."

Said Fernald: "This is a three-man party that I'm talking about."

"What three?"

"Jim Carver."

"Carver? He's a fellow that could make trouble, all right."

"Joe Bane."

"Joe back? Yeah, that's poison . . . trouble with Joe Bane."

"And Sam Loring."

The deputy sheriff turned with a start. "Sam Loring," he repeated, his breath hardly more than a whisper.

"Sam Loring," Fernald echoed. "All three of 'em, and they want my scalp."

"Who told you that?"

"I can't tell you that, but I'll tell you where they expect to collect it."

"Tell me, then."

"On the bridge over the creek, going out to Blair's place."

"I know it. The poplars make a good place to hole up."

"That's the idea."

"Sid Belcher was killed there."

"Yes."

"You know, Tom, that Joe Bane had an idea that you killed Sid Belcher?"

"I know that he had that idea," Fernald said. "But he was wrong."

"Yes, I guess that he was wrong. But still, that was his idea. All three of them going to wait out for you there?"

"Yes."

"When?"

"This evening, when I ride out to the house of Blair."

Ed Walters nodded. "What do you suggest?" he asked.

"Why, I suggest that I ride out of town just the way that I am supposed to do. I ride right on toward the bridge. You and three or four more of your best men, they can hole up in the rocks on the hill above the bridge. Ever been there?"

"No."

"I have, though. From the top of it, you can look right down among those little poplars, and you'll be able to see every move that the three of 'em make. Well, then, when they sight me and begin to unlimber their guns, before they start shooting, you rush 'em from behind. They won't have a chance to get to their horses before you're right in among 'em, and, when I hear your nags galloping, I'll sprint up the trail and try to get in on the shooting, if there is any. That looks to me like a fair sort of a trap."

"Only fair," said Walters.

"We've got to give 'em a chance to fight," argued Fernald. "You can't arrest three men just because they're hiding out in some poplars, can you?"

"No, that would hardly do."

"Give them a rush, and they'll start shooting . . . Loring will, anyway. He's a nervous fellow with his guns, they say."

"Too nervous . . . and too straight to suit me," Walters said. "You've dished up a mighty indigestible mess for me, Tom."

"Well, I suppose that I have. But think it over, will you?"

"I've thought it over already. I'll have to try to do what you say. But I've got to pick the men who ride with me this evening."

"Pick fellows who won't be afraid to shoot, and shoot straight."

Walters looked at his friend with a curious interest. "Tom," he said, "I think you like the idea of this here party."

"Well, I don't mind it," Fernald said. "It's a break in the monotony, at least."

"*Hmmm,*" said the deputy sheriff. He laid a hand on Fernald's shoulder. "Don't you get too much of a taste for it," he advised. "Blood, you know, goes to the head faster than whiskey."

"It's all right," said Fernald. "I'll never turn into a killer." But far back in his mind there was a grim bit of doubt in his own words.

VII

He went to the hotel and there laid out his weapons. He had a rifle with a shortened barrel, a rifle that threw a .45-caliber slug, and had a magazine containing fifteen of these shots. He selected that gun for the coming expedition. It shot twice as far and twice as hard as a Colt, and, although it had neither the accuracy nor the range of a rifle, the weight of its bullet would knock a man off a horse about as far as the lead would carry. He had a holster under the right side of his saddle that would accommodate this weapon. Then he took out from his armpits two Colts. They were the ordinary old single-shot pattern, throwing .44-caliber slugs. The triggers and the trigger guards were filed away, which made them both lighter and more handily balanced. These guns were fired by fanning the hammers with the thumb of the right hand. It was said that a few ambidextrous geniuses could fan two guns at once, but for Fernald, as for most men who had mastered the art of fanning, one hand at a time was enough. When the first gun was exhausted, the second revolver was thrown into the right palm with a speed that hardly interrupted the stream of shots. These guns held only five shots apiece. The sensitive hammer rested upon an empty chamber. Otherwise, the least jar in riding or even in walking might explode a bullet into the owner's leg.

When Fernald had looked over his stock of weapons, he nodded with satisfaction. The time had passed when he labored eight hours a day to perfect himself with guns and quick shooting. But he spent at least an hour a day in practice. For some time past, he had known that his life was in danger, although he was well aware that it had never been so in peril as now.

Jim Carver was an athletic youngster who had once been well known around Griffon for his long-distance skill with a rifle. He had brought down deer at almost incredible distances, and a man, who can shoot a deer at 400 yards, ought to be able to knock over a man easily at 200.

Joe Bane was a natural genius with weapons. Some of his nerve, men said, had been lost after his first encounter with Fernald. But now he might have recovered his original assurance, plus a good deal more, furnished by desperation. He hated Fernald. That much was sure. He hated him because he attributed the death of his partner, Sid Belcher, to the sheepherder of those days.

He hated him, above all, because Fernald had downed him on the only occasion when they had drawn guns on one another. Bill Ransome's intervention had accounted for part of the outcome of that fight, of course. But the ultimate victory was Fernald's. And results are what count. Joe Bane would probably go into the fight ready to die ten times over if he could sink one slug in the body of his enemy.

Sam Loring was the third fellow to take into account. Fernald knew all about him, and so did most of the other men in the Southwest. He looked like an underfed boy; when he smiled, he resembled a half-wit. But he had killed his first man at thirteen with a common penknife. Since then, the list had grown. Men attributed twenty-two killings to him, and he was hardly older than the number of men he was said to have killed.

If he had not killed twenty-two, he had at least accounted for half of that number. Besides, mere numbers did not count. What mattered was the peculiar fire and zest and cold cunning with which this fellow threw himself into a battle. He was considered a dead shot with any sort of gun; he had justified the reputation more than once.

When the States grew too hot for Loring, he drifted south into Mexico. When the country south of the Río Grande grew too warm for him, he came north again. And always there was a blood trail behind him. Yet so crafty was his work that there was no outstanding charge of murder against him. He was wanted, but not wanted badly—according to the letter of the law.

Such were the three against whom were to be pitted Ed Walters, and whatever sort of a posse could be raked up on the spur of the moment.

Fernald had many doubts as to the outcome. In the first place, Ed Walters was a good fighting man, but he was not a genius, like every one of the three who he would have to face if the plans worked out. In the second place, his posse would be a picked-up lot, more than likely to fortify courage with liquor before the pinch came, and whiskey meant bad shooting, in any man's language. There remained, as the rock on which the defense would have to rest, Fernald himself.

He stood in front of the mirror in the bedroom at the hotel and looked himself over, without vainglory, but as one taking stock of himself. He noted the thick padding all about the shoulders that looked like fat; his neck looked fat, also. Then he raised his arms and tensed them. At once, his coat was filled with iron-hard muscle that almost burst the seams of the cloth. And the cords at his throat stood out like rods.

No, he had not lost his strength. If it came to close encounter, he could prove to them that he had not lost the power of hand that once lifted Carver Rock. With a quiver of delight, he was aware of the strength in him. He felt that he could crush heads like eggshells, snap limbs like pipe stems. Well, it might come to hand-to-hand work, before the end.

Then he wondered why, with such a slight preparation, he was willing to ride out to the encounter. Ed Walters should have had time to equip himself more fully. A dozen expert gunmen were needed. Why did he prepare to go? Was it because there was in him something of the bloodlust of which Ed Walters had warned him?

There was a tap at his door.

He turned around, alert, on tiptoe. "Come in!" he called.

The room clerk appeared. "Miss Darden is down in the street in her runabout waiting to see you, Mister Fernald."

He nodded, put on his hat and overcoat, slung the short-barreled rifle with a shoulder sling beneath the coat, and went down the stairs. He was ready for the fight, and he would see Julie on the way to it. It was, as a matter of fact, about time for him to start. The sun was half down in the west. The sky was rimmed with fire, and in the zenith blew one cloud that was half red, half purple. The cool of the night breeze was commencing.

Julie Darden had the team at the sidewalk just below the hotel. She kept them well in hand, although they made little dancing half steps from time to time. She wore a linen duster, with the collar turned up high about her throat. She wore a narrow-brimmed hat that turned up like the hat of a boy. And she had on long gauntlet gloves.

But her beauty met him in the distance, as it were, and amazed him.

He stood beside her, with his hat in his hand. "What is it, Julie?" he asked.

"You know what it is," she said, her eyes, as always, grave and level against his.

"It's about our wrangle," he opined.

"Yes, it's about that, and something more."

"What?"

"Because I'm worried."

"About me, eh?" he suggested sarcastically.

"Don't take that tone, Tom," she besought him.

He stepped a little closer. His heart was as hard as a stone. "Let me tell you something, Julie," he said. "I like you a lot. I respect you. You're a real person. But you can't talk down to me. Not before we're married . . . or after, if it ever happens. I'm telling you now."

She waited, pulling in a little on the reins, as the horses fidgeted and the wheels made a half turn forward, then back again. As she waited, she was watching him steadily, thoughtfully. "I think that we'll marry, all right," she said, "and I think that we'll have a hard time. But I didn't want to see you today about the future. I wanted to see you about now."

"What about now?" he asked her, feeling a little ashamed of his outburst. Yet it was generally this way, a rushing love for her beauty and her fineness, and anger and revolt against her grim, man-like steadiness and character. She never gave way in the least. She was always herself.

"You spent a long time with Blair today," she said.

"What of that?" he asked.

She answered a bit surprisingly: "Blair's no good. He used to be all right, but he's no good now. Dad says so. A lot of people guess it. He's losing out. Once you wanted to throw in with him. Don't do it now."

He paused, then he answered coldly: "I have to run my own affairs, Julie."

"You're going in with him, are you?"

"I may."

She sighed. "I almost hate you, Tom, when you talk like this," she said.

He was silent.

Then she went on: "You have something big up your sleeve, but it won't come off, if you're with Blair. I know that in my blood."

"You keep to your instinct," he answered, "and I'll keep to facts and figures. I can work my way along, you know."

"Tom," she said, "can't you take a kinder line? Do you have to hit me so hard with every word?" Her speech was appealing, but not the tone in which she spoke.

"You knocked me down this morning," he said. "You want me to hold your hand tonight. That's like a woman, I suppose."

She shook her head. "I told you the truth this morning," she answered.

"What makes you so sure of that?"

"Because you took it so hard."

He was silent again, choked with angry guilt, and what was almost hatred of her.

She went on: "Listen to me. I know that you killed Visconti and robbed him of his money. In spite of that, I still want to marry you, if you'll have me. But I wish that you'd try to take a kinder line. I can't be soft and clinging, like a lot of other girls, and I wish that you'd come out in the open with me and treat me at least like a man partner in your affairs. That's chiefly what I wanted to say to you this evening. And I see that you're not in a mood for listening. So long, Tom."

She relaxed the pressure on the reins. The horses instantly shot away down the street and swerved around the next corner, leaving Fernald with his lips parted, a shout of recall in his throat. But he uttered no sound.

VIII

It seemed to Fernald, when he had mounted his horse and ridden down the main street toward the creek road that his position in the world had suddenly changed. Julie was right. She deserved to be considered as he had not been considering her. He had taken the high hand with her. Now she had told him, pointblank, that even a murder would not stand between her and her affection for him.

It staggered Fernald. He was no nearer, really, to telling her the truth, but the mere possibility of being able to confess to her made his heart swell. No, she was not like other women. She was by herself, out in front. He gritted his teeth and told himself that one of these days he would make her know how much he loved her.

Such were his thoughts as he rode out of Griffon and took the creek trail toward the Blair place. He kept the pinto at a steady jog trot, for that gait would eat up the miles fast enough to bring him to the bridge in the middle of the dusk, when there would still be time enough for straight shooting—at close hand.

That was what he wanted. To be picked off at a distance was neither creditable nor a fighting chance. But, close in, he could make the ten bullets of his revolvers tell heavily.

So he came over the hill above the bridge and saw the poplars turning the underside of their leaves in the night breeze with a dull glimmer. The bridge was in the shadow of them; beyond, the last light of the day gleaming upon the rocks among which Ed Walters and his men must have found hiding. Well, all had worked out exactly as he had hoped. This was the place. This was the time. Ed Walters surely would not fail him, even if he had to come alone to the rendezvous. So he jogged the pinto steadily on down the slope toward the bridge.

The overcoat was off his shoulders and strapped behind the saddle. The short-barreled rifle was thrust into the saddle boot. Fernald himself was leaning forward a little in the saddle, keenly balanced, and prepared for the first sign of trouble. He listened, however, for the sound of horses galloping down from the rocks of the hill beyond, the appointed covert, and his heart failed him a little when he heard and saw nothing.

But then he was amazed to behold a man ride out from the poplars and sit his saddle on the farther side of the bridge, waving a hand. Was it one of the three giving him a warning and a sporting chance of escape before the battle should take place?

The fellow was big enough to be Jim Carver, and Jim might well have had some such chivalrous notion.

As for Fernald, he was about to turn the head of the pinto and flee, before a rain of bullets was poured upon him, but he changed his mind. Something like the coldly compelling hand of fate took hold of him and drew him steadily on toward the bridge. The forehoofs of the mustang beat upon the wooden planking, and then he recognized the voice that called to him.

"Hello, Tom! It's me!"

That was Ed Walters's voice. A vast relief flowed through him like warm water over the aching body. He rode on up to the deputy sheriff. "What's up, Ed?" he asked.

"Nothing," said the other.

"Didn't you bring out any men? Didn't you find a thing here?" asked Fernald, bitterly disappointed, in spite of his relief of a moment before.

"I brought out three jim-dandies. And I sent 'em back again. Before I sent 'em, I seen the three beauties we were looking for down here among the poplars."

"You saw them here?"

"Yeah. I recognized Jim Carver by the make of him, and Sam Loring by the way he rides slanting ever since he got a couple of Mexican rifle bullets in the seat of the pants. The other might've been Joe Bane, by the cut of him, too."

"Why'd you send your men in then?"

"Because the three all drifted."

"To where? When did they drift?"

"About half an hour ago, son."

"Hold on, Ed. Where did they go?"

"Up the trail."

"Toward the Blair place?"

"Yes."

"What started them?"

"I don't know."

"You fellows were up there on the hill, holed up?"

"We were hiding tight."

"Didn't make a sound that the three of 'em could have heard?"

"No. Bill Meagrim's mustang started to sneeze, but Bill pretty near choked the poor horse and kept it quiet."

"The sneeze of a horse," said Fernald, "can be heard a mighty long way."

"Yeah. But you couldn't have heard this one for fifty feet. Bill heard the critter take a long breath, and grabbed its nose, just on a chance. It was mighty quick work. Well, when the three of them skinned out, I saw it was no use keeping the boys up all the rest of the night. So I sent 'em right back in by the short cut, and I waited here to give you the word."

Fernald nodded, his face a brown study. Then he asked: "How long after that choked sneeze before the three of 'em lined out up the trail?"

"Oh, about a minute. Maybe less. It just happened that they made up their minds to move and that. . . ."

"They heard that horse sneeze!" insisted Fernald.

"They couldn't've. And then, besides . . ."

"Don't argue, Ed. I tell you the straight of it. Now you line out and ride like the devil with me."

"Where?"

"To the Blair house."

"But what for, Tom?"

"To keep Blair from being murdered, if we're not too late already for the job that's in the air." As he spoke, he put the pinto into a strong gallop, rushed over the bridge, and heard with satisfaction the brief thunder of hoofs upon the boards as Walters followed him. He hardly knew why he was so sure that crime lay ahead of them, but the certainty was in his bones.

Ed Walters, whose horse had a longer and more sweeping stride, pulled up beside him, turned in the saddle, and shouted loudly through the dusk: "Hey, Tom! Whatcha know?"

But Fernald merely waved a hand at him. He knew nothing. But he guessed at death in the air.

They rattled across the gravel of the hollow. They strained at a trot up the steep pitch beyond, and then they could see the house of Blair before them. It was not a pretentious place, considering the size of Blair's fortune. It was simply the ranch that his father had owned before him. Discontent with ranch life was what had turned Blair into a banker. The same discontent had kept him from paying too much heed to the affairs of the ranch or the house upon it. He used it simply for a day or two of rest, when business was pressing him hard. There were no servants on the place. He came out here to be away from the interruptions of home and family, to be a careless bachelor for a time. Men said that he pondered, here, his deepest schemes. A trip to the ranch boded trouble for someone somewhere.

These thoughts came to the mind of Fernald as he galloped the mustang toward the place, but the second glimpse of it caused a wave of relief to pass over him, for he saw the gleam of a lamp through one of the darkening windows of the house, like a reflection in the black ice of water. That light seemed to give assurance that the banker was still there. When they came nearer, he could see, moreover, the wavering column of smoke that arose above the roof of the house. Yes, Blair was there, and cooking his supper. Fernald's suspicions must be wrong. He drew rein.

"There's no use going on, Ed," he declared.

"Maybe not for you," said Walters, "but I need a cup of coffee and I think that I can smell coffee boiling clear over here. Come on, Tom. I'm dead for coffee. Whiskey never bothered me none, but coffee is what this *hombre* craves."

Fernald, chuckling, still almost weak with the removed burden of suspense, laughed, and jogged the pinto on again. They came to the rack in front of the ranch house at the very close of the day, before the moon in the east could make its light felt, although it was near the full, and with the last rim of sunset color showing in the west. The mountains were sinking into darkness.

"Hey, Blair!" called Ed Walters.

There was no answer.

"Blair don't like company out here," Walters said, laughing again, as they tethered their horses, which stood in the fetlock-deep dust around the hitching rack. "He comes out here to be quiet. But he's gotta feed me coffee tonight."

"Blair!" shouted Fernald, frowning, paying no heed to the careless good humor of his companion.

Again there was silence. The two men looked at each other.

"He's gone out to the shed to bring in an armful of wood," Walters commented, but there was no conviction in his voice.

Fernald, for answer, drew out a revolver, and held it poised, the hammer under his thumb. "I'll try the door," he said gloomily. "Keep your eyes open, Ed . . . because I smell trouble." He went to the front door, turned the handle, and pressed. The door opened a few inches, then struck some partially yielding but heavy object and lodged there.

A little farther, Fernald thrust the door by sheer strength, the flimsy panels bending under the mighty thrust of his arm. Then, putting his head inside, he saw what he already had more than half guessed at.

A big man lay, face down, upon the floor, his arms wound tightly around his head. A streak of crimson ran across the boards toward the lower edge of the doorway and pooled there against the threshold. The features of the fallen man were invisible, but Fernald knew who it was. Blair was dead, shot through the brain.

IX

They crowded through the door then, with Ed Walters groaning and cursing beneath his breath. But Fernald was already busy examining the room. He turned the body, then lifted and carried it to the bed at the side of the room. There was still a bewildered look on the face of the dead man. Yet it did not seem possible that he could be dead. Not with the fire that he had built still roaring in the stove and the coffee that he had made still simmering. Some bacon was singing in a pan; it began to throw off dense, acrid clouds of smoke as it burned, and Walters took the pan off the stove.

"You're right, Tom," he said. "They must have heard or seen something when we were stacked up there on the hill. That's why they scattered and came back this way. You guessed why they'd come. What made you guess, Tom?"

Fernald shrugged his shoulders.

But the deputy sheriff insisted. "I've got to know," he said. "You may be a mind-reader, but there's more than mind-reading in this business. You knew why the three of 'em had come back here. You knew that they'd try to murder poor Blair. Well, you've got to tell me how you came to know."

Fernald looked at him with a grim annoyance. "If they turned around up the trail, where did the trail lead except to this house?"

"That won't do," said Walters. "There's something behind this and I've got to find out what it is."

"Why, man," answered Fernald, "it's simply that they tried to frame me with Blair . . . and then he double-crossed them. They guessed that much . . . Sam Loring is the sort of a rat that smells the tricks of his kind miles away. They spotted you fellows on the hill, and Loring must have put the story together in quick order. He and the others came back here to kill Blair for double-crossing them. And I hardly blame them for doing it."

"Did he sell them out to you, Tom?"

"Yes. That's what he did."

"Why should he?"

"Because he needed money, I suppose."

The sheriff still shook his head. He looked dubiously at the stove, which trembled with the flutter and force of the flames inside it. "There's one thing that looks mighty wrong to me," he said. "Sam Loring works alone. And he wouldn't list up with Joe Bane and Jim Carver just to get one *hombre* . . . not even if that *hombre* was you, Tommy."

Fernald nodded. "I think that you're right, there," he said. "Sam Loring isn't the kind to hunt with a crowd. And why he's doing it now, I don't know, except that both Joe Bane and Jim Carver think I'm special poison. But probably there's money behind the trick. They want to make dead sure of me . . . and they've hired Sam Loring by the yard for the job."

The deputy sheriff looked curiously at his companion. "How do you feel about it, Tom?" he asked.

"Bad," answered Fernald.

"I don't think you do. I never saw you looking more cheerful. Tell me the truth, Tom. This is like a good stiff drink to you, isn't it?"

Fernald shook his head. "Don't talk nonsense," he said. "Which one of the three killed poor Blair? That's what we've got to find out."

"If we can get our hands on all three of 'em," Walters said through his teeth, "I think that I could hang the whole lot of them for the job."

"You could?"

"Their whole line of action looks too rotten," said Walters. "How would it tell in court . . . the way they sneaked into the poplars, just the way you had said that they would? That sort of sneaking business would hang them in the eyes of any jury in this part of the country."

Fernald walked over to the bed and drew back the sheet that he had pulled over the head of the corpse.

"He won't tell you who killed him, if that's what you want to know," muttered Ed Walters.

"Jim Carver killed him," said Fernald.

"Does he tell you that?" Walters asked, scoffing at this pretended surety on the part of Fernald.

"Bane and Loring are old hands with a revolver. They both fan their gats, don't they?"

"Well, what of that?"

"That means that they'd be shooting not much more than hip, doesn't it?"

"And how does that help?"

"A lot. Somebody was standing outside the door when Blair came and opened it. The fellow on the outside leveled his Colt at the head of Blair. He was a tall man, because the floor of the house is a bit higher than the ground outside, and yet the bullet went straight through the head of Blair. Gun must have been held by a six-footer. And Jim Carver is the only one of the three who stands that tall."

The deputy sheriff nodded. "That's right," he said. "I'm sorry that it's Jim Carver, though. He used to be a decent kid. Nobody in the whole town had a word to say against him, until that night when you lifted the Carver Rock and broke the heart of Jim. And now . . . murder. It's a rotten business, Tom. I'm sick of it. I wish to heaven that I were doing almost anything else in the world."

He spoke with genuine feeling, and Fernald watched him in the manner of a man making a new judgment of an old friend.

"You're getting chicken-hearted, Ed," he told the other. "Jim Carver's gone wrong. He's spoiled. And there's no reason for it. He was born with a silver spoon in his mouth. He tried to kick me in the face when he thought I didn't count. He tried to insult me before the whole town. Then he welshed and crawled out of the wager that he'd made with me. He's been going downhill ever since. I have no pity for him, no more than he had for me. Now he's herding with man-killers. And he'll hang for it, if I have to trail him all around the world myself!"

Savagery came out in his voice as he ended. He sat down and brooded at the gleam of the fire that came through the cracks of the stove. Ed Walters was calmly pouring himself a cup of coffee.

"I know that you're right," he said. "And I'm not one to let Carver off. Only, it made me a little sick for a while . . . the blood on everybody's hands, I mean, and the dirty, small ways that are the beginning of murder."

Fernald nodded, glancing quickly up and to the side. "It's money that turns the trick," he said.

"Money?" echoed the deputy sheriff. "I guess that money had nothing to do with this. They didn't rob Blair."

"Money made Blair throw in with them at first. Because I'd thrown my business into a bank outside of this town. And then it was still more money that brought Blair back in line with me. He simply sold out the three of 'em. Yes, there's money behind the whole rotten business."

"You'll have to tell that to the judge," Walters said. "I don't understand all of this here lingo of yours, but I guess that the judge will understand."

"I'll tell the judge," Fernald said dryly. "I'm starting back for town now."

"There's no use casting around for a trail by night, I suppose?" pondered Walters.

"A night trail on the line of those three wildcats?" murmured Fernald. "I'm not such a fool, for one. I'd rather go bare-handed to a lion's cave than trail Sam Loring in the dark, or even by the light of the full moon."

"You're right," answered Walters. "I was just talking offhand. I wasn't meaning anything that I said. Loring and Joe Bane and Mister Murderer Carver all together . . . no, it wouldn't be safe to hunt them at night unless we had a whole regiment along with us." He finished his coffee and jammed his hat down over his ears. "Ready, Tom?"

"Yes. Ready."

"Well, let's start back."

"Not through the door, Ed."

"Why not?"

"One murder came through that door already today. Another one may come through now."

"You mean that they're watching the door from the outside?"

"They may be."

"Whatcha talkin' about?" Walters laughed. "If a man played every card as carefully as all of that, he'd never dare to turn around." So saying, he threw the door open and stepped out.

The step was hardly completed, however, before he whirled, drawing a revolver at the same time, and lurched back for the interior of the cabin. At the same time, the loud, ringing report of a rifle *cracked* upon the ear of Fernald.

Walters sprawled upon the floor; Fernald caught him by the collar of the coat and jerked him in as easily as though he had been a mere play figure stuffed with straw. Half a dozen shots in rapid succession splintered the door as he slammed it shut again.

The firing ceased. He kneeled beside Walters and stared into the white face that was upturned to him. "Where, Ed?" he asked.

"I guess they've got me," Walters said with an admirable calmness. "It's right through the wishbone, I guess. I'll get no more wishes, Tommy. Well, this is what comes to fools that go trailing a Sam Loring by moonlight." He smiled as he said this. But the smile was a dreadful effort. His faced gleamed with sweat. It was as wet and as sickly white as the belly of a fish.

Meanwhile Fernald had opened the coat of his friend and located the exact spot where the bullet entered. He turned the body and examined the spot where it had come out on the other side.

"If that had been a Forty-Five-caliber slug, Ed," he said, "you'd be dead in two minutes, but that little slug out of a rifle whipped through as fast and as clean as a tailor's needle. You'll be riding a horse again in a couple of weeks. Wait till I get a pad and a bandage on that there wound."

X

The dead body lay on the floor in a far corner. Ed Walters was lifted to the bed. Gently, though, Fernald touched him, yet Walters could not keep back a groan.

"Let it out," advised Fernald. "Don't lock that shouting up too tight, or it'll bust you."

"Yeah. It's busting me," gasped Walters. "I gotta let out a groan or two, Tom."

"Groan your head off," said Fernald. "It'll keep me from getting lonely . . . the sneaking rats! The low, snake-eating. . . ." He stopped himself, grinding his teeth in a frenzy of rage.

"Oh, it's all right," Walters said. "I can feel where the bullet hit me. You're lying when you say that I'll pull through. I'm a goner, Tom."

"Shut your mouth. You talk like a fool . . . like a regular weak-wit fool of a woman, Ed. You're showing a yellow streak. That's what you're showing."

"Yeah. And I'm scared," said Ed Walters. "I'm so scared that it makes me kind of sick at the stomach. Tom, I thought that I'd be more of a man than this, when it came to my turn to be bumped off!"

"Your turn hasn't come," Fernald argued. "The only danger you're in is of dying of fright. Pull yourself together, you overgrown baby, you."

"Yeah. I'll pull myself together," whispered the wounded man. "I feel a lot better, right away. You won't leave me, Tom?"

"I won't leave you," said Fernald. "Of course, I won't leave you. There they go again, the rats."

A fresh rattle of rifle shots began, and the slugs whipped through the flimsy walls, breast-high—then, again, hardly more than a foot from the floor. Twice the slugs rang loudly upon the iron of the stove. The stovepipe was clipped through and allowed a thin, steady stream of smoke to come out into the room.

"They want me pretty badly, Ed," said Fernald.

"Sure they do," said the other. "They want you mighty bad. The first two they got were only appetizers, I guess. What are you going to do?"

"I'm not going to stay here until they rush the house and set fire to it."

"You think they'll do that?"

"That's what I think."

"They wouldn't do that, Tom."

"Why not? Burn up all signs of their three murders and give them all a clean bill of health. What could be better than that?"

"I understand," said Ed Walters. "If Sam Loring gets that idea. . . ."

"He'll get it before long. He may have it now . . . only he's not sure how closely we can keep watch from in here. As soon as he finds how many blank walls we have around us, he'll walk up and blow us to the devil, living and dead."

Fernald stood by the stove, his hands clasped behind him, his eyes far away in thought.

"Tom, do something!" cried Walters.

"Yeah. I'll do something," said Fernald dreamily.

"What's in your mind, then?"

"Just a little idea."

"Tell me what?"

"They're covering the window and the door with their rifles, most likely?"

"Yes. Those are your only ways out."

"They wouldn't be apt to be watching the other end of the shack there, would they?"

"No, of course not. Why should they? There ain't any window or door there."

"Well, I'll make one."

"Make one?"

"You'll see what I mean. If I can make a hole in that wall fast enough, I'll get outside before they can bring their guns to bear on me. I'm going to try my luck at it, anyway. In here, we'll only be stung to death by wasps in the dark of the night."

A fresh *crash* of rifle fire came as he ended his speech. The bullets whipped through and through the house; again a noisy tattoo beat upon the stove.

But Fernald, stepping to the blank wall at the end of the house, carefully examined the boards. There was only a single layer of them composing the flimsy wall, and they were nailed, as a matter of course, from the outside.

"A horse could kick its way right through that wall," Fernald announced. "And I think I can throw myself through." He backed up several steps, then crouched and, like a football player charging the line, he drove against the wall, striking it with the tough cushion of his shoulder muscles, his head ducked down close to his breast for safety. The crash of the impact made the entire flimsy little house shudder. But it was a ripping, tearing crash, and the body of Fernald burst through a ragged hole out of the room and into the open moonlight.

He was more than half stunned, but, before he made the attempt, he had planned exactly what he must do if he were successful in breaking through. The force of his own thoughts—his plan—now guided him and kept him in motion.

Just up the slope, which continued at this end of the house, there were a number of rocks, and these worked into the brush and bigger trees that were packed well back from the ranch house. If the place had been lived in more regularly, the shrubbery could not have been allowed to grow, because it would have been used up regularly as firewood. But for years the brush had gone wild, and it was in the meager shelter of this that Fernald hoped to escape from the guns of his enemies.

On his hands and knees, his brain swirling from the shock that he had just passed through, he worked through the rocks and into the bushes.

Then he heard loud, angry shouting. He could make out the voice of Joe Bane, screeching like an enraged mountain lion:

"You fool, Jim Carver! You damned fool! You've let him get out!"

"I wasn't here," said Carver, roaring his response. "It wasn't where I was supposed to be. How was I to guess that he was going to walk right out through the solid wall of the house?"

"Use your brains, and they'll give you some idea now and then!" Bane cried, still furious. "Where is he now? And is it Fernald?"

"Aye, it's Fernald."

"Nothing's gained unless we get him."

"I know that. I think that he's there among those rocks."

"Work up the hill on that side. I'll work up it on this side."

Then, out of the greater distance, Fernald, as he worked like a snake through the shrubbery, heard a smaller, softer, almost a feminine voice that called: "Fernald! Fernald! Fernald!"

He was about to answer, but thought better of that impulse at once.

"Fernald!" called the other.

"Shut up, Sam!" yelled Joe Bane. "You're just giving him a screen to get behind, with all of your racket. D'you think that he'll talk back?"

"Fernald!" Loring cried again. "If you've got the soul of a flea, step out and have it out with me, man to man!"

"And me and Jim Carver will be honest referees, eh?" Bane sneered.

"You and Jim Carver will back up . . . you'll go clear back to the hollow, when I say the word. And that'll leave me to fight it out with Fernald."

"Now, don't you think he's a fool, even if you are," suggested Jim Carver.

Their big, powerful voices flooded and filled the hillside. They boomed at the very ears of Fernald, and he began to see that his chances of escape were very small, indeed. He had not brought a rifle out; he hardly could have managed that, with his flying exit. But he knew that revolver shooting was likely to be the height of inaccuracy in the moonlight.

So, grimly, bitterly he added his chances. He no longer tried to worm ahead through the brush. He could see, beyond the patch in which he was at that moment, a bright stretch of silver moonlight glittering on the clean faces of the rocks. That fairly ended progress in this direction. He was a little better off than in the house. From this position, he could watch the house and make sure that the trio did not rush poor Ed Walters in his helplessness. They were not likely to undertake that rashly, because they could not very well know how badly he was wounded.

"Fernald! Fernald!" came the mournfully appealing, high-pitched voice of Sam Loring. "Why don't you sneak up? Give me my chance at you, and I'll promise to see that you get a straight deal. I'll get Bane and Carver to back up and leave us alone to finish the deal." He added loudly, a moment later: "Fernald, you're not what they told me you were. I've never refused an invitation like this in my life. I'd rather die ten times over than back down. But you're backing down. . . ."

Red lightning of anger seemed to strike across the brain of Fernald. He found himself shouting furiously: "Back up your two running mates, Loring, and I'll come out to meet you fast enough!"

"He's there!" called the exultant voice of Carver. "He's in that patch of brush. I can almost see him. Joe, take your bearing on that patch of brush. We can light the grass and smoke him out into the open."

Fernald, his heart still and cold with dismay, listened.

And then he heard the piping voice of Loring crying: "You fellows back up, you hear? You fellows get off down the hollow. Fernald's a gentleman, and I'm going to show him how another gentleman keeps his word!"

XI

There was a moment of wrangling, the arguing voices of Jim Carver and of Joe Bane swelling and rising in protest. But then those voices retreated, and he knew that little Sam Loring was having his way.

He was amazed. He could not say whether he was more delighted or shocked by the success of Loring. The man seemed to know how to succeed in everything.

Through the air from the shack, now, came a succession of deep groans, long-drawn and shuddering. They were the sounds made by a man in agony and in weakness, his throat half closing as he lies relaxed at the point of death.

Hearing them, a sickness of spirit overcame Tom Fernald. He had seen death before, but never had he felt its presence so vividly. Ed Walters was grappling with exhaustion and with pain in that lonely house, with no hand near to help him. And what would happen if exactly such a wound should be delivered by the accurate gun of Loring, when he and Fernald fought together in the moonlight?

He could feel the surface of his flesh prickling and contracting slowly into gooseflesh. Then he heard the voice of Loring nearby.

"If you're in that brush patch, Fernald, and you mean fair fighting, step out in the open?"

Cautiously rising and looking around him, Fernald saw no place near enough to account for that voice, except a ragged tangle of big rocks nearby. Behind them the gunman must be concealed. Well, it was now or never. So Fernald, suddenly throwing his head high and his shoulders back, came out from the scattering shrubbery into the moonlight.

A slight form detached itself from the stones at once and waved cheerfully to Fernald. It was little Sam Loring, who said: "Hello, Fernald. Mighty glad to meet up with you like this."

"Thanks," Fernald said, "and the same to you."

"I've been wanting to meet you for a long time," said Loring. "You know the way it is. The way a whole school wants to see the new boy from Australia, eh?"

"Yeah, I know," said Fernald. "And here we are, at last."

"Here we are," said Sam Loring. "I'd like to have a fine long chat with you, Tom. But I can't. We haven't much time, I suppose, on account of poor Ed Walters lying in there with a hole poked through his ribs."

"Did you poke that hole through him?" asked Fernald.

"No, I didn't. I didn't do any of the rifle work. I ain't pulled a trigger all evening long," was the surprising answer.

"Not one?" exclaimed Fernald.

"No," replied Loring. "Not one. It's not my kind of work, huddling together with a lot of thugs to do a murder. Murder ain't my line, Tom. But I guess you'd know that without my telling."

"I believe you," said Fernald. "And a lot of lies have been told all over the lot about you."

"A lot of lies," Loring agreed hotly. "I've had my troubles with the boys, now and then, and I've sometimes had my share of luck in tagging the other fellow out before he tagged me. But I've never gone in for killings. People have lied a lot about me. Maybe you know how that is?"

"Yeah, I know how that is, all right," said Fernald. "But what's the main idea now, old son? Are you coming after me to build up your reputation?"

"Reputation?" murmured Sam Loring. "I dunno. I was just sort of curious. That was all. Maybe you know how it is . . . a man gets curious."

"I suppose that I know," Fernald admitted. He felt that this must be the strangest conversation that ever had taken place between two men who were very likely, before many minutes passed, to be doing their best to kill one another. He could not hate this new enemy. Rather, he felt as though he were in the presence of a quite irresponsible child. A coyote wailed suddenly out of the hollow of the valley, a shrill, prolonged sound that cut the air like a knife; closer at hand, poor Ed Walters was still groaning with every breath that he drew.

"That poor Walters," said the great Sam Loring, "is having a pretty hard time of it. He'll be wantin' water, by the sound of him . . . water and brandy . . . mighty bad, like some that I got in a flask along with me right now. I reckon that we'd better hurry up and get through with our little knockdown, Fernald. I hate to hear a man sufferin' like that and do nothin' about it."

It was amazing to hear the real concern that melted his voice.

"Fill your hand, then," snapped Fernald.

"Me fill my hand?" .

"Yes."

"Me make the first move?" Loring cried, something like grief mingling with anger and surprise in his voice.

"Why not?" said Fernald. "If you're so curious about me, fill your hand, and we'll soon have the party started."

"I'll see you damned first," Loring said with great heat. "You think that you can talk down to me, do you?"

"I'm not trying to talk down to you. I'm just inviting you to the dance. That's all."

"I don't take no first steps," said Loring. "I'm a finisher, but I ain't a beginner. You make your move . . . and I'll try my damnedest to answer it."

"Thanks," said Fernald. "That's all right. But I don't see the game that way. You'll have to play it by my rules. I'm not taking any concessions from anyone."

"You're a swelled head," snarled Sam Loring. "That's what you are. But listen to me. There's that coyote yappin' down the valley. Suppose that the next time it blats, you and me make our move together."

"Sure," Fernald said. "That's all right with me. The next time it yips." He paused. They faced one another in a moonlight that was suddenly dimmed, for a thin cloud had blown over the moon, and Fernald, from the corner of his eye, could see the silver ship sailing through the sky, now darkened and tarnished, now emerging and flinging from its bows clouds of glimmering spray. On the horizon, out of the duller parts of the sky, the stars swarmed; at the zenith they were few and dim except for one blazing planet. Jupiter, no doubt.

And ten paces away from him stood the slender, boyish silhouette of the manslayer, Sam Loring, who rode endless miles and took his life in his hand because he was—"curious."

There was something about all of this scene that was as absurd, as unreasonable as a dream, to Fernald. And then the high-pitched cry of the coyote struck his ear. He reacted under it like a fine set of springs from which a weight has been removed. The revolvers whipped from their armpit spring holsters into his hands, and, as they came out, he made, according to his custom, a single little quick, quarter-step forward.

He saw, at the same time, that he made these instinctive movements, that the great Sam Loring was already beaten. He was behind—he was perhaps a thousandth part of a second behind, and no better than a dead man.

But then the dim light and that little quarter-step forward undid Fernald. His foot came down not on level ground, but dropped into a hole six inches deep. The involuntary gesture to keep his balance caused his right hand and the gun in it to jerk upward. He fired ahead of Loring, but he knew his bullet was wild. Even as he knew it, a little cat's tongue of flame licked the lips of Loring's gun, the Colt was wrenched by a giant hand from Fernald's grasp and hurled back against his head.

He fell into spinning darkness on his side and back. The sky above him was swinging rapidly around and around, with a motion that gradually slowed. Presently it would stop altogether, and then he would be able to do something. But no! Before that happened, the second and following bullets from Loring would rip through him.

Then a shadow leaned above him; he saw the glint of a gun. For that glint he reached, found it, tore it out of Loring's fingers with consummate ease. The jerk pulled Loring into arms that mastered him with a single effort.

Like a child he had seemed in silhouette, like a child in actions and speech, and hardly more than a child was he when the terrible, bone-breaking grip of Fernald came upon him. He wilted. One groan, one gasp broke from his lips, then he was a limp hanging weight. Fernald arose with it. He felt that he should be dead; instead, he held his conqueror lightly in his hands.

Not that Loring had fainted. No, he was still conscious, and his keen, fearless eyes dwelt upon the face of the bigger man with a sort of resigned wonder and expectation of what was to come next. But his arms were paralyzed; the fingertips of Fernald had bruised flesh and nerves deep as the bone.

Fernald's own brain was still partially obscured by the shock of the blow that he had received. But now, as it cleared, he heard the pounding of many hoofs deep within the valley and, next, a sound of men shouting in the distance.

That cleared his mind entirely and at a stroke. Riders were coming. They must have heard the sound of the two shots, and for this reason they had called, far off. They could not very well be adherents of either Jim Carver or Joe Bane. They must be men, then, who would stand on his side. The tables were reversed, and he was the total master of the situation. Carver and Bane would be sneaking off in the distance. He, Fernald, remained upon the scene with a victim in his hands.

He shook Sam Loring, but not with a harsh grasp. "Sam, you understand what I'm saying?"

"Yeah. I can hear you, all right."

"You know what I mean to do with you?"

"Break me in two and eat me on toast, I reckon," Loring answered without emotion.

"There's a horse yonder. Over there behind the rocks . . . I can see the head of it."

"Yes. There oughta be a horse there. That's where I left my nag."

"Go over there and get on it then, and ride like the devil. Some men are coming up this way that look like they had something on their minds. Get out, Sam, and the next time you travel, you pick out a better pair for company."

"You mean you're turning me loose?" asked Loring.

"That's what I mean. Get out, Sam. I've got nothing against you. It was luck that dropped me first, and then it was luck that turned you over to me. I don't play my luck to a hangman's rope. So long, Sam. You better get going."

"I better had," Loring said.

He paused for another instant, as though something of importance remained unspoken by him. But then, with a shrug of his lean, crooked shoulders, he turned and went toward the rocks, limping a little and rubbing a bruised shoulder on which the grasp of Fernald had rested.

XII

Before Fernald reached the door of the shack, armed riders

swept up the slope and poured about him. Guns were pointed at his head.

Then a great bearded man was shouting: "It's all right! That's Fernald, thank God!"

"Fernald, with a bullet through his head!" cried another.

"Tom, Tom!" cried the voice of a girl. "Are you badly hurt?" And there was Julie Darden swinging out of the saddle and running to him. He caught her by one wrist and kept her at arm's length.

"I'm all right," he said. "I don't look pretty, but that's all. I'm doing fine. Just a nick in the scalp. Hold your horses, Julie."

She gave him, through the moonlight, one keen, probing glance, and then, with a sigh and a nod of satisfaction, he saw the trouble melt away from her face. But the memory of that first distraught look of hers would never leave him. His heart rose and swelled with the thought of it. But that earlier impression caused him to look instantly away from her toward the giant of the beard, he of the husky, familiar voice.

He was not so close, that rider, and the moon was darkening behind clouds. But Fernald knew him. By a powerful instinct of hatred and disgust he recognized once more that converted sinner, Bill Ransome, hero of the smallpox plague among the Comanches.

After that, the whole flood of people poured into the cabin sweeping him along, asking a thousand questions at once, and then standing stupefied before the desperately wounded deputy sheriff and the dead body of poor Blair.

A weariness of words came over Fernald. He let them clamor and gasp while he calmly washed the blood from his face, and allowed Dean Ellison to tie a cloth about his head to stanch any fresh flow of blood.

Julie, he noted, was not one of the talkers. She was too busily engaged in taking charge of Ed Walters, and he saw that Walters quickly began to look after her as a badly hurt hound looks after the all-wise master that tends it.

Some of the men had found the hole that was smashed in the end of the wall. They gathered about that, wondering, muttering their theories.

Fernald was saying to Dean Ellison: "What happened, Dean?"

"I was out with Ed's party," said Ellison. "I went back with the rest of the boys, and, when we got into town, there was big Bill Ransome, all heated up. One of them pet Comanches of his . . . the rotten hoss thieves! . . . had listened in on a little talk between Jim Carver and Joe Bane, planning how they'd get hold of Sam Loring . . . no less . . . and lead him to you and see how fire and dynamite got along together. Murder was in the air, according to that Comanche. He was one of them deaf mutes, but the foxy lad, he could read lips, and he read Bane and Carver to a T. And Bill Ransome, he starts riding for town, and he comes all the way of a hundred miles inside of twenty hours. How come? I thought he hated your heart?"

"Oh, plague take Ransome and all of his ideas!" snarled Fernald. "What he does makes no difference to me."

"Take another shot, Ed," someone was saying.

"I don't need another," Ed Walters insisted. "I feel a lot better. It was the pressing of the bandage that was hurting me, I guess. Since Julie changed that, I feel fit to ride a hoss, pretty near."

"Then, you tell us what happened. Fernald, he won't talk."

"I dunno all that happened, except that Tom and me come up here and find Blair lyin' murdered across the inside of that door there. You can see some of the blood on the floor still. Then, as I started out, they put a rifle ball through me . . . the dirty blackguards that was lying in wait . . . I mean Jim Carver, and Joe Bane, and Sam Loring."

"Sam Loring didn't shoot you, Ed," said Fernald.

"You know that?" muttered Walters. "Anyway, he was with 'em, which makes things black enough for him, if the law ever taps him on the shoulder . . . that little poison rat! And here we was together, with the rifle bullets drilling the house clean through every jump and the old stove ringing like a dinner bell. There was nothing for us to do. They had the window covered and they had the door covered. They had us trapped. They could sneak up and touch a match to the house and burn up their third man, and all the evidence along with him." He reached out a somewhat unsteady hand and pointed. "So Fernald, he just walked through the solid wall there, and went out and entertained all three of them thugs, until you boys came cantering up the valley and scattered 'em. A mighty close play all around, I'd call it."

Fernald was saying to Ellison: "Did Ransome get the boys together?"

"He did," said Ellison. "He did . . . and Julie Darden helped. She had heard of something wrong, and she was right on the spot when Ransome got in. She soon had things whooping up, and it was her idea to hurry the gang right back out along this road to see what might have happened. You and Walters were overdue in town by that time, anyway." He added, in a lowered voice, as one much moved: "Maybe you don't like Ransome, and I know some reasons why. But he's played a friend to you tonight. And what Julie Darden thinks of you . . . that goes without saying, or any brass band to announce her, either."

Fernald nodded. "Thanks, old son," he said. "You boys have given me a good break just about when I needed it."

"What happened to your head?" asked Ellison.

"Why, as I was walking over the mountains," said Fernald, "I just bumped into a careless eagle. That was all."

He let it go at that, and Ellison gave a quizzical smile, and asked no further questions. A wise man in the ways of men was Ellison.

The other arrangements had to be made at once. Such of the party as returned to Griffon would send out conveyances to take in the body of Blair at once. Ed Walters would be brought in as soon as the pain of his wound permitted him to stand the journey.

Jay Topping, who had studied medicine, gave it as his opinion that, if the trip were made slowly, the patient could stand it at once, but the morning following might be a better time. He and two other men would remain to nurse their deputy sheriff.

Julie Darden came to the side of Fernald. "You stay here with them and rest till the morning, Tom," she recommended. "You're done up. You look all finished."

He stared at her. "Done up about what?" he asked irritably. "I'm not done up. I'm as fit as ever. This scratch along the head . . . it doesn't amount to a thing."

"Are you as fit as that?" she asked.

"Yes."

"Then come outside for a moment with me and Bill Ransome."

"I don't want to go anywhere with Bill Ransome," Fernald said decidedly.

But she had him by the arm, and somehow he could not resist. Out he went with her, and, at a nod from her, Ransome followed. They stood just around the corner of the house; within, they could hear the voices of the others clearly, except when several spoke in a roar together.

The subject of their argument, just then, was the ragged hole that Fernald had torn like a projectile through the rear of the shack. Many protested that no man could have done such a thing. Ed Walters, his voice sharp and high with angry fatigue, was arguing that he had seen it with his own eyes.

But the three outside of the house heard these things as out of a great distance. They had a nearer and larger concern with one another.

For, as soon as they were together, the girl said, her hand still upon the arm of Fernald: "I know that the time has come when you two can't keep apart any longer. You have to be friends."

"There's nothing," said Ransome, "in the entire world that I'd rather call myself than a friend of Tom Fernald's. I've hurt him, and he's helped me. But the day may come when I won't arrive too late on the spot to make you glad that I've come."

"You came in time tonight," said the girl. "Except for you. . . ."

"No," broke in Ransome. "I didn't come in time. I was too late, tonight, though Fernald won't tell us so. But I saw the shadow of him off in the distance, holding another shadow by the nape of the neck . . . and then turning the other shadow loose. He had the game in his hands before we reached the place."

"Is that true?" asked the girl, frowning at Fernald. "Who was the other shadow?"

"A friend of mine," Fernald answered with a shrug of his shoulders. "Little Sam Loring."

"Sam Loring . . . the murderer!" she cried.

"He's a thousand miles from a murderer," insisted Fernald. "But I'll tell you, Julie, for the last time . . . I'm through with Ransome. He tried to do me a grand good turn today. I ought to be grateful, but I'm not. We've both done some good turns for the other fellow. Tonight just balances the account, as I see it. And that leaves me free to say what I think, and what I think is that I never want to lay eyes on his face again. Ransome, I don't like you. I don't like the look of you, or the things that you do, or anything about you. What you call religion, I call rot. If you're not a hypocrite, you're a fool. To me, you've been a crook. You've damned my reputation for life. You know you have. And it's hard for me to keep my fingers off your throat when I'm this close to you. Julie, don't hang onto my arm. I can't stay near him. He chokes me."

He shook off her detaining hand and turned hastily away, the angry blood singing in his ears.

But, behind him, he heard the girl saying: "I'm not through, Bill. I'll try him again, and again, and again. And finally, I'll make him see things my way, I know. Will you try to believe me when I say that?"

"No man in the world could listen to you without being persuaded," said Ransome. "I'll trust you, and God bless you for trying, Julie. It's the thing that's nearest to my heart."

XIII

The little newspapers of Griffon got out extras in honor of that evening's great occurrences. They hawked them through the streets of the town, the ink wet and ready to smear under the thumb, but although every soul in Griffon knew all about the affair by this time, never was the maxim more clearly illustrated that we love most to read what we already know. For everyone bought and everyone read. Not content with one paper, they bought both, and read and re-read, biting their lips with intense interest.

Fernald, stretching in his bed between cool sheets, very tired but very happy, listened to the cries of the hawkers in the streets below and knew that a crown had been put upon his fame and name. He had appeared first as the humble shepherd, then as the dangerous man-killer, then as the man of mysterious wealth, but now, finally, he would appear before the eyes of the public as a pillar of the law and an upholder of the deathless rights of man. They would tell, for more than a day, how he had fought for Ed Walters in the murder hut there among the hills. And they would not forget that Sam Loring, his captive, had been allowed to escape.

Eyes closed, a faint smile curving at the corners of his lips, he tasted his future life. For that was what his future life would be now. Griffon was expanded for him and colored with a sunrise glory, for his days of greatness were just beginning in a flame of triumph.

How much it meant to him—public opinion—he had never dreamed before. For so many years he had been shut away from everything except open contempt, and then, with the coming of his celebrity as a man of wealth and might of hand, there had been the ugly rumors afloat about him—the rumors that Bill Ransome had started.

Finally, here was Bill Ransome himself riding 100 miles in the hope of doing him a good turn. To be sure, Bill had only done it out of what others might call Christian spirit, but Fernald knew very well that that was not the name that would be given to Bill's act by the majority of people on that range. They would term it repentance. They would say that Bill was striving to undo a little of the harm that he had already wrought against Fernald. No, the picture was too perfect for words. Everything fitted ideally together.

He would never forget the ride into Griffon from the Blair house. He would never forget the quiet murmurs of the other cowpunchers as they looked at him and stifled their comments, lest they should appear to be praising blatantly. But in their attitude there was the strong red blood of a reputation that could not down, unless he chose to cut his own throat. He would never choose that.

There was a rap at the door; he called out, and the proprietor came in, grinning, nodding.

"Seen the evening papers, Mister Fernald? Well, they've got

out some extras I thought you might like to see. They got an account of how Dusty Wells has made a neat little strike up in the Gerson Hills. Kind of exciting reading." He laughed, the foolish and pleased, high-pitched laugh of a little boy.

"Thanks," said Fernald. "I'd like to read about old Dusty. He's been deserving a different sort of a break for a long time. I'm glad that he has it now."

"He's got it now, all right," said the proprietor. "By the way, seeing that you're sort of used up. . . ."

"I'm not used up," Fernald contradicted. "Only, I'm a little tired. Had some long riding the last few weeks."

"Yeah. Just a little tired. I know. Just a little tired." He laughed again in the same foolish, pleased way. Then, from his pocket, he pulled out a pint flask. "Occurred to me that I had some bourbon that's fifty years old, Mister Fernald. I want you to take this and soak some of it into your bones and see if it don't make you feel a lot better. This will rest you a lot quicker than sleep ever will."

"That's mighty fine of you," murmured Fernald. "Sit down and have a glass with me."

His invitation was hastily accepted, and, while the liquor was being poured, his thoughts drifted back to the same ruddy face—a good deal younger then—suffused with wrath and roundly cursing a certain small boy who had done badly a certain job of weeding in the vegetable garden. That small boy had been little Tommy Fernald. But now he was Mister, and nothing that this hotel could produce was too good for him. The thought soothed him marvelously. It was better than a hot bath for a tired body.

There was a little talk—about Blair, about Ed Walters, and, above all and finally, about terrible Sam Loring. Was it true that he had been helpless in the hands of Fernald?

"Listen to me," Fernald said. "Sam Loring isn't helpless now, no matter what he may have been before. He's a free agent. He's not carrying around any wound to cripple him. I've an idea that I'll meet him again, one of these days, and that he'll shoot both his guns hot before he's through with me."

The proprietor, amazed, shortly afterward said good night and left in a hurry, obviously to spread around the latest story—and this time from the very lips of the oracle.

Fernald, with a faint smile and a faint frown, picked up the papers. The frown was for the thought of Sam Loring, which was never quite out of the back of his mind. Something would come of that fellow—and before many days. A Loring does not easily wear the gloom of a first and only defeat. But the smile was for what he found in the newspapers. It was about as he had expected. The whole vocabulary was there. Poor Blair's death was hardly mentioned, except as means of further praising the hero of the hour. Ed Walters was simply the foil that had drawn forth the tremendous effort of Fernald. The breaking of the house wall—that was the chief point, the originality and the Herculean strength—and then there were the usual passages describing the earlier life of this "prominent citizen" and his rise to power, his wealth and success, his modesty and courage, his brilliance and quiet behavior, his strength.

It was all lavished upon him. Then it was said again, in a more flowery manner; finally, in an editorial, Griffon was called upon solemnly to congratulate itself heartily for having such a man.

In the midst of this pleasant reading, he heard a mere whisper of sound from the window. Then, from the corner of his eye he saw a shadowy form standing inside of the aperture. The next instant he had a gun in his hand and was sitting up. But a quiet voice said to him: "It's no good, Fernald. I'm not fighting with you twice tonight."

Out of the shadows came Sam Loring, his thin face ghostly

white and drawn, as though a body wound were sucking out his strength of nerve and bone. He came and rested a hand on the edge of the table at the foot of the bed.

"Hello, Sam," Fernald said, troubled, but feeling that the man was not to be feared so long as this humor lasted. "I'm glad to see you." And he put his revolver away under his pillow again.

"What happened?" asked Sam.

"When?"

"You had me beat," Sam Loring said, "and then you stumbled."

"I stepped into a hole. That's all."

Loring nodded. His dark eyes in his death mask of a face never left off reading away at the soul of Fernald. "You had me beat," he repeated.

Fernald shrugged his shoulders. "No fight's over till the finish of it," he said. "I might have missed, anyway, even if I hadn't stumbled."

"You had me beat," insisted the lifeless voice of the other. He took off his hat and showed the crown. It was slashed across as though by a knife stroke. "That's how much you missed me," he said.

Fernald said nothing. There was nothing to say.

"You tried for the head, and you would've got me," went on Sam Loring. "I'm only here . . . because of a hole in the ground. Not because I'm fast . . . not because I can shoot. I'm here only by an accident." He laughed soundlessly. "I'm only a ghost, by rights. I'm nobody at all," Sam Loring announced.

Again Fernald was silent.

"I got to thinking it over," said Sam Loring. "I had to come in and tell you what I knew. I thought I didn't have any nerves. Now I'm shaking. I'm like a girl. I'm like a silly, sick girl. I ain't any kind of a man at all. I just thought that I'd tell you that your slug didn't entirely miss its mark."

"Listen," said Fernald.

"Sure, I'll listen."

"Take that glass and fill it to the top with whiskey out of that flask." The thing was done. "Now pour that down your throat."

Loring blinked. Then, as though at a doctor's orders, he turned off the mighty dram.

"Now," Fernald requested, "lie down on that other bed and give the blanket a turn around you. Nobody'll find you here. I'll call you in the early morning before anybody's stirring around Griffon. You need a rest."

"You want me to rest here in this room . . . your room?" Loring muttered hoarsely.

"Yes, that's what I want."

Loring came closer. A wild light was in his eyes. "You mean that you want me to stay here, Fernald?"

"You bet I do. You turn in and sleep. I'll see that nobody troubles you. Nobody troubles my friends . . . in Griffon."

"Friend?" repeated Loring.

"Yes," Fernald said cheerfully, "if you'll shake on it." And he held out his hand.

XIV

All the night he could hear the breathing of Loring, groaning as he slept. It reminded him, in a way, of the groans of Ed Walters, after he had been wounded. This was a much lighter and fainter sound. There was the hurt of the soul rather than the body to account for it. Ed Walters would recover from his wound and be as sound as ever, but Loring never. He was stabbed to the heart.

Loring was not really bad. He simply had been led astray by the Nordic love of adventure and the shock of danger. He had fought. Other men had gone down before him. Given another age, he would have been a shining example of the knight errant—one of those famous little men, in the days of armor and ponderous swords, whose exquisite skill made up for weight of shoulder muscles. He would have wielded one of those swords that had magic in their touch. But Loring lived in a wrong age and he was, therefore, a social outcast. He had learned his lesson, too. Some of his pride had been stolen from him. And he had ridden a distance, through dangers, to get to another man and simply say: "I am beaten. You conquered me fairly."

Well, a fellow as honest and open as that had something great about him, something worthwhile that ought to be saved. Society had put its curse upon him. But Fernald would save him.

He felt like a king dispensing justice. Long ago, in a school text, he had seen a picture of such a king, St. Louis, of France, seated in the open under a tree and giving his judgments. And Fernald . . . was he not the king of Griffon? People would accept his judgments of people and of things. In an extra-legal sense, he was the head and the crown of the place.

He could hardly sleep through the night, he was so filled with this sense of his own power. He found himself smiling with a fierce joy into the darkness above his face. He found his muscles quivering and straining with ecstatic impulses. After a time, he dozed off and slept for an hour or two. But his sleep was broken all the rest of that night.

Then the morning came, first gray and stealthy, the time for him to waken this dangerous guest of his, this man who all of Griffon would so gladly hang by the neck until he was dead. He saw gravely that he was taking an enormous responsibility upon his shoulders. He was guaranteeing the life and limb of Sam Loring with his own life and limb. But he felt a stern, cold confidence, like the stern, cold light of the dawn. Then the sky was rosy, then golden.

Sam Loring stirred suddenly. His faint, groaning breaths ceased. He sat up with a start and looked wildly around him. First, he looked out the window and listened to the sounds of life. Then he stared calmly at Fernald.

"Why didn't you do it last night?" he asked. "You might've done it last night with a bullet. That would've been a lot better than to get it today with a rope!"

But Fernald smiled upon him, in the fullness of his confidence. "I listened to you breathing in your sleep, last night, Sam," he said. "You whimpered and whined like a wolf, like a sick wolf that's been thrown out of the pack. That's the way you live, like an animal. You haven't any friends. There's nobody that wants to be with you, because you've been outside the law. They haven't had many big things against you, but, just the same, you've been a hunter and one of the hunted all your days since you were a kid. That's the life of a beast. I want you to settle down and be a man among other men. You hear me talk?"

The childish, bright, calm eyes of the other watched him without a response.

"I'm going to take care of you and give you a start in Griffon," Fernald stated. "D'you like this town?"

Loring stood up from the bed. "Do I like this town?" he said. "I ain't the one to ask questions about the town. Any town's too good for me. Like this town? I tell you, man, any town's heaven that'll let me stay inside of it. You say that I been living like an animal. I know it. I'm the only one who knows how much like an animal. I been living like a fool. Now and then two or three people would step aside for me . . . now and then I'd hear men whispering behind my back. I knew they were afraid of me. That was my happiness. You know what kind of a happiness?"

"Tell me," said Fernald.

"Like the happiness of the man who beats his wife. He has to have somebody afraid of him . . . his wife or his children, even.

That's the sort of a fellow I've been. I'm sick of it, rotten sick of it." He went over to the window and stood there, the shade up. "I want them to see me up here in your room," he said. "I wanna crowd to get together. That's what I want. And there the crowd starts. There's some that's seen me. There's some more, too. They're running together like chickens when they see a hawk." He broke into a half hysterical address to people who could not hear him. "I could be a hawk to you!" he declared fiercely. "I could make you run together, and I could scatter you again, too, when I stooped!" He turned to Fernald. "What do they know of sleeping out with nothing but one flannel shirt between you and the snow? What do they know of setting your own broken leg, and then crawling for roots and trapping rabbits and field mice for weeks and weeks till you dared to take the splints off? What do they know, those fat fellers down there, of things like that?"

"Did you set your own broken leg? Did you do all of that?" asked Fernald.

"Yeah, I did all of that. I can bear up against pain," Loring said. "I can bear up against danger, too, and crowds. But I'm tired of bearing up. I've been beaten by one man. What's the use of trying to pretend that I can bully a whole crowd, when one man can beat me?"

Up from the street Fernald, as he dressed, could hear the rising rumble of the crowd's voice. He was barely ready, when a dozen men came with heavy footfall down the hall. They paused outside the door of his room, and the voice of the proprietor called out: "Hey, Mister Fernald! Fernald!"

"I'm here," said Fernald. He went to the door and opened it.

Every man in the hall was wearing a grim expression—and guns! They looked past him, over his shoulders, toward the place where Loring sat, smoking a cigarette.

"We thought we saw Loring," began the proprietor, and then,

with his own eyes, he actually did see the man. He gaped, and all around him looked amazed.

"Sure, you saw Loring," said Fernald. "Come in and meet my friend, any of you boys who don't happen to know him already. Come in, Cress. I want you to meet my new partner, Sam Loring. Sam wants to settle down in Griffon, if Griffon wants to have him. This is a good enough time for Griffon to speak up and let us know its mind."

They came trooping in—an awkward squad and presented their hands, one by one, to Loring. Some of them, when they came close, obviously were measuring the little man with their eyes and were surprised by the result. Fernald watched carefully. And he studied Loring. The man had a girlish brow, smooth and low and broad, pale as a stone. Only his eyes were remarkable in their brightness, in the calm, detached clarity with which they looked into face after face. He no longer seemed small. He began to look like a giant, over-topping all the others. By all those present, this moment would never be forgotten.

"What's Loring going to be doing with you?" asked the proprietor, the last to leave.

"He's going to run my cattle ranch for me," said Fernald.

But when they were alone, a moment later, Loring said: "I don't know the hoof of a cow from its horns, Tom."

"You know a man from a fool, though," Fernald said. "And about the cattle, you'll learn. Do you want the job?"

"I want to do anything I can . . . under you," said Loring. "If only you can get me through the first day or two. But I'm not through yet. These fellows all looked as though I might turn into a dynamite bomb. They don't see me settling down inside the law."

"No," admitted Fernald. "We'll have to wait for a day or two before we know how the boys feel around the town. But we've won the first round of the fight, and that's the most important part."

On the whole, he was pleased, but he was far from certain as to the final results. He saw that there were very grave possibilities ahead. These townsmen had been curious, impressed, and much moved by the close presence of the gunman. But they had come up ready to shoot him down like a dog. What would the course of the day bring?

They went down to breakfast together. Instantly the dining room filled with murmuring men who made only a pretense of eating. They were too occupied with the sight of the great Sam Loring.

They spent the rest of the morning together, strolling in the streets, and they were back in the hotel room later on with Fernald in a greater quandary than ever. For he had received smiles on every hand, but his companion had been stared at as though he were a wild beast, walking to heel, to be sure, but with a tiger's possibilities still in him and scarcely on the leash.

Then, at eleven in the morning, came the important message. It was from Darden. It said: SHERIFF CLEVE BENDER IS SICK, AND HE'S RESIGNED. SOME OF US ARE MEETING AT MY HOUSE TO RECOMMEND TO THE PEOPLE A SUCCESSOR FOR CLEVE BENDER. YOU'RE THE MAN WE HAVE IN MIND. WILL YOU COME OUT AT ONCE AND TALK TO US?

XV

He had felt the esteem of the people before. But this was the proof of that esteem. For there had always been a saying in that county that a good sheriff meant good days for everyone. A bad sheriff or an inefficient one meant hard times. It was too much a hole-in-the-wall country. Yeggs, cattle rustlers, all sorts of criminals came to this district and hid out. They could slip across the Río Grande in a pinch. But the pinch seldom came unless there were a veritable man-hawk enforcing the law. Ed Walters had done his section well. But the chief sheriff of the entire county had a different job. He had to enforce the law over a district larger than some of the original thirteen states. It was an office universally looked up to over the range. And now they wanted Fernald for the place.

There would be no question about the matter. When Darden and his friends wanted to put a man into office, he went in quickly.

Neither was there any question in Fernald's mind about his ability to handle the position. He had ridden every inch of the county, at one time or another. He knew the people. They knew him. He had a reputation to use, and he would use it.

Besides, he now had a Sam Loring. It seemed to him like the direct will of heaven that he should have picked up Loring and made a friend of him at just this juncture. When manhunter Loring went out to serve a warrant—well, it would be served on the victim, living or dead.

He explained his point to Loring; he saw the face of the latter light a lamp in a dark room. Then they rode out together toward the house of Darden.

When they were still at a distance, they could see riders and buckboards making for the same goal, turning in toward the broad face of the Darden house. When they came up in their turn, they saw a long line of horses at the hitching rack; others were tethered in the big, open sheds. For the day was hot; there were only a few ragged wisps of clouds and the wind was not stirring. The dust they raised rose straight up in the air and hung there motionlessly. Behind their galloping, dim ghosts seemed to stretch, fainter and fainter, slowly dissolving.

The Darden house was alive with people, with footfalls, with loud voices. And Julie Darden, in a dress of bright blue silk, was on the front verandah, moving here and there, greeting people. Heads turned to look after her as she went along, and those heads nodded in admiration. She represented all that a woman should be, to most of them. So did she to Fernald. At the sight of her a hot wave of joyous possession came over him. She was his. She belonged to him. So did the place of sheriff in that great county. So did his wealth in lands, in cattle, in hard cash. So, above all, did he own the esteem of the people. They looked up to him. He was young, but he was the uncrowned king.

When he came up the steps, Julie Darden met him, grave and unsmiling. But she shook hands with Loring and found her smile for him. She said that she was glad to meet him, and that, of course, she had heard a great deal about him. He looked at her with his childish, overwise eyes and made no answer at all. Then he stepped back, and Fernald wondered why. Then Julie was talking to Fernald, standing close, looking gravely up into his face. Her voice was so low that he could barely hear it.

"Tom, I could stand anything else. Your money, and what it's based on. I could stand everything else. But I can't stand this. They want to make you sheriff. They're in there to decide it, but I know that it's already decided. They're going to make you sheriff, and yet you could be accused of murder and theft. I can't stand it. Tom, I wish you joy and glory. You have them both today. But I'm saying good bye now to everything that we planned between us. I can't marry you. I'd feel like a black hypocrite, smiling at you as though I believed in you as the others do."

Every word tore through his heart like a bullet. On his lips he forced and maintained a stiff, mechanical smile. But his brain was wrecked. He had known that he cared for her, but he had not known how much. There never had been an adequate measure. But now the measure was provided, and he understood.

He merely said—"That's interesting."—and then he walked on past her white face.

His own face was cold and wet. He found Loring at his shoulder as he reached the front door.

"Did she knife you . . . account of me?" asked Loring.

"You've nothing to do with it," Fernald said.

Darden met him, his eyes shining. They darkened when he saw Loring. "Do you think this is the place to bring Loring, Tom?" he asked.

"I have to bring him here," said Fernald.

"Well," Darden murmured hesitantly. "Oh, well, bring him in, then."

They entered the old dining room. There were fifty men there, and, when Fernald looked them over with a dim eye, he saw that every important name in the county, well-nigh, was represented. They were all here. Not an interest of any size was omitted. Lumbering, mining, sheep and cattle raising, farming, all were here.

Yes, if Darden had got together such a host, it was plain that they would be able to do as they pleased for a sheriff. These men could vote the county blind for whatever cause they saw fit. And, as he glanced around the big iron room, there was only one face that it was a shock for him to see. That was the face of Bill Ransome.

Why had Darden called this man in? Yet he understood, after a moment of afterthought. For if Fernald within the last few years had grown from a poverty-stricken shepherd and general no-account into the leading citizen of the community, so Bill Ransome had grown from gambler, highway robber, and ruffian into the most thoroughgoing Christian on the range. He did not preach with words but with deeds. The saving of the Comanches was not his only good deed. Yes, Bill Ransome had advanced to such a point that he must now be considered in every act of public policy.

Fernald smiled faintly and grimly. For he remembered how the present standing of Bill Ransome and his own success had both been rooted in the happenings of a single night.

Darden was busily calling the men to order, and, as they came to attention, he turned to Fernald and said: "Tom, we asked for you to come out here. But we didn't 'specially invite Sam Loring. Will you tell us why he's come?"

So perturbed was Fernald in spirit, so did the voice of the girl still ring in his ears, that he actually smiled a little at this blunt question. And he said: "You know, Darden, that men can go straight or crooked according to the chances that come to them. Here's Sam Loring who's done some things that would be better left undone, I suppose. But still he's a fellow who amounts to something. They accused him of murder last night. I can swear that he had nothing to do with that. He had an argument with me, and he played the gentleman straight through it.

"What are you going to say about Loring, after all? That he's braver than most men . . . that he's lived more freely than most . . . and that he's made up his mind to give himself up to the law, if the law has anything against him. But, before he does that, he wants to know . . . and I want to know . . . if the people of this county want him for a member of the community. Will you men answer that question?"

There was a heavy silence after this, and then the veteran, Dr. Willis, stood up straight and tall and lean among the others. "Loring has the name of a gunfighter and a ruffian," he said. "Why do you ask us to take him in, Fernald?"

Said Fernald: "When you were a youngster, Doctor, you sowed your own wild oats. You did it fighting Indians and Mexicans, and running up against the border gunfighters. You spent a few years at that, and I'll wager that you look back on them as the happiest years in your life. But times have changed. There's more law today and less adventure. Fellows who go out looking for glory today don't find Indians and glory . . . they find guns and steel bars. Suppose that you had been born thirty years later, would your own record be so clean as it is today?"

For a moment, the doctor scowled darkly. Then suddenly he laughed and made a gesture of surrender. "For one," he said, "I'll withdraw any objections. I vote Loring in . . . if a man like Fernald believes in him."

"So do I," said Darden. "We'd take Fernald's endorsement of a doubtful check. Why shouldn't we take his endorsement of a man he knows better than we know him?"

Then a sudden murmur of agreement ran around the room. The coolness toward Loring melted. It had been thicker than bars of ice the moment before. Now it dissolved quite away and an air of good feeling pervaded the place.

Fernald turned to his new friend. "Sam," he said, "they've taken you in. You belong to Griffon from now on. They wanted your scalp before, but now you'll find that they want your friendship and they're willing to trust you and believe in you. Go on out and take a breath of a new kind of air. I have something of another sort to say to them."

The keen, clear eyes of Loring gleamed as they rested for an instant on the face of Fernald. Then he turned and stepped silently from the room and, when his back was turned, something cat-like in his way of moving sent a shiver through more than one of the men who watched him going.

After the door closed, Darden said: "We've made a good beginning here. Now we can get on to the main business. We have most of the larger interests in this county represented here. A good many of us want Fernald for sheriff. If there's anybody who stands out against him, I want to hear him speak now."

Gradually all eyes shifted toward big Bill Ransome. He rose slowly, and, leaning with his big hands upon the back of the chair before him, he said: "You look at me, friends, because you're sure that I must have something to say against Tom. I've spoken against him before. That's the first time and the last. God help me if I ever attack him again. I can't be sorry that I said what I thought. But in the meantime, he's piled up a good many months of honest work. He's showed his mettle as a man and a Christian. My hand is with his hand as hard as I can lift."

He sat down, and there was a loud murmur of applause.

Darden, in turn, stood and waved his hand for silence; Fernald, with a sick heart, watched him and knew that the time had come to speak of the dead past.

XVI

When the room was again silent, Fernald took instant advantage of it, and something in his voice and in the set suffering of his face riveted the attention of every one there.

"It seems that you've cleared the way for me, Darden," he said. "There's no voice against me, and the way's open for me to be set on the road for the sheriff's job. But there's one thing against that . . . the thing is what I have to say to you today. You can't make me sheriff . . . but you can put me in jail." He paused to draw breath and let the old scene pour back into his mind.

Rigid sat his listeners. Only Bill Ransome dropped his forehead into the palm of one great hand and covered his face.

Then Fernald went on. "Go back to the night when Pete Visconti, the money-lender, disappeared. I'll tell you what happened. I'll make it all clear. I came out from Griffon to my small place, that night, with a little over two hundred dollars in my pocket. It was a bad day, rain and hail rattling on my slicker, but I hardly cared, because I had in my pocket enough to pay off the interest I owed on three thousand dollars that I had borrowed from Visconti. But out of a rain gust, just before I came to my place, came Bill Ransome and stuck me up, and I handed over my money, like the sheep that I was."

Bill Ransome raised a tormented face. "That is truth," he said. And he dropped his head once more. The seal had been placed on everything that Fernald was to say. Men leaned forward a little, breathless, scowling with intensity, hardly breathing.

"I got to the cabin," Fernald explained, "and there was Visconti, waiting. When he found that I didn't have the money, he damned me, flew into a rage, and swore that he'd foreclose on me at once. That was ruin . . . years of work wiped out. But I had to take it. It never occurred to me to hit back at that time in my life. Then luck stepped in. I thought that it was luck. Visconti's horse was lame. He took my pinto to ride home. I heard the horse bucking and came to my door to watch. Well, that pinto was a tough customer for a man who didn't know his tricks, and Visconti couldn't know them, and the pinto wound up by pitching Pete Visconti right through the door of my shack. His head hit the doorjamb . . . he lay on my floor, dead.

"At first, I was stunned. Then I was glad because no one was alive to collect that three thousand I owed. Immediately after that, I saw that people would say I had killed Pete because of the money I owed him. Just then, as I was standing there, through a trick of the wind, I guess, I thought that I heard horsemen coming up the trail. And I went cold, but all at once my coldness was not fear. I got a rifle from the wall and went to the door. I was ready to shoot to kill . . . but the trail was open. I went back inside, got Visconti on my back, carried him up into the rocks on the hills, and buried him under a rock slide. I came back and cleaned up some more. I felt safe. Visconti was gone, and there was no way to trace him to me. He had no relatives and there was no one to trace the clues. Nothing remained to show where he had been except his lame horse. So I led that horse back across country to his house and left it there in the pasture. But by that time I was thinking of the money he was said to have hidden around his house . . . a whole fortune. I hunted his house for it. At last I thought of the well and. . . ."

"By thunder!" broke in an excited voice. Heads turned. The interrupter sank lower in his chair.

"I found the money," went on Fernald, "and covered my trail, and went home, and counted out four hundred and fifty thousand dollars on the table in my shack, and then I heard a sound and looked up and saw the face of Bill Ransome at the window. He had been to Griffon and lost the money he got from me. He came in and demanded the lion's share of this loot. He guessed that I had got it from Visconti. Well, I found a chance to jump him with my bare hands. And by luck I mastered him. He was down and about choked. . . ." He paused and looked at Ransome.

"And then," Ransome cried in a deep, strange voice, "the God, who I have tried to serve since that day, stepped between and spared my life. Fernald spared me, though I was to testify once against him, as you all know. He spared me, and I'm here to tell you that all I know of his story he's repeated truly."

"Ransome left," Fernald continued. "The rest of the story . . . you people know. I went gradually into business. I had luck. I managed to invest all that money without raising too much suspicion as to where I got it. I've doubled that money, and more than doubled it. But there's a dirty taint of stolen goods on the whole property that I own. Only one thing is clean . . . that's the sheep walk that I had when I just started out. I've told you the story, gentlemen, of the fellow you wanted to make sheriff. When they come to jail me, I'm willing to go. But jail and not the sheriff's job is what I get."

With that, he turned and walked out of that stone-still assembly.

Out to the hitching rack he went and fumbled there, for a moment, with the hard knot that he had unwittingly tied when he arrived.

It was old pinto that he was riding. He led the faithful pony to the watering trough and let it drink, vaguely pleased to see it bury its nose deeper than the bit. Then, when it had finished, he mounted and turned the head of the horse toward the entrance lane.

Not until then did he see Julie Darden waiting before him, a Julie no longer glowing, but with a white face that gleamed with tears.

"They've sent me to call you back," said Julie Darden.

"Who sent you, Julie?" he asked.

"They all want you back," she said. "They say that you did no more than any man would have done. And . . . I say so, too. And thank God there's no bloodstain on your hands, Tom. Thank God for that!"

"I'm going home, Julie," he said. "I can't face people just now."

"If you're going home," she said, "you haven't far to go. This is your home, Tom. My father wants me to say that."

"D'you want me for a charity boarder, Julie?" he asked.

She stepped closer and laid a hand on his. "Is it charity from me?" she asked.

"From you?" he said. "You're through with me, Julie. That's what blew a hole in my brain."

"I was through with a trickster," she said, "not with a man who had the clean courage of the truth about him. Tom, I feel humble, and like a child before you. Get down from the saddle. If you won't stay here, I'll follow after you, if I have to go on foot."

He dismounted. He was in a dream. And, with her, he walked back slowly toward the big, open-faced house. What lay before him he hardly could guess, except that somewhere he felt sure there would be happiness that was clean of all regrets.

ABOUT THE AUTHOR

Max Brand® is the best-known pen name of Frederick Faust, creator of Dr. Kildare, Destry, and many other fictional characters popular with readers and viewers worldwide. Faust wrote for a variety of audiences in many genres. His enormous output, totaling approximately 30,000,000 words or the equivalent of 530 ordinary books, covered nearly every field: crime, fantasy, historical romance, espionage, Westerns, science fiction, adventure, animal stories, love, war, and fashionable society, big business and big medicine. Eighty motion pictures have been based on his work along with many radio and television programs. For good measure he also published four volumes of poetry. Perhaps no other author has reached more people in more different ways.

Born in Seattle in 1892, orphaned early, Faust grew up in the rural San Joaquin Valley of California. At Berkeley he became a student rebel and one-man literary movement, contributing prodigiously to all campus publications. Denied a degree because of unconventional conduct, he embarked on a series of adventures culminating in New York City where, after a period of near starvation, he received simultaneous recognition as a serious poet and successful author of fiction. Later, he traveled widely, making his home in New York, then in Florence, and finally in Los Angeles.

Once the United States entered the Second World War, Faust

abandoned his lucrative writing career and his work as a screenwriter to serve as a war correspondent with the infantry in Italy, despite his fifty-one years and a bad heart. He was killed during a night attack on a hilltop village held by the German army. New books based on magazine serials or unpublished manuscripts or restored versions continue to appear so that, alive or dead, he has averaged a new book every four months for seventy-five years. Beyond this, some work by him is newly reprinted every week of every year in one or another format somewhere in the world. A great deal more about this author and his work can be found in *The Max Brand Companion* (Greenwood Press, 1997), edited by Jon Tuska and Vicki Piekarski. His next Five Star Western will be *Acres of Unrest.*